'Has lingered in my mind all year, not least because one of the main characters is a dingo.' *Australian*, Best Books of 2015

'Some of [Daisley's] most vivid writing...Moving and brilliant.' *Australian Book Review*

'*Coming Rain* shimmers with dusty red heat...Tune in to the distinctive rhythm of the prose and you'll enjoy the rich, subtle rewards of a really good book.' New Zealand *Listener*

'A challenging and brave book...At once cruel and gentle, graphically violent, including to animals, yet tender and beautiful.' *Sunday Star Times*

'This late beginner continues to make his distinguished, solitary way, not least in reclaiming the rural societies of a half century ago, rendered so vividly that they seem keenly of the present, rather than past curiosities.' *Australian*

'I consider it a masterpiece...*Coming Rain* deserves its accolades.' *New Zealand Herald*

'Astonishingly good...The writing is spare, the landscape and relationships haunting—a beautiful and unforgettable read.' Stuff.co.nz

'There are moments of aching tenderness and heroism that will enrapture readers to the very end. Highly recommended.' *Writing WA*

STEPHEN DAISLEY was born in 1955 and grew up in the North Island of New Zealand. He has worked on sheep and cattle stations, on oil and gas construction sites and as a truck driver, among many other jobs.

His first novel, *Traitor*, won the 2011 Prime Minister's Literary Award for Fiction. *Coming Rain* won the Ockham Prize in 2015. Stephen lives in Western Australia.

Stephen Daisley
A Better Place

TEXT PUBLISHING MELBOURNE AUSTRALIA

The Text Publishing Company acknowledges the Traditional Owners of the country on which we work, the Wurundjeri people of the Kulin Nation, and pays respect to their Elders past and present.

textpublishing.com.au

The Text Publishing Company
Wurundjeri Country, Level 6, Royal Bank Chambers, 287 Collins Street, Melbourne Victoria 3000 Australia

First published by The Text Publishing Company, 2023

Cover design by W. H. Chong
Cover art: *Wounded at Cassino* by Peter McIntyre, National Collection of War Art, Archives New Zealand
Page design by Rachel Aitken
Typeset by J&M Typesetting

Printed and bound in Australia by Griffin Press, an accredited ISO/NZS 14001:2004 Environmental Management System printer.

ISBN: 9781922458681 (paperback)
ISBN: 9781922459978 (ebook)

A catalogue record for this book is available from the National Library of Australia.

FSC
www.fsc.org
MIX
Paper | Supporting
responsible forestry
FSC® C018684

The paper this book is printed on is certified against the Forest Stewardship Council® Standards. Griffin Press holds chain of custody certification SCS-COC-001185. FSC® promotes environmentally responsible, socially beneficial and economically viable management of the world's forests.

Dedicated to the memory of
Lance Sergeant Len Seaman. DSM; 22Btn; 2NZEF.

Buried in Raetihi Cemetery, Parapara Road,
Aotearoa, New Zealand.

DISCLAIMER

This is a work of fiction. Of my imagination.

The rain was lifting; thin sunlight coloured the soaked paddocks of the Waiatarua Valley.

MAURICE SHADBOLT, *STRANGERS AND JOURNEYS*

No, there aren't any others.

PATRICK WHITE, *THE SOLID MANDALA*

The old musterer was standing on a high ridge. Dogs everywhere. Two horses behind him, a mare and her foal. Leather reins over his right shoulder. A pair of German binoculars around his neck.

He was bareheaded. White hair, cropped short, and a rough beard. Faded coat, grey bush shirt. Moleskin trousers held up with a wide belt and, below the knees, bowyangs. His worn boots covered in pale mud.

The metal bit rattled in the mare's mouth as she looked back to her colt foal. No rope. No rein, bridle or hackamore. Still suckling, he followed her everywhere. The old man considered this a natural thing. The young horse would settle in his presence. Recognise his smell and how he was unhurried with his mother. Respecting her ability on the hills. Respecting her being there with him. To carry him like she did.

He would bring them food in winter. Bread. Look at her feet after a long day. Whisper to her as he did this. Tell her what he had read in the newspapers. Rub mutton fat and creosote into the splits in her hooves with both his thumbs. Stockholm tar.

Her foot placed on his knee, her chin resting on his back.

Listening to him. Ears going back and forth. Understanding nothing except his tenderness. His decency.

The colt would also come to trust him entirely, with all his courage.

The old shepherd Roy Mitchell was seventy-eight years old. He had never married. No.

People in the district would often say he was not quite the same after he come back from the war. There was a twin brother, Tony. Killed on Crete in 1941.

The hut he built when he come back was on a bit of flat ground above the Mangawhero Creek. He called it his whare. Corrugated-iron chimney on the south wall. A run off water tank on the north. Black maire firewood cut and stacked on the verandah.

The land was steep, mostly uncleared country. Deeply cut with heavily timbered gullies. Scarred, with the bush sickness on it.

Nearby, a catching yard for young horses. Ropes and leather harness hanging over the rails. Raised kennels above the track. The kennels were north-facing with dry folded sacks for the dogs to sleep on. Water bowls made from cut-down drums.

In 1942, Roy had driven seventy-five miles through the North African desert to see a litter of ten pups. Just to see them. Someone from the 5th Field Artillery had told him about them. Drove back to the New Zealand lines after that.

Always kept filled, the water bowls. Never forgotten.

The last woman who saw him naked was in Northern Italy. Trieste 1945; 98 Venezia Giulia on the Street of Whores.

'Gesu,' she whispered and made the sign of the cross. 'Madonna mia.'

He continued to stare at her.

She nodded, held up four fingers. 'Quattrocento lire.'

'Four hundred?'

'Si,' she replied. 'Four hundred. No cibo mangiare. My children do not eat since two days.' Her four fingers became two, and she took off her coat. Took off her dress.

'I don't want to know about your children,' he said.

She bent forward and stepped out of her underwear. Her pubic hair was strong and black and her hipbones were pointed between the stretched skin of her pelvis. You could count her ribs. A pulse beating in her throat. 'Tu parli Italiano?'

'Some. I speak some.' He was just twenty-five, a sergeant since El Alamein. He reached out for her hand. There were red venetian blinds in the windows of her bedroom and a wooden crucifix on the wall above the bed.

She accepted his hand.

Told him to be quiet as he came.

The next morning, he left her all the money he had. The coins carefully stacked upon the notes on a table by the door.

A row of hooks on the wall. A raincoat hanging from one of the hooks. On the floor and against the wall, two pairs of children's shoes on sheets of folded newspaper. Without food, they stop crying after two days. Talking, after five.

He closed the door behind him.

At the wharves off the Via Tedeschi, the military docks were surrounded by lines of waiting soldiers. He recognised a lot of them. Some would wink and turn their heads towards him as they greeted him. Nod, Roy. If they were not from there, they would often just say, Taranaki.

A chalkboard propped against a bollard: SP1/NZ, 18Btn /22Btn/25Btn/28Btn NZEF. HMS *Dominion Monarch*.

It was an ordinary thing for these young men to wait in lines. They were soldiers. They waited.

After about twenty minutes Roy was at the head of the line. He was beckoned forward by a young officer seated at a portable desk. Roy stood to attention before him. Saluted. 'Sir.'

'Surname first, please.' The officer did not look up from the clipboard on the desk. 'Christian next, or at least your initials.' Holding his arms, looking down. Nodding as he spoke. 'Rank and unit after that. Thank you.'

Roy did not know what to say to such petulance. Remained silent.

'Well?' the officer said.

'Sorry, sir. I'm not sure I know what you're wanting here but my name is Sergeant Roy Mitchell. Taranaki. West Coast, Wellington. 22nd Battalion. 2nd NZEF.'

The lieutenant gripped his arms more tightly. A red and a blue pen before him; he aspired to the green ink of government. He could also smell him, this old soldier who did not answer properly. Absolutely stank of old sweat and alcohol. And a whore. Their dreadful perfume. The lieutenant flicked a page and continued to run his finger down the lists. Tapped the sheet and ticked the margin.

'Let's forget about that. There you are. Six years overseas?'

'Sir.'

'All theatres? Greece? Crete? Lost a brother at Maleme, I see. Twin brother?'

'Sir.'

'He is registered here as A. R. Mitchell. DOW. Is that right?' The lieutenant paused, looked up at him.

'Tony his name, sir. Anthony on the regimental lists. A. R. Mitchell. Anthony Robert. Died of his wounds on Crete. That's right, sir.'

The lieutenant was frowning as he continued to read. 'You were later posted to North Africa. Were at Tebaga Gap, Ruweisat Ridge, El Alamein, One and Two. Sicily. The Italian campaign. Wounded at Cassino, I see. Later repatriated to Trieste where you rejoined your battalion in 1945. The 22nd. Is that right?'

'Sir.'

'Hold on,' he said. 'I have lost my place here.' All impatience gone.

'That's all right, sir.'

The young lieutenant stared at him and nodded. He pretended

to keep reading for a bit. He had not lost his place. 'There we are. Safe trip home now, Sergeant Mitchell.'

Roy saluted and turned away.

It was indeed called *Dominion Monarch*, the troopship. The Yugoslav partisans in Trieste were pleased to see them go. They had gathered at the docks and stood in groups at the northern end of the wharf to bid them farewell. Some of them were passionate men and said goodbye to the New Zealanders by raising their clenched fists towards them, bent from the elbow and thrusting up and down. They were also yelling obscenities in Serbian and Croatian. Greek, Arabic. The insults were graphic, often involving their mothers and donkeys. Some were in Italian, the lingua franca of Trieste.

After a while one of the 22nd Battalion aboard the troopship yelled back. 'Fuck your fucking dead.' He was from Raetihi anyway.

Other Kiwis had begun showing their naked buttocks to the partisans on the docks. Probably Charlie Company boys. The Cowboys, they called themselves.

Two battalion officers came down from an upper deck and told the soldiers to stop what they were doing, and eventually they did.

Crete 1941

The first of the 642 Junkers 52s had been flying above the Aegean Sea since before dawn. Short-arm crosses on their sides. Iron bodies. Corrugated wings. Three fine rotary motors. The black swastika on their tails.

The JU 52 transport plane was known by many as Auntie Ju and beloved by the men of the leading assault company of the German Parachute Division, the Storm. Luftlande-Sturm-Regiment. Der Fallschirmjäger. Fine young men, and supremely confident. Most of them would be dead by the end of that first day.

Generaloberst Karl Student said it would break your heart if you let it. Instead, he ordered the massacre of the villagers at Kondomari. The destruction of Kandanos.

A ruthless man in revenge. He did not let the enormous number of the deaths of his young paratroopers break his heart. He let their deaths show that he was indeed a child of Frederick the Great. A true National Socialist.

The coastline of Crete appeared below them and the jumpmaster smiled, closed his eyes and made a fist. Raised three fingers. 'Jungen.'

The young men looked back at him, their jumpmaster, as they shed height, levelling into the attack-run above the airfield.

Their platoon leader Zugführer Hauptmann Johann Von Schiller stood and took the spliced connection rope from his mouth. Hooked it onto the central overhead static line, his wrist action strong and certain.

One hundred fifty metres.

The other paratroopers rose up as he had, reminded themselves again of who they were. The first section, first platoon of the first company. AAMG Strike Battalion West. 11th Air Corps. Meindl Group West. Der Adlerkrallesh. The Talons of the Eagle.

One hundred metres.

They all wore the buttoned Fallschirmjäger over-smocks. Knee pads and the distinctive shaped helmet: Reichsmarschall Hermann Goering's division. The Luftwaffe eagle decal.

His expression had not changed, but it was Von Schiller's intense honour to be the first to jump into combat for Operation Mercury. His pride somehow enhanced by the modesty of his movements.

Ninety metres.

Tuesday, 4 May 1941. Their immediate goal: Maleme airfield and the bridge across the Tavronitis River.

The weather conditions on Kreta were good. The jumpmaster had checked before take-off. Midday temperatures around twenty-two degrees Celsius. Now fourteen with a light southerly breeze. Dry. It would not rain again this summer.

Eighty-five metres.

The British colonial troops on the island were of little consequence. Many of them had shown themselves to be cowards in Greece, terrified of the Stuka. Running in circles at the screaming.

Seventy metres.

They would be swept aside as they had been before. Ten days to take the entire island, and the airfield was essential. Maleme.

Sixty-five metres.

It was difficult to be heard in the noise and vibration of the JU 52. They used hand signals for the most part. He turned, nodded and winked at the young Fallschirmjäger behind him.

All well trained. Prussian boys. Saxons too. They were given to this. Ropes, snatch lines in their mouths; hooking on, waiting for their turn.

Falling towards their combat height. Some laughing in their eagerness to jump. Others smiling as they dry-retched.

Sixty-three metres. Auntie Ju began singing to them. It was of the altitude; of their being there.

They were coming in from the east. Falling still. The rising sun behind them. Sixty-two metres. How much sooner? How much lower?

Hauptmann Von Schiller checked his watch. One minute before 8 a.m. Luftwaffe time: precise. The gliders would have gone in one minute earlier. The jumpmaster's go button was still red; when it turned green, they would jump.

Sixty metres.

Height above ground confirmed. Sixty metres.

Green.

Go. Their lowest jumping height. Combat height. Von Schiller dived without thought. Arms outstretched in the pose they all knew as the crucifix.

The chute snapped open and he looked to where, in about ten

seconds, he would land. Put his feet together. Below him Maleme, the airfield. Victory certain. Falling. Three seconds before he landed. Two seconds. One two.

It was then the bullet hit him. An English round: copper-cased .303 lead ball, making contact with the crest of his hip and spinning him around.

Roy Mitchell, unshaven and unwashed, a New Zealand soldier from the North Taranaki hill country, had missed what he was aiming at. He was aiming at the head.

The German spun in the harness of his parachute, a few metres above the airfield.

Roy reloaded and this time he aimed at the boots. Fired again and hit the falling man in the middle of the chest. Blew out his heart. Worked the well-oiled breech of his rifle, palmed the bolt closed and called for his twin brother.

'Tony?'

Roy was coming forward. Bayonet fixed. Aiming yet at the dead man he had just shot.

Johann Von Schiller, Zugführer der Fallschirmjäger. A decorated veteran of the Fort Eben-Emael drop; Iron Cross first class. Killed by a barely literate New Zealander from the Northern Taranaki backblocks.

The German had been born in Königsberg, East Prussia, in 1915 and was twenty-six years old. Newly married. He and Klara had gone skiing on their honeymoon and taken photographs of each other. She was pregnant when he left.

The wind had taken the parachute canopy and dragged the body into a line of olive trees along the banks of the Tavronitis.

Roy lifted the rifle to his shoulder and shot the dead German again. And then once more, for good measure. Five rounds gone in the magazine. That should be enough, he said. Four into him. Change magazines and reload, son. Knew he was going a bit overboard. With four.

'Tony,' he yelled out again to his brother. The parachute canopy had wrapped around some branches. Become entangled in rocks and yellow grass.

'Tony.'

'Roy,' Tony called back as he ran to join his brother.

They used knives to cut away the harness of the dead paratrooper. Deft, instinctive strokes. Many of the rural New Zealand soldiers kept a knife on their belts throughout the war, just as they had before.

Roy's woollen khaki trousers were hacked roughly off at the knees, oil-stained and covered in white dust. Both pockets of his shirt were unbuttoned. Black-and-white New Zealand flashes crumpled up in his epaulets. A red diamond on his left shoulder. A round helmet, the British model, still pushed back on his head. Four large ammunition pouches strapped across the 08 issue pack on his back. Filled with flares, grenades and cans of Norwegian sardines. British tobacco. Matches wrapped in waxed paper. The certain signs of a frontline soldier.

They were almost identical, the twins. Roy and Tony. Thick black hair on forearms, chests and legs. Dark eyes, square front teeth, white in their faces. Roy was slightly taller.

Otherwise you wouldn't know. Some who knew them said Tony was the more sensitive of the two. Shy bugger, really. A better rugby player, but he was not quite right. A bit different, if you know what I mean? Especially about ordinary things. He liked the art gallery in Whanganui. Who would think? Speaking with rivers. Tukutuku panels in a church by the *awa* that sang of windows to the world. He called it something else.

He was staring now into the face of the dead German. The blood spider-webbing over his cheeks, disappearing into his blond hair. The eyes looking at Tony.

Roy spat to one side. 'You right?'

Tony nodded, as Roy stripped the German's watch from his wrist. Pulled the blond head forward and tore off the binoculars. The helmet came away in his hands and he threw it to one side, did not look at the eyes. No point. The pale hair. The bullet holes in chest and hip and back. The blood he had coughed up over his face.

'These'll do me.' Roy pushed the binoculars into his pack. 'German binos. Zeiss. See for fuckin' miles.'

The German's mouth was open. He must have been calling out when he died.

Tony took the wallet from his chest pocket. A wad of Greek drachma and the photograph of a young woman. *Vergissmeinicht* written across it. A shining face.

Roy looked at his brother holding the photograph. 'It means forget me not,' he said to Tony. 'Must be his wife or his girlfriend, y'know?'

Tony remembered him coming to a shot stag on the high tussock country. The plateau lands at the back of Waiouru. Ruapehu, Tongariro, Ngauruhoe above them. Immediately cutting its shaggy throat to stop the suffering. Slicing open the stomach and allowing the wet intestines to fall smoking into the cold tussock grass.

13

Taking the head. Counting the points. The skinning of the animal. Roy always ensured the back steaks were taken. If they had a long walk, they would sometimes roast parts of the liver on a grass fire before they left. It was an old-fashioned thing to do. Tasted like jellied blood, steaming in the high air. Deer blood, burning your mouth. A thing from the old country, Roy had said. The liver of a stag is strong meat.

Salt if you were lucky.

'Captain Davin, Div Intel, told me that. Vergissmeinicht means forget me not.'

Tony dropped the photograph onto the dead man's chest. He knew what it meant. Took the money, stuffed it into his pockets. Placed the wallet next to the photograph and wiped his blood-wet fingers clean on the captain's uniform.

The sounds of running men approaching. Dangerous men. Rattling equipment. A company at least of the hated Fallschirmjäger. Germans barking orders like dogs. Shouted orders, instantly obeyed.

On their left flank, Tony saw an MG34 machine-gun team go to ground. The number two loading a fresh belt of ammunition into the gun. Pushed the dust cover shut and slapped the gunner on the shoulder. A burst of 7.62 mm gunfire exploded through the air around them.

Tony knew immediately he had been hit. Three terrible blows like a madman with a hammer on his left shin and foot. He looked down, and his entire left foot was gone. About ten inches of bone and ankle completely shot away by the machine-gun fire.

There was no pain at first. He saw it lying about six inches away in the dirt, his foot. Still in the boot, jagged bone-ends sticking out. The boot he had polished that morning. Laces done up in the ladder fashion. The folded top of a khaki woollen sock, straight and British. The blood gushing out of what was left there. Spurting everywhere.

'Roy?' Tony said, hearing his voice crack. 'Jesus, Roy.'

He saw the beating of his heart in the ragged flesh and knew he had to close off the main arteries. He bent forward, tore up handfuls of dirt and grass and pressed them into the mess where his foot had been. The welter of blood between his fingers slowed. He could feel the pulpiness of the flesh, the sharpness of the bones.

And now the monstrous pain was beginning. The appalling agony from his missing bones. He closed his eyes and vomited.

Roy had not seen this. He had not seen his brother being wounded. Instead, he had crawled forward from where they had been looting the dead paratrooper and taken cover.

The enemy fire hitting the ground and rocks and trees around them. Thudding into the body of the Fallschirmjäger hauptmann he had killed. Ripping him further apart. The noise, overwhelming. More harsh orders being shouted on their flanks. Gunfire. Exploding grenades.

'Tony,' Roy yelled towards where he had left his brother, 'we have to go, mate.' Shrapnel sprayed over him from another grenade. 'Tony? We have to, they're coming on both sides, mate.'

Silence yet from his brother.

Roy waited, counted to ten. Jumped up and began sprinting away from the listening post. Came to a nearby tree line, stopped and turned to cover where he had just run from, looking back. No movement. Tony was not following. A relief of sorts.

'Tony,' he called out, softer. He started to run again. 'Tony.' He knew that this time he was calling for himself and not for his brother.

Tony would never have done that. Abandoned him. He would not. No matter what. They called him Rowdy in the 22nd Battalion because he was so bloody silent. With all his shy silence, Tony would never have left him to die.

Roy was dripping sweat as he ran, blinking rapidly. After a minute or so, he sank to his knees and vomited. Coughing as the burning bile came up.

Above him, more waves of German transport planes were coming over the island. The same Junkers JU 52: three motors and corrugated bodies; swastikas everywhere.

The sounds of German machine-gun fire growing in the south. More fighting coming from the direction of Heraklion. Shooting and explosions. A major assault by the Germans.

So much had changed since yesterday. The news of Manny's arrest.

Early that morning, before light, they had been sent to the forward listening post known as Whangamomona, located on the high ground above the Maleme airfield.

Roy had originally been assigned another rifleman but it was him, Manny bloody Jones, and Manny had been locked up for causing a fight in a café in Kastelli. Not out of character. Manny Jones being AWOL and in trouble was a regular thing. He had snuck out of their defensive lines saying that he was going into the village for a root and to get pissed.

Fuck the fucking listening post, he said. It will still be there tomorrow.

With Manny gone, Tony had gladly taken the opportunity to replace him and go out onto the listening post with his brother.

Their section commander, Danny Reppel, kept them apart as best he could. Brothers being killed was a difficult report to give. Twins worse. A mother reading that message was not something he wanted to see or think of.

Danny had been a mail delivery boy in Wellington during the first war. He said you felt the women's cold fingers when they took the cable. He said you could see the dread in their eyes. Their little boys running about barefoot on the lawn. Falling over suddenly as running children do. Laughing at a gushing hose. Washing on the line. Many families had lost as many as four boys. Some six.

The Luftwaffe had been bombing for the last few days and it had become more intense the morning of the attack. 'The usual hate', they called the regular bombing and strafing runs by the Germans.

But on the morning of the attack, the intensity of the Stukas increased. Waves and waves of them coming over. Protected by the damned ME109's Messerschmitt fighters.

After that, it seemed the entire sky filled with parachutes. For as far as you could see. Different colours too, who would have thought?

Roy was dry-retching as he ran through the olive trees. Following a rough track towards the bridge and the battalion lines, he passed a red-brick shed and continued along an avenue of lemon trees. More rows of grapevines in heavy leaf, the tendrils seeming to reach out and tangle in his boots.

He stopped, bent forward and retched again. Long bursts of

machine-gun fire still coming from near the airfield. He waited, his hand braced against a tree.

Tony had not followed him from the listening post. His brother. His twin. Tony would not have run away from him. No, he would not.

'Sie. You.'

Tony looked up.

An enormous German paratrooper stood above him, his face expressionless beneath the brimless helmet. He did not blink. Unsmiling and aiming his 9 mm MP40.

Tony closed his eyes and bent forward over his destroyed leg and began to recite the words of Psalm 23, the soldiers' psalm. Though I walk...*I can no longer walk*...into the valley of the shadow of death I will fear no evil for Thou art with me...*God's light at my opened door.* Though I walk through the valley of death. *I cannot walk.*

Tony heard the sounds of crashing stones coming closer. He stopped praying and opened his eyes.

Another paratrooper was running towards them, head down. He was also dressed in the baggy blue and grey Fallschirmjäger fatigues. Sleeves rolled up. But this one was wearing a Red Cross armband. A medical pack slung over his shoulder. A young face with pimples on his top lip. A German boy, twenty, twenty-one.

He slid to a stop beside them and greeted his comrade, then, noting his age and rank, he stood again. Amended his greeting to the formal style, one of respect. As you would a senior rank.

They spoke in German for a few moments, fell silent and both looked at the wounded New Zealander. The older man indicated their dead zugführer.

The open wallet, the photograph on his chest covered with bloody fingerprints. The hauptmann was also missing his binoculars and wristwatch, the beloved helmet thrown to one side. The open mouth; the hair, which had been allowed to grow much longer on the top of his head in the fashion of the time.

These fucking New Zealanders killed the captain, the older man said. Shot him four times and took everything he had. Looted him and used their knives to do it. They all carry knives, like bandits.

He grunted and again aimed his machine gun at Tony. Braced his legs to fire a burst.

'Otto.' The young medic held up his hand. 'Otto, bitte. Wait.' Knelt beside Tony. Shielding him with his body as he examined his wound. Blinked at what he saw.

To his left, half a metre away, the foot, still in its English boot. The blood beneath it. Jagged and terrible bones protruding.

He looked at Tony and made a face—not so bad—and applied a tourniquet above the knee. Nodded as he tightened it like a belt and the blood stopped oozing from the dirt-packed wound.

'Ist nichts…' he said. 'A scratch.' He was not looking at Tony.

'My foot.' Tony said. 'Ist?'

The German medic closed his eyes, shook his head. An angry red pimple above his top lip, another in his eyebrow. This young man, still a teenager.

The older man watched them. Tenderness angered him.

Kindness angered him. It made him think of other things. And he didn't like being told to wait by a lower rank. A younger man, probably a medical student before the war. One of those university types anyway.

The medic had once again turned his back to him, kneeling between him and the wounded New Zealander. Held up a hand without looking back. He opened another field dressing and used the cotton wool to clean away the grass from the wound, exposing it properly, the devastation. Unrolled a packet of instruments and surgical scissors. The suture needles would not be required. There was nothing left to sew up.

He used the sterile scissors to cut the remaining pieces of uniform and sock away from the mess. Took a water bottle from his belt and washed away the soil clinging to what was left; the shattered bones. Then he held a fresh dressing tightly against this flesh.

Checked again, the timing of the tourniquet. Looked at his wristwatch and then up at what this young New Zealand soldier was doing not to cry out. Biting down on his hand in the web between the thumb and his first finger. Biting into this to remain silent. Blood in his mouth. His upper teeth had met his lower teeth and bitten through.

The German medic murmured, 'Lieber osmann.' And did not even know why, really. An ancient term of respect. Darling man. He began to prepare the morphine injection. Two ampoules from the tin. The sterilised needle.

Otto muttered something obscene and spat as he slung the MP40 over his shoulder. Called the medic a weak university cunt and turned his back to scramble out of the hollow beside the riverbed. And, not looking back, he disappeared towards the village of Kandanos and the sounds of machine-gun fire. Children calling out for their lost mothers there. Victory much more certain.

Tony felt the sting of a needle in his thigh and the pain eased almost immediately. Morphine was the most beautiful drug. God invented morphine for wounded soldiers. And bullfighters. Penicillin came from Jesus.

The Fallschirmjäger medic pressed another shell dressing onto the wreckage of Tony's lower leg. Blood still oozed from the edges. He dusted the torn flesh with sulphur powder. Anaesthesia of sorts. Pressed the field dressing over the bleeding stump. Strapped it. Allowed any painkilling drugs to work. This wounded soldier.

A thorough man, the German medic checked that Tony was fully asleep before he cut away the last of the shredded tissue. Did the really painful things to the boy. Dug out all the foreign matter from the bones. The muck he'd stuffed into them to stop the bleeding. The medic washed the stump again with water and iodine and placed a large swab over the end. Fitted a Feldgrau portable stump splint over that.

Looked at his watch again and eased the tourniquet. Blood seeping out from what was left of his leg. Retightened it and the blood slowed. Again, he wrote the time on a card tied to the identification tags around his neck.

A field hospital would soon be established near the drop zone. Medical command HQ would send their sanis, the stretcher bearers, to take him back. The boy medic retrieved the English rifle. Fixed the bayonet and thrust it into the earth. Placed the hauptmann's helmet on the upended butt, a marker for the sanis to see.

He turned the sleeping soldier onto his side, propped a blanket against his back. Patted his shoulder as you would a friend. Knelt and looked towards the sounds of machine guns and explosions, where his regiment was fighting and dying. They would also need his help.

This New Zealander had lost his leg. The boy thought he might die, and he did not even know who he was. His name tags read: Mitchell. A. O rh Pos. Methodist. He was a Methodist too. The sanis would come for him.

It took Roy another twenty minutes to get back to the Taranaki Company positions near the bridge above the Tavronitis.

Lewis guns from HQ companies had been set up among the steel girders. Slit trenches and fire positions, carefully located. Bren guns closer to the front line.

'Halt!' the forward sentry called out.

Roy dropped flat on his belly. He saw the round British steel helmets. Recognised the voices.

'It's me,' he called out. 'Coming in from the Whanga listening post.'

'Is that you, Roy? Rowdy? You there?'

'Just me. No Rowdy. He's not with me.'

Silence. They all waited. After a while someone else said, 'Come in, mate.'

'You sure I'm right to come in?' Roy yelled. 'Don't shoot me you bastard. I don't remember the bloody password.'

'Come in, Roy. Where's Rowdy, then?...Tony? I say rugby.'

Roy ran towards their lines.

Ken Corbett, behind the gun. Broad shoulders and big arms.

Strong hands. A natural machine-gunner, he invariably located the best fields of fire without ever even being told. A cheesemaker from Kaimata. Would you believe it?

'...And you say lock,' Ken called out as Roy ran past him. 'That's the password, mate. I say rugby and you say lock.'

Peter Clarkson, his number two, frowned and shook his head. 'Ken,' he said. 'Mate.'

Ken, mouth open to say something more, stopped when he realised what Peter was trying to tell them. Rowdy was not coming back.

Peter Clarkson was a perceptive man. Even if he did come from Normanby in South Taranaki. Hector Gray country. Peter adored horses and dreamed of becoming a racehorse trainer when he returned to New Zealand after the war. Grown too big to be a jockey himself, he knew every winner of the Melbourne Cup since 1861. Golden Slipper too. He could tell you the weights they carried, their racing colours. The jockeys, the owners and especially their trainers. The race-day numbers they wore.

He always said the turning point in his life come with the 1930 Melbourne Cup. Phar Lap, number one and carrying a massive 9 stone 12 ounces. And yet he still won, the bloody rough bastard. An enormous heart, this horse. Red silks with hooped white and black arms. Pikey aboard.

Peter, born in 1920, was ten years old when Phar Lap won and that was that, really. It was White Nose the next year but he carried three stone less. Forty-two whole pounds. Number twenty-two of twenty-four. Why do you think they named him that? he would ask, smiling. Fucking White Nose?

Another who volunteered.

Roy could see his section had dug into the leading slope around the bridge. The rocky ground had made the digging difficult and they had been unable to get below a few feet. To compensate for this, they had piled up walls of rocks and sandbags around their rifle pits. They were known as sangars, these makeshift ramparts. The men would soon become experts at their rapid construction in the deserts of North Africa and, later, throughout the Italian mountains.

As Roy passed through the lines he noticed Bert Sutton in his large and well-made sangar. Bert was squinting at him. Wondering like the others where Roy's brother was, but he knew enough to say nothing. Bert was a tall man, six foot seven at least. A timber-mill worker. He had fair hair and blue eyes from his Scandinavian dairy-farmer grandparents. A tender heart. They said he might have been selected for King Country rugby before the war if he had a little bit more of what they called the mongrel in him. Could not see properly. Bad eyes. That was also unfortunate.

'We dug a shell scrape for you and Tony, Roy,' he said. 'Over there.'

Roy saw him pointing to another pile of rocks about ten yards to his left.

They all knew Bert called himself a socialist. Most of them believed he didn't even know what that meant. He had once met and worked with the man John A. Lee in a sawmill on the Kawana Track up the Whanganui River. Near the flour mill on the road to Pipiriki.

When they were working, the steam-driven saws screamed so loudly cutting through the tree bodies you could not hear yourself think. They would say that: you cannot hear yourself think with the noise of the fuckin' saws. So it was that one lunchtime Lee said

26

that maybe it was not the saws but the tree that was screaming.

'What?' The workers stopped eating for a moment.

'For what is being stolen from it,' John Lee said into the silence. 'Have you ever thought about that, Mr Sutton?'

Bert loved to tell them the story. 'The screaming being the other way around?'

Bert would tell them that a great respect to all others was shown by Mr Lee, also dearly loved by his mother and sisters. He witnessed their courage. His insight, respect and tenderness in such matters attracted many lovers in spite of the arm he lost in the First World War. Many believed he talked too much, but still he was beloved by many. Bert Sutton's father had shaken his hand and asked who would say such things? The tree screaming and not the saw? What damn communist fool would even think this?

Right now, Mr Lee said, it is still happening in our country. People are begging for food. Sleeping in the long grass and in shop doorways. Under park benches. His own sister had lost her husband in the war. They had five children and she became a whore to pay the rent. This should not happen.

He was, Bert said, an angel with one arm. John A. Lee. A blessed man. He said people should not have to beg to exist anywhere. Ever.

'No, no, no. Lee was just another land-stealing Bolshevik prick,' Geoff Phillips yelled out from behind some rocks in a nearby firing position. 'A red cunt.' He had been listening to Bert.

'They want to share everything,' he said. 'Fucking socialists, all right. Don't ever try to be better because we all can share everything anyway. What's the fuckin' point, eh, Bert? To even try?'

Geoff Phillips's family owned twenty farms from Hawera to Oakura. Fight you at the drop of a hat if you disagreed with them, and had a grandfather who was proud to say he had ridden with the Taranaki Yeomanry at Parihaka. Had framed souvenirs in his study. A kete and a pounamu mere. We took their fucking things and their fucking land, he would say. Don't you worry about that. What else do you think it was? Kindness? We took it. Simple as that. If they objected, we killed them or put them in prison until they became docile. Do as they were fucking told and laugh as we did it. We took their things and their land. That's it. We won.

Old Mr Phillips seemed to enjoy the fighting itself. Hurting other men. Making them become weak men. Free competition was, he said, you and me. Face to face. Come on, you cunt. Now. He would say such things. Win before a punch was thrown. A musket sold. The man was knighted by the King after the First World War. Became a justice of the peace in his old age. Smiled at the camera. Became a member of parliament and had a road named after him. Ended up owning twenty farms. Became fat, impotent, died of a heart attack in his bed.

'Lee made the most of his missing arm,' Geoff Phillips said. 'My father told me he shagged himself to a standstill, the one-armed communist cunt.'

'Come on, Geoff. Be fair, mate.'

'They are just lazy, jealous bastards. The whole bloody Bolshevik pack of them. Wanting what the rich already have. What we worked hard for. Wish I was at the riots on Queen Street.'

Geoff was killed later when a British tank ran over him in the dark on Operation Crusader in Libya. No one had called a warning. The devastation a human body suffers when a tank runs over it is quite horrific. Blood explodes out of the anus and the mouth. Almost like when you stand on a fallen tomato in the garden. No one had told them about this. What tanks did.

Roy reached the firing position the boys in his section had prepared. He settled down into the hollow behind the wall of rocks and laid out his .303 rifle pointing back from where he came. Sat with his back to the wall and drank the last of the water in his canteen. Took some deep breaths. His hands were shaking as he ate some bread and a handful of sultanas taken from one of the ammunition pouches. He knew he would have to report to their platoon commander as soon as possible. He would ask why he'd been out there with his brother.

Jesus, why did Tony have to come? Manny Jones should have been with him at the listening post. Manny Jones was in the detention camp on Prison Road. Found so drunk and beaten he could barely speak. Whispering that he didn't give a fuck anyway.

He had been wanting to pay for half an hour with the café owner's daughter in Kastelli. To give her one, he said and clutched at his groin. Asked repeatedly, how much for your daughter?

The local men had attacked him. He fought back but was too drunk to put up any sort of a defence and was soon kicked into the gutter. Where, they said, he belonged. He had told them to get fucked and spat blood at them through his broken teeth as they walked away.

Roy took his rifle from the rough parapet of his shell scrape and removed the magazine. Opened the bolt and removed it also. Took a cotton rag and cleaned off the black residue in the breechblock. Oiled the bolt and blew air into the front sight.

Manny originally came from somewhere up the Waitotora Valley. Small, hairy and sharp-featured. It was said he looked like his father, a known poacher and a thief in the district. Raven-black hair. Not above a bit of burglary himself. He would go with his old man on trips when he was old enough. Less suspicion, see, his father would say, having a kid on the horse with you. Smile, you little cunt, people trust kids. Smile, Manny boy. He called the police wallopers. The jacks, too, he sometimes called them. Bad as us, he often said. Bad as us.

Cleaning his rifle, Roy looked over at the fourth rifleman of their section, young David Brookes. He was returning Roy's stare. David was nineteen, fair-headed, soft brown eyes, tall and lean with wide shoulders and the tentative smile of the easily hurt. A gentle voice. He blushed readily and was generous to a fault. Exactly the sort of young man bullies love. Manny especially enjoyed hurting him.

David Brookes had been a junior railway clerk in New Plymouth before the war. He was studying governmental accountancy at night. Another who enlisted when war was declared.

At basic training his modesty at the communal showers and latrines was noticed immediately by the older men. The way he covered his groin, his private parts, with both his hands.

Manny Jones smiled as he recognised this. Said, oh-ho yes. Laughed and called him Sister. Sister Boy. Look at my cock. It is getting hard just looking at you.

Manny would be killed three years later, 1944, a night advance up a ridge above Casa Elto. And it was David Brookes, Sister, who went out to him. Brought him back.

Who would have thought?

He destroyed a machine-gun position with grenades that night for the man who had named him Sister Boy. Did not think twice. Led the remainder of the section up the ridge after he had rescued Manny. Awarded the DCM for these actions and although terribly wounded he would survive the war. Killed five Germans with his bayonet. The ones who were alive after the grenades.

David never called Tony Rowdy. They had become friends during the early years of basic training. They were often seen leaning towards each other when they laughed at something. Comfortable enough to be silent also. Knees touching. Hands on each other's shoulders for a long time. Staying quiet. Holding hands.

There was nothing more Sister could have done to save Manny's life. The mine had exploded between his legs. His intestines became a terrible shroud of blood and raw flesh. His bowel and bladder gone. No genitals left.

David held his hand. 'The bloody Waitotara Valley.' He knew where he was going.

'The valley,' Manny replied as he whispered, 'Our father.' Began to recite the psalm. The flesh was gone, all the way down the insides of both his thighs to his knees. You could see the white of his long thigh bones. He had been shot twice in the chest and once in the throat. Sister would say he had tried to smile as he died; was struggling a bit at the end. He never told them that he had said, thank you, David. There was no need. Held his hand. I'm sorry. That was all he said.

Roy finished cleaning his rifle. Reloaded. One up the spout. Safety on. Fixed his bayonet. He knew he had to report back to the officer in charge. He stood and, slightly bent over, began walking back towards where the platoon HQ would be.

As Roy passed his slit trench, David climbed out and stopped him. 'Roy,' he said. 'Where's Tony?'

Roy looked away from David. Stepped around him, kept walking.

'Roy.'

Roy would not look at David. Sister Boy. Could not.

'Roy?' Sister stepped in front of him. Stood up, chest to chest, like boxers do. He had clenched his fists.

'Is Tony all right?'

'I don't know.'

'Tell me the truth now.' David's voice was low. 'Please…is he all right? Is he wounded? Was he killed? Did you leave him behind? Did you?'

'I don't know, David.' Roy looked like he wanted to be sick. Shook his head and walked off in the direction of their HQ. More hunched over now, and looking at the ground. Carrying the .303 Enfield rifle in his right hand.

The platoon commander, Lieutenant Ross, was crouched in the bottom of a trench. He was desperately trying to get radio signals back to brigade. Kneeling next to a wireless set and holding the headphones to one ear. Mouthpiece in the other hand. Cursing and shaking his head and saying, fucking thing. The sound of artillery in the distance.

Roy slid into the trench, and the lieutenant looked at him. 'Who the hell are you? What do you want?'

'Private Mitchell, boss. Just in…from the listening post. Whangamomona above Maleme.'

Ross looked at him. Had no idea what he was talking about. Saw he was probably all right. 'Go on.'

'A heavy drop, boss. German paratroopers. Must be a company plus. Overran the listening post.'

32

The lieutenant could see the black smoke boiling up from somewhere near the coast. An oil storage tanker had been bombed. More German planes were coming in from the north.

'Go on,' he said again.

'From the air. Not the sea. They are all over Maleme. Jerry paratroopers. Mainly regrouping and getting organised. Seemed to know what they were doing, though.'

Lieutenant Ross yelled back at him, almost deaf from all the explosions around them. 'You had someone with you on the listening post, didn't you, Mitchell? There were two of you. Did the other bloke get back all right? Where's he?'

'No. I had to leave him behind. He was my brother, boss. Tony.'

Lieutenant Ross stared at him. 'You should not have been together. Brothers should not ever be together on forward positions.'

'One of the section was detained.' Roy hesitated. 'Locked up in Kastelli.'

'Yes, I heard about that. Manny Jones,' the lieutenant said. 'In trouble again?'

'Yep. Manny. That's the one, boss. We swapped.'

'The man's a bloody menace.' Lieutenant Ross nodded and stared back at Roy and decided this was not the time to ask again about his missing brother.

'We better get back to battalion HQ,' he said. 'You'll have to come with me.'

That low, confident sound of the JU 52 motors came above them again. They had become almost continuous, the Luftwaffe transports coming in at their impossibly low heights. Clouds of the escorting Stuka dive bombers above them. Screaming into the attack. Someone nearby yelling…bombs gone…bombs gone… take cover.

Explosion after explosion and the ground shaking around them as the dive bombers intensified their attacks on the 22nd Battalion's positions near the Tavronitis bridge. The raining down of dust and stones. The noise deafening.

Roy and the lieutenant were at a crouched run, heading back towards company HQ.

They reached the sandbagged entrance of the central bunker just as more bombs began exploding along the edges of the defensive perimeter. The earth shaking. Moving beneath them.

Someone in the bunker yelled out, a New Zealand voice. 'If that fuckin' noise was meant to scare me…it worked. I just shit in my pants.'

A pause and then laughter ran along the lines of dust-covered soldiers. They were all taking cover in the trench lines leading to the bunker. Another voice was proclaiming: Jesus Jesus Jesus I will sin no more. That terror humbled them all. That fear they had all come to know. One of the older men had advised them to name their fear, if it helped.

Someone said, 'Well, I won't be doing that at Auntie Poppy's funeral. Shitting in my pants. Oh no. No good at all. Who would even do that? Shit in their own pants? I just did and named it Obedience. I did. Named my shit. Called it Obedience.'

Some were weeping as they laughed. They were simply more frightened than they had ever been in their entire lives. Would never say so.

Roy was with Lieutenant Ross near the entrance. Waiting for the company OC. Someone who knew what to do.

The CSM from HQ approached them. Nodded to Roy and saluted Lieutenant Ross. 'Sir.'

Yet another wave of Stuka dive bombers came over them. Grimacing boys repeating words to each other among the screaming explosions.

The CSM, Bill McCready, who the men called Mother, spoke calmly to Lieutenant Ross. 'Best get back to your front platoon, sir,' he said. 'The bloody Germans have made four drops. The OC was killed earlier. The 2IC has taken over until we can get a replacement.'

'Sar' major,' the lieutenant replied.

The CSM smiled at the young men. They might be all right.

'Await further instructions is probably the word, sir. I believe brigade will order a fighting retreat but we just have to wait and see. In the meantime we must take up defensive positions. Wouldn't you agree, sir?'

He had that smiling calmness under fire the older NCOs always seemed to have.

As they ran back to their platoon and section lines, they saw another dead body. Platoon Sergeant Beechworth. Caught in the open by a German fighter earlier that morning as he was running ammunition to a forward Bren gun position; must have been the second wave of German air assaults.

The dead man lay on his back, one arm torn off at the shoulder. Opened chest. Four ammunition boxes around him. Scattered magazines. His khaki battledress covered with blackened blood. Open eyes, open mouth filled with flies. He would forgive a soldier anything except lateness.

Two Brens were firing to their front: short bursts interspersed with .303 rifle shots. Grenades. Bursts of machine-gun fire. The Fallschirmjäger returning this fire. Their grenades flying through the air.

They arrived back at the forward platoon's lines just as a flanking platoon of the enemy had advanced to within fifty yards. The Germans had split without a word spoken and began to assault the New Zealand line in a simultaneous attacking move, firing and dashing forward.

A well-coordinated tactic coming from well-trained men. Did not have to ask what to do. Calling out to each other in their harsh language as they prepared to run and as they ran; took cover and returned fire. Encouragement and location calls. Identifying their fire and movement.

The New Zealanders were shooting at them through the olive trees.

A messenger runner came forward from battalion HQ. He was carrying orders from the brigadier to the battalion CO. Radio comms were down. He passed the message to Ross. The written order came from brigade to pull back.

Positions southwest of the Tavronitis bridge were being prepared for them. *Act forthwith* was the hastily scrawled command.

Ross called out to the troops in his platoon. 'Prepare to fall back.'

Silence for a moment from the boys and then someone replied. 'Boss? The airfield?'

The lieutenant ignored him. 'A staggered retreat, boys. Just like the drills in training. Groups of four, while the rest of us provide cover as they go.'

'Boss,' Roy said. 'Wait on.'

'Do as you are ordered.' He sounded impatient.

'Look, boss. Hang on a sec. Look.' Roy pointed to his front. Leading elements of another group of German paratroopers had come from their extreme left and advanced into the forward bivouac area of some Royal Navy Air Arm tents they had encountered earlier in the week.

They were a support unit, not combat trained, and had been taking cover during the fight. Roy saw some of the young Englishmen looking at each other as they raised their arms tentatively in the air. An extremely young officer was holding a newspaper above his head in a gesture of surrender. Ex-public schoolboy by the look of his indolent manner. He shrugged and smiled, almost in apology. Attempted a lazy salute.

One of the watching New Zealanders muttered, 'Fuck me. He's saluting the cunts.'

'That'll change.'

Roy watched as an older Fallschirmjäger, a sergeant major with a scarred face, approached the surrendering Englishman and backhanded him across the face. Knocked him to the ground and spat on him, the newspaper flying out of his hand. The German kicked the gasping and astounded English boy twice in the stomach, turned and spoke to his fellow soldiers, then kicked the Englishman again. Gestured towards the New Zealand defensive lines.

'We have to fall back,' Lieutenant Ross hissed. 'Come on, Mitchell. Orders.'

'Hold on sir,' Roy said. 'Look what these bastards are doing to the Brits. Hold on. Look at this.'

The Germans had begun to kick the remaining Englishmen in

their backsides. Cuffing them like schoolboys, pushing machine-pistol muzzles into their backs, indicating to them to keep their hands in the air and to run towards the New Zealand lines.

'Can you see this, boss?' Roy said. 'The bastards are using the Fleet Air Arm boys as cover.'

The young Englishmen were running awkwardly, hands still raised, and they could hear their faint cries: 'Don't shoot mate, it's us.'

They were terrified. Some were openly weeping. Most were only boys, fifteen, sixteen. Apprentice chefs. Kitchen hands. Clerks.

Lieutenant Ross watched for a moment and then ducked down onto the floor of the trench. 'Oh Jesus,' he said. 'What should we do?'

Roy glanced down at the crouching officer. It seemed obvious to him. He worked the bolt of his rifle and shot the leading Englishman in the chest. The one who had saluted, and been spat on for his trouble.

He said, 'Sorry, mate.' Reached down and pulled the lieutenant to his feet. 'C'mon boss, we got no choice here.' He nodded towards the English as he shot the aggressive German bastard with the scarred face.

Roy reloaded and continued firing. More English lads were dropping. 'C'mon boss. You have to shoot the poor bastards.'

Lieutenant Ross was stunned and seemed unable to think for a moment. The hand holding his revolver at his side.

Yet another platoon-sized body of Fallschirmjäger had arrived in support of their comrades. They took cover behind a small terraced wall about two hundred yards from the New Zealand position, established a fire base and then spread out behind what was left of the other squad and the English boys.

These fresh German paratroopers also began advancing at a trot. They were in a staggered, extended line. Their speed. Their savage running. Where to focus their attack? Shouting to each other as they did so. Firing as they ran. Throwing grenades.

A German grenade hit the back of their firing trench and dropped to the ground. Wooden handle. Head like a can, it began spinning as Roy watched, smoke hissing from it. It was about to explode when Billy McKay from 7 Platoon tore off his helmet, dropped it over the fizzing grenade and jumped on it. He looked directly into Roy's eyes and winked.

'I am a man from the King Country,' he said and braced himself against the side of the trench. 'A cowboy and a fuckin' Indian.'

When the grenade exploded, he was thrown onto his back and came to rest against some ammunition boxes. The dust clearing. Both his feet had been blown off. Blood gushing from the ends of his shattered legs.

'Oh Jesus,' Petey Johns yelled, 'oh Jesus,' as Billy McKay began to convulse.

'Billy?' Petey holding him, covered in his blood and that grey-white dust, as he died from the shock of the grenade, the massive blood loss. 'Jesus Christ, Billy.' It was bright red, the blood.

'Look out, boys.' Lieutenant Ross yelling as another grenade exploded on the lip of the trench and yet more machine-gun fire shredded the sandbags behind them.

Two of the attacking German paratroopers appeared above them and began firing into the trench. Three New Zealanders were hit before Roy shot back. He got one of them in the chest, knocked him backwards. Lieutenant Ross shot the other one with his revolver. He had recovered enough to fight.

'Walk, boss. Come on.' Roy kept the rifle to his shoulder as they changed their position and made their way further back along the platoon trench. He was aiming the rifle even as he worked the bolt to reload. Changed magazines. Covering them. Shadowing his lieutenant. 'Walk, boss.'

He looked back and saw that one of the dead German's legs had fallen back over the edge of the trench. A rubber-soled jump boot. Not the jackboot. He stopped, and for some reason counted the crisscrossed lace holes in the jump boot. Twelve. There were twelve on each side, making a total of twenty-four. A lot to lace. Looked to where the legless body of Billy McKay lay still, his friend kneeling beside him. The boy musterer standing on his helmet, winking and saying that shit about cowboys and Indians. What a thing to say. Fuck me.

There were no more Germans coming. But their dead and wounded were all around them, the poor bastards. Blood on the ground and up the walls of the trenches. A lot of it. Splashed everywhere with the close-in shooting and exploding grenades.

It was best to wash the blood off as soon as you could. It gummed up the working parts of your rifle. Turned black and set brittle after about four hours.

As they retreated along the communication trenches leading to the rear, a sergeant from the 18th Battalion met them and spoke very calmly to Lieutenant Ross.

He had come over from a Canterbury Otago formation. An older man, he did not take his eyes from the lieutenant's face as he spoke to him. A steady gaze and savage face. In his slow and deliberate way of speaking it often looked like he was smiling when he spoke.

He was not smiling. It was just that old-fashioned way many of the high-country people had about them. English was often their second language after Gaelic. Very respectful, quite soft.

You could be forgiven if you thought the sergeant was wondering about other things. The possibility of snow falling during pre-lamb-shearing or how the freeze could break their hearts. The dead snow-covered lambs in tussock hollows. Mustering a thousand acres. The worth of a good dog. Soft words and three hundred dead lambs. Without raising his voice.

'We'll get around to their left, slow them down a bit for you, sir,' the sergeant said.

'McRae.' Lieutenant Ross nodded. 'Sergeant. Thank you.'

'You blokes should regroup and get back to battalion. Freyberg is at brigade HQ. And Kipp too, if I am not mistaken. We'll be right then. Your battalion commander is leading a counterattack but they probably need him back at brigade.'

The sergeant fell silent and continued to look at the lieutenant. Bit his bottom lip.

'Was there something else, sergeant?'

'Well.' The sergeant paused. 'There's an artist fella here too. Non-combatant and a bit out of his depth. Look out for him, will you? A New Zealand painter with a Scottish name. Comes from down our way and I promised his mother I'd look out for him.'

Talking was more exhausting than walking sometimes.

'McIntyre?'

'That's it, McIntyre. Might be all right one day with a name like that.' He smiled and winked. 'Otago boy.'

'Very good, sergeant,' the lieutenant said. 'But he'll end up in the North Island if he has a heart. The King Country.'

'The King Country,' Roy repeated, thinking of Billy McKay losing his feet.

'He has a heart,' Sergeant McRae said.

McRae disappeared with a small group of the Canterbury Otago men. After about ten minutes or so, more automatic fire erupted to the southeast, in the direction they had gone. Heraklion. Explosions and the noises of German machine guns. Long bursts and silence.

The sounds of a heavier gun started. The whistle-howl of artillery shells. More explosions. Somehow the Germans already had light artillery on the ground. Probably the bloody Leichtgeshütz 40 firing from a hidden position.

Roy looked at Lieutenant Ross. They recognised the deep coughing sounds of the 75 mm anti-tank gun. First heard them in Greece. The Fallschirmjäger had probably dropped them into Crete using their triple-canopy parachutes. Once assembled, loaded and aimed, the gun gave them real firepower. It was known that some of the Fallschirmjäger called it der Miststück. The bitch. Others knew the gun as Leibe Lotte.

What was left of the Canterbury Otago section they had spoken to earlier came scrambling back down the trench towards them. Covered in blood and wounds, and four of them were missing. Killed. They had stopped a major German outflanking attack but were overwhelmed by yet another body of Germans advancing from a drop zone near Retimo.

The sergeant stopped and spoke to Lieutenant Ross. 'Fair-sized German body, boss,' he said, still speaking slowly in spite of the carnage.

'Sergeant.'

'Coming in strength. Hundred-plus fighting men. Too big for us. We are pulling back to our battalion lines now. We stopped them but lost four of our blokes up there.'

He paused and looked at the ground. It was the most he had said for a long time. 'The Germans are not far behind us, boss. Get ready.'

'Righto, sergeant. Don't worry. Thanks for your help.'

The sergeant nodded, said, 'Boys,' and the Cantab Otago were gone behind him. Some of the Southlanders with them. The Blanket Boys, the Cantabrians called them. It had something to do with their rugby forwards, they said.

Roy looked around as he heard the roaring engines of British tanks. Two Matildas from the 7th Tank Regiment pushed forward in an attempt to retake the airfield. An Allied counterattack coming from brigade? Grating gear changes and a metallic clanking; moving slowly along the riverbed followed by two platoons of Scottish infantry from the 51st Highland Brigade.

A tremendous clanging and howling of German machine-gun fire ricocheting off the Matildas' steel armour. Two high-explosive Leichtgeshütz rounds hit the leading tank and its left track was unravelling, billowing white smoke, then another 75 mm shot exploded against the engine casement and the tank burst into flames.

The top turret was flung open and three of the crewmen began pulling themselves out. One of them on fire.

All three were immediately shot to pieces by the Fallschirmjäger machine-gun crews.

The other British tank had stopped and was desperately trying to reverse. Stuck, it attempted to go forward again but could not. Reversed, and that too was of no use. It was a sitting duck, all but stationary.

A fresh 75 mm round from the Leichtgeschütz hit the Matilda. The fuel tank caught alight, flames roaring from the rear engine compartment, smoke engulfing the tank.

Roy saw that at least one of the crew had emerged and was sprinting away as fast as he could.

'They look fucked to me,' someone in the section said. 'The Jocks. Look at them. They are gone, mate.'

'Steady, boys,' Lieutenant Ross yelled out to his men. 'Hold on now.' They were watching from their trenches and they became silent.

'Boys.' He waited a moment before repeating the earlier message from brigade command. 'I have orders that all 22nd Battalion men are to fall back from the Maleme airfield and from the river. Reassemble at Division Staging Point One.'

Roy looked at the lieutenant. The body of Billy McKay lay in the pool of blood where his legs had been. A groundsheet draped over his head and upper chest left the stumps of his legs showing, uncovered. The coagulated blood gleamed like red toffee.

'Leave the dead,' Lieutenant Ross said. 'Carry the wounded.'

The soldiers said nothing and began to pull back. Nodding, grim-faced, towards the lieutenant. They knew he had no choice. Covering each other, assisting the injured. Some men had their mates over their shoulders, in the fireman's carry, until they could get a stretcher for them.

Once they had retreated from the riverbed and the burnt-out tanks, the remnants of the 22nd Battalion continued making their way towards the southeast, where they knew a pass would take them over the White Mountains to Sphakia on the other side. The evacuation harbour.

After about half an hour, an Assault Pioneer section directed them to a rocky track that led into the foothills.

They had been following the track, steadily trudging up the side of the mountain, when New Zealand lead scouts reached a creek coming down from the mountain and crossing the track.

It was a perfect place to refill their canteens. The water falling down the mountainside had formed a small pool. There was a plateau of grapevines above that. A retaining wall and pond. The order was passed back. Take a ten-minute rest break in the riverbed. Resupply all canteens.

As they rested and began to re-water, Roy approached Lieutenant Ross.

'My brother, sir?'

Ross stared at him, frowned.

'He didn't follow me. I have to go back for him.'

'No, Roy,' Lieutenant Ross said after studying him for a few more seconds. 'We have to keep going. Our orders are to get over the mountain pass to Sphakia. We'll wait there for further orders, but I think it will be Greece all over again. Hopefully they'll ship us out to Egypt straight away this time. Alexandria.'

'I have to go back. He's my brother, sir.'

Lieutenant Ross nodded.

They both looked up as a Messerschmitt 109 roared over the column, seemingly out of nowhere. They recognised its shape instantly: the black short-arm crosses on both wings. It rose straight up and turned to level into a perfect strafing run above the New Zealand column. Two 20 mm rockets exploded on the sides of the track and lines of 7.92 machine-gun rounds flayed the ground around them. Plumes of white dust. Smoke lines from tracer rounds still floated along the high-sided riverbed.

Once again taking cover together.

'You do what you have to, Mitchell,' Ross shouted. They were inches apart but the noise was ferocious. 'If you must go back for your brother, you must. Jesus Christ, man.'

Roy Mitchell nodded. He looked up. The German fighter had gone, more than likely returning to base to refuel.

'We will regroup at dark somewhere near the summit and wait for orders from brigade.'

'Boss.'

'Otherwise, you can meet us over in Sphakia. We should get there day after tomorrow.'

Roy nodded again. 'Boss,' and got to his feet.

'Be careful, Roy. Don't be too long. Day after tomorrow.' He repeated himself. 'Day after tomorrow. Sphakia. You got it?'

A bottleneck had formed at the watering point of the creek. Nobody was overseeing the resupply and it had become a little crowded and chaotic. Lieutenant Ross soon restored order. The men spread out and waited their turn. Many so exhausted they simply fell asleep where they sat. Others began rolling up whatever tobacco they had and gratefully sucked the smoke into their lungs.

They had been there for about ten minutes when one of the scouts from their flanks came scrambling down from the slopes into the creek bed. 'Don't drink any more water, boys,' he hissed at them in an urgent voice. 'Bloody dead Jerries in it.'

The drinking soldiers stopped and frowned at him. One of the young men spat out his mouthful. 'What?'

'Dead Jerries in the creek. There's a bloody pond up there. Two of them caught up in the reeds.'

'Germans?'

'They can't have been able to get out of their chutes. The poor bastards.'

'Dead in the fucking water?'

'Fuck me Jesus.'

An old platoon sergeant from Alpha Company had come forward to see what the delay at the watering point was. When he saw the look on the young soldiers' faces, he quickly put his index finger up to his lips in a hushing motion.

It was Sergeant Johnny Kane. Grey hair. Bit of a limp from an old knee wound. 'Shh. Keep your voices down, boys,' he whispered. 'Calm down now.'

They looked at him.

'What's wrong?' he asked.

'Sarge,' one of the younger soldiers said. 'Campbell here said there are dead Germans in the water. And we have been drinking it.'

The sound of dry-retching.

Sergeant Kane looked at him, took the canteen from the young soldier and lifted it up to his nose. Sloshed the water about. Smelled the brim, paused and drank.

'You can taste them all right.' Still speaking in a whisper. Smacked his lips. 'Dead Germans.' Winked and sloshed the canteen again.

The younger soldiers were staring at him. There was not a hint of a smile on his face as he continued. 'They taste a bit like unsalted pork,' he said. 'If they are fresh, mind you. Anzac soup.' He made a thoughtful face as if considering the flavour. 'And boot polish.

47

Would you fuckin' believe it? Now, dead Turks in the water? They taste like cloves. Then, after a week, like fish. You know the ones? Like they been in the sun for too long. Long time no sea. Ha-ha. Squeeze the lemon juice over them to cover up the smell.'

The young soldiers continued to stare at him. One of them had let his mouth fall open.

'Now this water?' he said. 'This water tastes like holy water. Things are alive in it. Like a whore's cunt. For now, at least. So drink up while you can, boys. Anzac soup is all right.'

Most of the younger soldiers became silent, revolted by the old sergeant.

Some of them poured out their water.

Lieutenant Ross had gone forward to check on the progress of the column. He slid down into the creek bed. The OC of Support Company was helping organise what was left of the battalion.

'What's the hold-up? Sir?' he asked. 'Is there a problem?'

'Speak to the sergeant, Ross,' the OC said and hurried forward to the front of the column followed by some Assault Pioneers.

'No problem.' Sergeant Kane offered his canteen to the lieutenant. 'Drink, sir?' He did not know the officer.

'Good,' Ross said, took the canteen and drank. The younger soldiers stared him. Said nothing.

'Bit tangy.' He looked at the canteen before giving it back to the sergeant. 'We have just got word to push on over to Sphakia as quick as we can, you men. Tell the rest to fill up. It might be a while before we can water again. Look lively now.'

Kane nodded and saluted. Some of the younger soldiers were unsure what to do next.

'Come on, lads,' he said. 'Looks like you've seen a ghost.'

They were being waved forward by another group of Assault

Pioneers who had gone ahead to clear the ground of mines. They didn't seem to appreciate the well-worn infantry joke about them eating only pies made from ears.

The bulk of the New Zealand column continued climbing past some old olive trees and the stands of prickly pear which seemed to be everywhere. The hill on both sides of the track had been terraced with stone walls and the beloved grapevines were in full leaf.

The severely wounded were being carried on rough stretchers and the other injured men were being helped by their mates. No one still alive was left. Their progress was slow and they had fallen behind. Lieutenant Ross would circle back to them in support to urge them to keep going. The able-bodied men of the main column continued up the mountain. Their fully wooded .303 rifles were mostly slung. Bren guns and the bulkier Lewis gun with the water jacket had been hoisted onto shoulders. Two men carried a .50 Boyes rifle.

Once they reached a plateau just below the summit, the battalion halted and the men simply collapsed, exhausted, on the ground where they had stopped. The land fell away towards the 22nd and 28th Battalion headquarters to the west. Beyond that the 5th Brigade. They were travelling directly south and had reached the pass through the White Mountains. The soldiers slept where they lay.

After the unexpected New Zealand withdrawal from Maleme, the German commander of the airborne assault was delighted. Badly wounded during the Plantanias drop, he immediately understood that the confused retreat of the NZ 22nd Battalion from Maleme was a stroke of good fortune. What did Napoleon say about luck? Resupply from the airfield was crucial to their eventual victory. They had not even cratered the airfield before these New Zealanders ran away. Unlike their fathers, they were still children at war.

Colonel Eugen Meindl, known as Papa by his men. An old-style Imperial German officer, he was honourable and arrogant. These contradictions gave him the certainty of the Prussian. The ordinary soldiers respected him because he shared their hardships. Never shirked any danger. Any wound. Any food.

Meindl spat out a mouthful of blood and immediately ordered the occupation of the airfield. The taking of all defensive positions. This airfield was vital, but they must also take any high ground surrounding the airfield. This was essential. All soldiers know this, he said.

When he jumped, he had been shot three times by the New Zealanders, a race he had first encountered in Belgium during the first war. Tried to warn the senior commanders at OKH, Operational High Command, about the New Zealanders. Very similar men to the Australians and the Boers. They were savages, he said. They had once overrun an artillery battery he was attached to in Belgium during World War I. They shot and bayoneted everyone in sight. Even the wounded. Don't be fooled by their terror in Greece, he told them. They are adaptable. If they were anything like their fathers, they would fight back. Look out then.

On the first morning of Operation Mercury, Papa Meindl jumped with his men.

He was shot in the belly and twice in the chest before he hit the ground. The same uncivilised New Zealanders he had warned OKH about.

The Fallschirmjäger scout emerged from an olive grove on the road to Canea. Empty lengths of white rutted roads in both directions. He knelt and turned his head to one side to listen for a moment. He was good. The moving of his head as he listened was like that of an animal. He was known in German as Späher. Careful as a cat, he was almost invisible against the trees. True Späher usually belonged to old forestry families. The best German forward scouts were always Späher.

Roy watched the scout. He lay on his back on the slope above the road, his feet pointing downwards amid the tall yellow grass of the hillside, and watched every move of the German scout below him.

A sound from behind him. The whistle. Morepork. Ruru. One-two, three. A New Zealand bird call. Roy flinched. Shut up, man. He knew that any movement would immediately betray his location to the German scout on the road. He remained still.

Yet another questioning call…morepork? This time it was almost laughing at him. Asking if Roy remembered who he was.

He knew he could not refuse again, and replied with the

same call. Moved his head slowly.

Above him, another New Zealand soldier in the long grass. A corporal from the 23rd Otago Battalion. A fucking pain in the arse with his whistling ruru. Three rifles by his side. The corporal winked and pointed uphill. Made an obvious and bold show of looking back up the slope and gesturing as he did so. Inviting Roy to copy him.

The Fallschirmjäger scout immediately spotted this movement. Crouched and carefully watched the soldiers pointing uphill. Both the men had turned and were looking where he was looking. They were doing what he was doing; they must be friendlies.

He began to make cautious, beckoning hand signals to the comrades behind him. Three more Fallschirmjäger emerged into the road from the olive trees.

From the corner of his eye Roy noticed one of them raise his hand as shade and peer up the slope. He said something to the scout. Shouted alarm and pointed. Raised his MP270 machine pistol to fire.

The Otago soldier turned slightly and shot him, then used his other two rifles to shoot the remaining three Germans. Sudden and catastrophic explosions of sound. Reloading only once. It had taken no time at all and he had not missed.

Silence returned. Four dead paratroopers sprawled across the road.

Roy could see that each of them had been shot through the upper body. Chest or throat. One hit in the head. He was not wearing a helmet and it had taken the top off. An occasional spasm or nervous reflex was their only movement now. Blood pooling in the pale wheel ruts of the track.

Retaliatory gunfire erupted from the trees and bushes along the roadside cover. But it was simply cover fire and they were firing blindly. It wasn't long before the shooting stopped.

Roy and Otago did not move. They waited until there was no movement at all coming from the olive trees. The four dead German paratroopers lay in the white road. Their kneepads made them look like children.

Nothing more was said. He did not call ruru anymore.

Roy and the man he knew as Otago continued to lie unmoving in the long grass. They waited there for the remainder of the afternoon. The day faded slowly until it eventually gave way to a warm Mediterranean night. A rising westerly wind.

It had been dark for about an hour when Roy heard Otago leave. He made a faint, sliding sound as he moved through the grass on his backside. The rattle of small stones. And he was gone.

Roy lay on his back and looked at the sky. The northern moon was rising and the stars were strange: not the same as the southern sky. The Three Sisters of Orion's Belt remained. They were on his right and not his left. Like all country boys who grew up without electricity, he knew the alignments of the stars. Their changes. He saw the angle of Berenice's hair and above her the Great Bear. The unknown Lesser Bear. He missed the familiar night skies of their childhood. The nine stars, as Tony had once pointed them out to him. The dog stars and the Southern Cross. The lighthouse of home. They also knew the cycles of the moon. There was nothing else to look at. The making-up of stories after dark.

Roy waited until he felt the dampness of the night dew settling on his face and chest. He crawled to the ridge top and dropped down behind it. Skirted the base, cut around the roadside and began to make his way towards the flank of the road that led back towards Pirkos and Maleme.

There was little light and after a while he stopped behind a stone wall. Slowed his breathing and waited. Listened. Studied the dark shapes of the surrounding Cretan hills and tried to remember how they looked in the daylight. Waited as the sun rose. He could just make out the slight hollow where they had been. The listening post. The Whangamomona listening post where he had left Tony the day before. Waited as the sun rose.

Roy could see the remains of the nylon parachute still tangled in the long grass. Even the humped body of the German captain remained. Bullet holes in his chest. On his side. Black flies were already crawling over his face. The burial parties had not come for him yet. They were still fighting for the island.

He saw Tony's helmet on the ground. His rifle had been pushed, bayonet- and muzzle-first into the earth on the leading edge of the hollow. A Fallschirmjäger helmet on it. Playing cards scattered on the ground when the Germans came. Depressions in the earth where someone had knelt. Blackened lines that were sprays of blood. Wads of cotton wool stained red and black. A discarded yellow, white pad and grey shell dressing. Three bottles of water sterilising tablets. Larger coagulated pools of that deep black-red blood. A dropped MP40 magazine.

Roy continued to stare at the ground where so much had happened. Saw the impressions of several different types of boots. The drag marks of field stretchers. Unrolled bandages. The hollows made by kneeling men. Broken morphine ampoules and a small pile of vomit in the sand. And then he saw, unmistakably, his brother's foot.

He had seen this thing all of his life. Still in its boot. Shattered bones shot away. Part of a puttee, some sock and some of his ankle showing through. Black hair on it. His brother's foot. He thought of Tony putting on his rugby boots at the Raetihi showgrounds. They were playing the King Country Colts come down from Te Kuiti.

Roy sank to his knees. Put out one hand to support himself. Candlesticks. That is what they called the mucus that ran into their mouths from their noses when they were kids. Candlestick snot. You could suck it into your mouth and it was sweet. Like pus.

Tony could run faster than him. He would sometimes even let him win and pretend he hadn't as they raced past the toi-toi bushes and mahoe to the swing bridge.

He couldn't do that now, though. Run. Or beat Roy. Not without that foot. He would have to hop. It looked like someone had tossed it over there in the long grass to be out of the way.

Roy was unable to move for a bit. Then he leaned over, his head about to touch the ground. Weeping.

The ghost of Tony was bending his arm up his back as they fought. Reluctant yet triumphant, just like the marble statue they had once seen in an art gallery Tony insisted they visit. The Wrestlers. Roy snorted that they looked like they wanted to fuck each other. The pair of them. Wrestling naked like that. But Tony had said it was a very beautiful thing. He had wondered aloud if they were also brothers and laughed at Roy walking out and saying he had just about heard enough for one day.

Roy buried his brother's foot as the sun continued to rise in the sky and then he placed a stone on it. It was like a headstone, he thought. He was still weeping as he said aloud it is not a headstone, it's a fucking footstone. Would you laugh at that, Tony? Oh Jesus I don't know what else to say. But I will beat you in a race to the swing bridge now. You will have to hop.

They had been playing two-handed euchre when the paratroopers came. He looked over at the dead German officer they had shot and looted. The sounds of flies buzzing in and out of him. The bastard with the binoculars and photos of Klara asking him to never forget her. Drachma in his pockets to buy what? Those terrible flies sounded like a newspaper being shaken out and read and shaken out again. That rattle. His carcass had begun to stink.

Roy didn't know how long he sat there looking at where he had buried Tony's foot. It must have been about half an hour. He closed his eyes for a moment and shook his head. There was no use staying on. He knew Tony would never have survived such a wound. He must be dead.

He crawled out of the listening post and continued along the side of a narrow ridge until he could see down onto the Maleme airfield itself. The Germans had taken the field and the constant comings and goings on the runway were like a kicked-over wasp nest. Ground marshals and support crews everywhere. The JU 52s landing with more men, weapons and supplies. The mountain troops: Der Gebirgsjäger of the 109th Assault Battalion disembarking from the transport planes. On another runway, Heinkel bombers were landing to be refuelled. The Stuka JU 87s. Bf 109s with their yellow noses lining up to take off.

He could see the Maleme airfield boundaries being further secured by Luftwaffe ground crews. Fresh, luminescent lines being painted onto runways for night operations. Flags and posts, boards with numbers. Squads of soldiers digging gun pits and communication trenches. More concertina wire being walked into position along the eastern perimeter. Minelaying teams at work. Bare-chested surveyors with theodolites and measuring staffs. Dark glasses and rubber straps around shaven heads shining with sweat. Platoons of soldiers assembling in ranks behind the surveyors.

Yet more JU 52s had landed and BMW motorbikes with sidecars and MG34 machine guns were being unloaded from the rear of the planes. Batteries of light field artillery.

'What do you plan to do, Taranaki?'

That same half-whispered voice of Otago behind him. He must have crawled right past Roy in the night; would have watched him as he did it and must have seen his grief over Tony. Never said a word before these. Repeated them now.

'Eh, Taranaki? What do you plan to do?'

Otago was so well hidden as to be almost invisible among the rocks on the hillside. Among the bushes and long grass. The stands of prickly pear. He only moved when the wind moved.

'I was looking for my brother,' Roy said.

'Your brother, Taranaki?'

'I lost him yesterday morning.'

'You did?'

'Yes,' Roy said. 'I did.'

A pause, and then he said, 'Me too.'

Roy didn't know what else to say.

In the late afternoon, the wind became stronger. It turned onshore and Roy could see the small white-crested waves in the Aegean. He did not remember running away from the listening post but he knew he must have.

Roy waited and continued to watch the airfield as night fell. Floodlights came on along the Maleme runway. The German planes were constantly landing and taking off through the night. Spotlights crossing the black and cloudy sky above them. His eyes were becoming heavy. It had been a long and terrible day.

When he woke, it was just before dawn. A cold wind coming up from the east. The rising sun making a washed colour above the central Cretan mountains. It was still dark in the shadows of the land below him.

A faint, unmistakable sound began rising up to him. It was coming from the southeast: the Maleme airfield. A rhythm of haka. The Ruamoko cadence. The growing voices of young men joining and speaking separately and as one…Laughing: Ahh…ha ha. George. A most ancient Ngati Porou call. Their voices asking for your head.

There was no mistaking it. It was overwhelmingly the men of Nga Kaupoi, of the 28th, C Company. They were being led by Awatere in the rain. That was all that needed to be said. It was not raining. Their haka before going into battle. It was something to hear all right. There on Crete. He began to see more clearly the area where the troops from C Company of the 28th had assembled prior to the assault. A bit of flat ground covered with olive trees.

They were going to go for the airfield itself. An impossible task, to retake the airfield. They must have known they were going to die.

Jesus Christ. They were attacking.

'Look out,' Roy breathed as he saw a body of young men leap to their feet with fixed bayonets and charge a machine-gun position near the airfield. They had not hesitated. At the same time, another group of about thirty men, also C Company, ran straight at the German entrenchments in an almost suicidal attack. A third section on the left flank also attacked with fixed bayonets. A simultaneous three-pronged attack against dug-in positions. More men from the 28th had made their way forward and were preparing to follow up the attack if called upon. The Rotorua men: the Penny Divers, Ng Ruku Kapa, supported them. No one hesitated.

Roy and Otago could see how they ran at the enemy.

This counterattack had been needed twelve hours earlier. It was the commanders' fault, but they did not seem to care about that. They would not have lost the airfield at Maleme if the 28th had been deployed earlier. They were being slaughtered now. Their suicidal bravery, even in the words of the Fallschirmjäger, who were given to Prussian understatement in such matters, was remarkable. Uncomplaining and without hesitation.

Roy could see how they were being engulfed in a series of explosions and raking machine-gun fire. Clouds of smoke and shell bursts.

'They are being wiped out,' Otago whispered. 'Jesus.'

The dust cleared after the first terrible salvo and Roy saw what looked like pieces of khaki-coloured sacking scattered on the field. The remaining men had gone to ground in the devastation of the German fire. Many of them torn apart. Terribly killed.

He heard their voices coming up on the wind. They were calling to the others to remain strong and fall back. The voices of his childhood. Get out of the lines of fire. Roy saw two men leap up and run to retrieve one of their wounded comrades. Another was holding his mate around the waist. Trying to walk him back. It was no use and Roy saw how they were shot down. The German machine guns did not stop.

Light artillery shells also began exploding among the attacking soldiers. The fire was being walked in. Expertly directed.

What was left of the assault force had begun falling back. More soldiers from battalion HQ had come forward and formed a staggered cover line for them in retreat. Bren guns were once again pushed out to both flanks as they fell back to join the remnants of the battalion. They were being massacred.

'Oh no,' Otago said. 'No, no.' He had just seen some movement on a nearby ridge.

Almost directly across from them, separated by a deep gully and partially concealed behind some rocks, German fire control officers. One of them was looking through binoculars towards the charging New Zealanders and speaking into a radio mouthpiece. The other was bent over a map. What looked like a protractor in one hand, a range finder in the other. Calling map coordinates and distances out to his partner.

'Do you see them?' Roy whispered.

'I do,' Otago replied.

Roy watched Otago disappear into the gully and come up below the German observation post. He had moved quickly. Almost like a mustering dog through the bush.

'Bitte. Kameraden,' Roy heard Otago call out. 'Bitte. Kameraden.'

The two Germans stopped what they were doing. Exchanged glances and stood up. Looked down towards where that voice was pleading with them in such heavily accented German. Please. Comrades. Please.

61

They peered over their camouflaged stone parapet. Otago shot them both through the head.

The mortar fire stuttered and ceased.

More Allied troops were coming up from the 5th Brigade, being pushed forward and assembled into a staging area. This initially caused a terrible confusion as the men from C Company had not expected reinforcements.

Roy watched as the Wehrmacht Mountain Troops crossed the runway of Maleme. Der Gebirgsjäger of the 109th Assault Battalion, responding to the earlier attack by the 28th Battalion. The mortar fire. They formed into section-sized groups and began a fighting advance beyond the airfield wire. Went to ground and continued to pour a withering fire at their enemy, forcing the New Zealanders to abandon any thoughts of further attacks and continue their withdrawal.

Brigade orders were being passed down to all battalions and companies: immediate evacuation from the island of all Allied troops.

'You better get back to your unit, Taranaki,' Otago said to him from where he was lying. 'They might need you. It looks like they are pulling back. You better get back too.'

'What about you?' Roy asked.

'I'll be down in a bit.'

'You not finished?'

'No.'

'You all right mate?'

'Yeah. I'm all right,' Otago said.

Roy waited.

'Go on now, Taranaki.' Otago gave out the morepork whistle to farewell him.

'See you.' Roy smiled and slid back down the hill.

No reply.

Roy descended to the track that led to Galatos and began walking as fast as he could in the direction where he thought the remnants of his unit might be.

The track, broken by streams in many places, became narrow and rocky as it led into the White Mountains. He began to climb and felt it becoming colder. Lieutenant Ross had told him they would try to get over to the other side of the mountains. Sphakia, he had said.

It was about another half an hour before he encountered a Fallschirmjäger patrol in the foothills.

He heard them speaking to each other before he saw them, and dropped down off the track to take cover behind some boulders. The Fallschirmjäger confidence of talking aloud while on patrol was unusual. Almost all of them were carrying 9 mm MP40s, their light machine pistol. One of them was carrying the MG34 Spandau machine gun over his shoulder. No mistaking their battledress smocks and kneepads. Three or four grenades pushed into their belts. Light packs and extra bandoliers of ammunition crisscrossed over their chests. He watched as they turned to go downhill.

He waited another fifteen minutes before he emerged from behind the boulders and continued up the track. As he climbed, he began to see discarded packs and British helmets. Blankets and wooden crates. Empty magazines abandoned beside the track. The detritus of a retreating army. It also confirmed he was on the right path. Three corpses were rolled in groundsheets and abandoned by the track, partially covered with rocks. Flies buzzed up from them as he passed.

He kept climbing until it became dark. He was alone and did not light a fire, simply lay down beside a stone wall and slept. Somehow he remembered an old Methodist dictum that the truest of paths always leads through mountains. Another saying that it is a long road that has no turning.

The next morning, he rose and ate a handful of dried fruit, some squares of saved chocolate and half a biscuit. The last of his rations. He drank the last of the water in his canteen.

Fingers of light as the sun began coming up above the eastern ridge of the island. After a few moments, Roy continued climbing. It was midmorning before he crossed through the pass and began to descend towards the fishing village on the coast.

He reached the outskirts of Sphakia around midday. A Kapiti platoon occupied the forward positions. Two Bren guns had been set up on both sides of the road. As usual, the heavy Vickers .303 with its water-cooled barrel was located above them.

'Who goes there?' the forward sentry yelled out.

Roy threw himself to the ground as a burst of machine-gun fire ripped overhead. Firing even as they challenged him. Jesus, the murderous Kapiti bastards.

'Who is it?'

'Roy Mitchell here. Taranaki Company. Stop shooting.'

'Prove it,' came the reply.

'What?'

Silence. Then: 'Fucking prove it.'

'I don't know what you mean.'

'Say a mountain.'

'What?'

'Like Ruapehu,' the Kapiti sentry called out, 'you bloody clown. Ruapehu. Tongariro. What's the other one?'

'Fucked if I know,' Roy said.

'Ngauruhoe,' another voice sighed. 'Jesus, Taranaki.'

'What?' Roy yelled back.

Another burst of Bren-gun fire over his head.

'What are they?' A third voice from the Kapiti position.

'Mountains,' Roy said. 'They are mountains.'

'Who you with again?'

'Taranaki. Wellington. The 22nd. Like you.'

There was yet another pause before Roy heard someone laugh. 'Fuckin' Taranaki cow cockies.'

'Come on, then.'

Roy stood up and ran into the New Zealand perimeter.

Men from the 6th Wellington were lying in reserve. They were backing up the Kapiti boys. One of them winked to him as he passed. Called out, 'More bloody stragglers from the Taranaki platoon. Can you smell cow shit on his boots, Trevor? I can.'

Roy smiled. Old rugby taunts to be laughed at.

'Your lot's back there in the village.' One of the Kapiti boys pointed behind himself in the direction of the streets. 'Down by the beach I think. The jetty.'

An explosion rocked one of the buildings. The Germans had begun shelling them again. 'Keep going, son,' the man called. 'Keep going.'

Roy immediately ducked and kept moving along one side of the street. Crossed another bomb crater and kept running. Taking cover from the German fire. Staggering at times through the rubble-filled streets.

He kept moving until he eventually found what was left of his section near the wharf. They had taken over an area one street back from the water's edge, behind the remnants of what looked like a textile shop. Multicoloured bolts of cloth had been ripped apart and lay around everywhere. Lengths of blue wool. Outside the shop, a streetlamp was festooned with long dark-purple ribbons. Next to that, a devastated restaurant. Burnt timbers fallen into the street. A white and blue sign in Greek. Doors askew and a collapsed wall panel.

Lieutenant Ross was sitting at a dust-covered outdoor table near the front door. Staring off into the distance as if he was a million miles away. He was surrounded by shredded umbrellas and bolts of cloth. A bottle of Ouzo and a glass before him. A white pack of English cigarettes. Senior Service. A brass ashtray. Silver Fern wax matches.

'Boss,' Roy called out to him.

He looked up. 'Private Mitchell?' Smiled. 'Good to see you. Take a seat. Drink? How did you get on with your brother?' It was as if he was back in New Zealand. Afternoon smoko with the shearers. He pointed to the bottle of ouzo.

'No sir. Thank you.' Roy sat down.

'Aniseed flavour,' Lieutenant Ross said. 'The ouzo. I don't think I have ever tried it before.'

Roy rested the front sight of his rifle back onto his chest. Waited. The lieutenant was drinking one glass after the other and chain-smoking.

Roy watched him lighting a new cigarette off the one he had just finished. Some of the men called this fucking the monkey.

He had big, capable hands, Lieutenant Ross. They were not shaking. He had believed in God once, took his mother to the

66

Anglican church in Kai Iwi every Sunday and they sang hymns together. Not everyone can kill another human being up close when it comes to it. Few could, apart from Sister.

'Did you find your brother?' he repeated as he smoked.

'No sir. I did not.' He would never speak of finding and burying Tony's foot.

'No?' Lieutenant Ross looked at him. 'You better go and find the rest of your mates, then.' He drank another glass of ouzo.

'Boss.'

'They'll be somewhere back there, I think. Back of the bloody shop back there. Fucking mess everywhere.'

'Boss.' He had wanted to use his first name, but did not. He had known who he was before the war.

Roy stood and turned to go.

'Oh, Mitchell.'

Roy stopped and turned back to him.

'We have to prepare for evacuation by sea when the rearguard comes in. The remnants of 14 Platoon. Tomorrow morning, from what I can gather.'

'Boss.'

Roy found the front door to the smashed textile shop. Ribbons of cloth hanging everywhere. He entered and crossed into the rear cooking area: what had once been the kitchen of a restaurant. The first thing he noticed was a small fire burning against a brick wall. Smashed-up furniture thrown into a corner ready to be used as firewood. Ten naked chicken carcasses hanging from five bayonet handles pushed between the bricks of the wall. Their feet tied with green and blue communication wire. Two per bayonet. No heads.

A tripod of metal rods had been arranged above the fire. A row of opened tins alongside a cooking pot. Two loaves of flat bread and cannisters of German coffee. Another filled with stolen cognac.

Bert Sutton had taken over the cooking duties for now and was stirring the pot. Potatoes, carrots and celery. Some red lentils and barley they had found in the restaurant's storeroom. He said he would chop up the chickens and add them later. Boil them all together and you can't go wrong. Handful of salt.

Someone had said, you are a fucking useless cook and should stop doing it, you cunt.

Bert splashed some cognac into the pot and took a swig himself. Shuddered. Jesus.

Someone had placed an upturned British helmet full of eggs near the fire.

'All right,' he said. 'All right.' Took another swig of the cognac.

Roy heard his own boots crunching as he entered the kitchen. The men stopped what they were doing and looked at him.

'Roy,' Ken Corbett said.

'Ken.'

They were all staring back at him. No one wanted to ask about Tony. After another minute of silence, Ken cleared his throat. 'You hungry, mate?'

'Who called the cook a cunt?' Peter Clarkson yelled, and the rest of the section chorused: 'Who called the cunt a cook?' Even the men whose eyes were closed. Repeating together the refrain, the stupid and yet adored lines.

'To me, boys.' The alarmed voice of Lieutenant Ross rang out suddenly from the road. 'Five Platoon.'

The half-sleeping men woke instantly and leapt up. Grabbed their rifles, machine guns and grenades. Ran through the textile shop into the street beside the bombed-out restaurant. Some still in their socks.

Lieutenant Ross was standing in the street next to the table where he had been drinking ouzo. He drew his revolver, cocked it and pointed it at the approaching soldiers. Quite sober now.

'You there,' he yelled at the three men coming towards them. 'What are you doing?'

Two New Zealand soldiers from the 28th Battalion were bringing in a Fallschirmjäger prisoner.

The German's left ear was badly torn. He was not wearing a helmet and one hand was wrapped in a rough white bandage. His collar and shoulder were drenched in blood and both eyes had been punched black. His nose was broken. Blood smeared across his cheek. His blond hair was also matted with blood and filth, clumps of it torn out.

They had brought him in after a sweep. One of them, an unsmiling Nga Puhi man, name of Hohepa. A Mowera boy was still holding the German's epaulet as he spoke. They were from the Northland Company of the 28th Battalion. The Gum Diggers. Te Nga Kiri Kapia.

They stopped about six feet from the lieutenant. He lowered his revolver.

'He thinks he is a bit special, this pakeha,' Hohepa said. 'I can finish him up if you want, boss.'

Hohepa was holding an American .45 automatic pistol in his right hand, cocked. Pointed at the ground. God knew where he'd got it.

They watched as the German paratrooper drew himself

to attention and raised his chin. Tried to click his heels as he addressed them. 'I speak English.'

What was left of the platoon had gathered behind Lieutenant Ross. They all stared at the tall German. The swollen face, broken nose; the blood and the torn ear.

'I speak English and I demand your immediate and unconditional surrender.'

'See,' Hohepa said, 'he told us this when we first grabbed him. Said we should surrender to him. So I told him say that again, pakeha, and he said it again.'

'And?' Lieutenant Ross asked.

'Well, we gave him a hiding then,' Hohepa said.

'Is that how he got the black eyes?'

'Yep. Well, he fell over too.'

'Did he say anything else?'

'He reckons that they can never be beaten and would die for victory and their Führer.'

'They do?'

'I told you. I speak English. You must give up now. Surrender to us.' The German said, interrupting with some pride.

'See?' Hohepa said. 'This pakeha.'

'We would die for our leader,' the Fallschirmjäger prisoner said.

'All right then.' Roy raised his rifle and shot the German between the eyes. 'You fucking arrogant prick. How dare you say that to us?'

Lieutenant Ross ducked and turned. Pushed Roy's rifle up. 'What the hell are you doing, Mitchell?'

Roy stepped around the outraged lieutenant and stood over the fallen German. Shot him again in the head. Worked the bolt and reloaded automatically.

'Sorry, boss. I thought he was going to escape.'

The dead man's boots were making small furrows in the sand as he died. Two blue-black holes between his eyes. Brain tissue oozing from his skull. The colour of human brains exposed is like freshly caught octopus on the dock.

'As you were,' the lieutenant said softly. He was white-faced, staring from Roy to the body and back. The dead German who had been demanding their surrender. Proud of his ability to speak English.

'No fuckin' chance of that,' Manny whispered from among the group of soldiers.

Someone threw a sheet of corrugated iron over the body. Then another, as the first one didn't cover him properly. Three or four bricks crashed on top. Weights to keep the iron sheets in place.

Bert cleared his throat. 'Come on boys. That soup must be close.'

He turned and walked back into the wreckage of the building they had emerged from a few minutes earlier. Roy joined the other soldiers as they followed him, grumbling about his cooking.

Lieutenant Ross found the chair and table where he had been drinking ouzo. He sat, and lit another cigarette.

The two Nga Puhi boys who had brought the German in stared at the convulsing body for a moment. Then at Roy. Stepped away, turned and began walking back towards their lines.

'Ka pai? You good?' Hohepa said to the other man who just shrugged, looked away and kept walking. Nodded in the rough direction of their company position.

As the sun went down that evening, Roy and the remnants of the Taranaki Company made their way from the bombed-out textile shop to the designated evacuation points on the Sphakia beachfront.

They formed up, remaining one street back from the water's edge until called forward by the battalion guides into what they called staging points. No smoking, no talking. Stand by and stay alert for any immediate or alternate action. Military order.

At midnight, Royal Navy motorboats slipped quietly into the Sphakia bay and stood off about a hundred yards from shore. Shut down all motors and rode the tide in the Mediterranean darkness. Waiting.

After about an hour, torch signals began flashing to the waiting men onshore. The motorboats started up almost as one and all made soft idling sounds in the rising tide. The British fleet had radioed back from Gibraltar to commence the evacuation.

At the water's edge, more whispered orders, directions and encouragement. The launches could not come in any closer to the beach due to the high, sandy bottom and they had avoided any existing loading docks. It was believed they would be targeted by the Germans.

Up to their chests in the warm salt water, rifles held above their heads, they waded out to the motorboats, and were pulled aboard by sailors with English accents. Saying things like there you are, son, wee lad, and you are wet as a fucking shag, mate.

The British sailors gave them mugs of cocoa, slices of bread and butter and marmalade. Blankets. Pats on the back. Roy thought some of them spoke like his grandfather had, that same English accent. Called him lad.

Tony was still unconscious when they carried him to the casualty clearing station at the southern end of the Maleme airfield.

He awoke in an enormous aircraft hangar. Two football fields long and another wide, filled with wounded men. The concrete floor, painted with numbers and lines, smelled of oil and fresh paint. Petrol. He was lying on a field stretcher with a Luftwaffe blanket draped over him. There were no planes.

Occasional spikes of agony coming back to his leg. The morphine the medic had given him was easing.

Other wounded men were being laid out around and either side of him, narrow walking spaces established between each of the rows. Hospital stands with saline and blood drips, lines of rubber tubing, medicine trays mingling with the industrial smells of chlorine and ether. A strong faecal smell of exposed intestines and bowels. Pools of blood and vomit on the cement floor. The occasional slap of buckets of water being thrown on the mess. Sweeping sounds.

Some of the soldiers were groaning, others yelling in pain. Cursing. Still more were silent or drugged into sleep.

In the distance, constant machine-gun fire. Explosions and the tremendous roaring of planes. Black smoke rising.

Tony tried to remain as still as possible to minimise the growing pain in his leg. It soon became impossible to think of anything else and he put his hand across his mouth so as not to cry out. Heard their father saying to him and Roy: hold on. Him, of all people. The coward father who could not speak without weeping. He could taste blood in his mouth.

A group of German medical staff were moving towards him. Leading them, a young triage doctor wearing a white coat over his grey and black Wehrmacht uniform. No cap. Shiny black hair. A stethoscope around his neck. He carried a torch in one hand and a steel rule in the other.

This frowning doctor was making terrible, necessary choices for each of the wounded men. As he spoke, an assistant was writing down what he said in a large notepad. Suggested treatment: medicines and options.

Another orderly wrote a corresponding number on a tag and tied that to the big toe of the wounded.

If the toes were gone, or both feet or the legs, he tied the tag to the handle of the stretcher they were lying on.

When they reached Tony, the doctor greeted him with a formal nod. Picked up a clipboard and read the notes the sanis orderly and the combat medic had made. Watched the agony playing across Tony's face.

He saw how he had ruined his own hand. Someone lifted the blanket and cut away the remaining dressings. Removed the temporary field splint. The doctor shone the torch on what was left of his leg. Nodded. Looked at the notes the field medic had written on the tag. Nodded again. Gave an order to the assistants.

Reached down and took Tony's hand from his mouth. Held it for a moment. This was unusual; the orderlies looked at each other.

Tony was lifted and carried into an area of the hangar where an operating theatre had been set up. White screens. Bright, pulsing overhead lights and generators. Transferred onto an operating table, a needle inserted into his arm and a black rubber mask placed over his mouth and nose. He felt the cold hissing of chloroform and heard the question in English. Your name? Your mother's name? The year she was born and to count back down from ten. Past six, nothing.

The German surgeon then amputated what was left of Tony's shattered leg at the knee. It was better there. More likely to heal. Cutting through the cartilage and ligament of the knee was quicker than through bone. Did not need the saw anywhere near as much.

The surgeon would carry out ninety-five amputations that first Wednesday the 21st of May 1941. One hundred and six the following day.

Before the war, it was rare to have more than three a week in the Central Berlin hospital where he had done his internship.

The anxiously awaited rearguard of the 22nd Battalion NZEF reached Sphakia before first light the following morning. They were all that were left of those who had been covering the battalion's retreat over the mountain.

As they entered the fishing village, it was still dark. The sounds of small waves breaking along a pier wall. Guided by the lines of white tape laid out by the Assault Pioneers, they were taken to the evacuation beach and ferried out to the waiting troopships. The convoy got under way as soon as they could and the ship's hastily turning screws curled up phosphorus from the sea bed. A green-yellow trail that followed them across the Mediterranean towards Egypt. Africa was not far away.

At daybreak the following morning Roy could smell Alexandria well before they landed. The septic tanks of the ancient city had been constructed to wash directly into the sea along with household rubbish simply thrown into the waves. Easy and convenient, with the ever-cleansing ocean. The refuse and waste floated out for a mile and surrounded them.

The city seemed to emerge from the great body of land behind her. All gold and purple shadows. Smelling of shit. Of rotting fruit. Dead animals in the street stalls. Tall minarets, great mosque domes and wide avenues of palm trees. Trading houses and jacaranda trees. Floating in the air between the sea and, as all true believers said, Paradise. Alexandria became Alexandria.

The ship's engines stopped and the Royal Navy destroyer *Fiji* slowed in the water. Her decks were crawling with soldiers and she glided gently towards her berth in the Victoria Docks. Royal Navy tugs came alongside to help push the troopship into the disembarkation wharf.

Market boats had also come alongside to greet her and the troops were leaning over the sides. The traders below holding up baskets of fresh fruit. Fish. Chickens tied by their feet. Bags of citrus fruits.

Some of the prostitutes of Alexandria had also come out. Paid for rides on the fruit and vegetable boats. Many showed their breasts to the sailors while standing on boxes of lemons and oranges. Some also lifted their skirts, turned and bent over to expose their backsides. Pulling apart their buttocks and smiling back at the soldiers as they did this.

A naval motor launch arrived. It was flying the British Ensign and an English marine officer stood on the prow. He was holding a bullhorn and dressed in parade blues. A white pith helmet held firmly in place by the marine chinstrap. He raised the bullhorn to his mouth and began speaking to the traders in fluent Arabic. At first, he adopted a conciliatory, almost obsequious tone and seemed to be appealing to their better natures. He was trying to explain how their presence was impeding the progress of the ship into the harbour and its successful docking. As he spoke he also paid respect to Allah and His prophet Muhammad, called for peace and blessings to be upon him.

The bartering merchants simply ignored him. Some told him in Arabic to go fuck his mother. His sister also. And that he resembled a camel's limp penis anyway, after it had fucked his mother. They seemed to forget he understood their language. Simply continued to ply their trade with the smiling soldiers and sailors leaning over the ship rails.

The British officer fell silent. He looked for a moment as if he might burst into tears and then he nodded and dropped the bullhorn onto the deck. Opened his eyes and took the issue Webley .45 revolver from the blancoed holster at his belt. Fired into the air. Once and then again. A third time for authority. Held the pistol up still, blew a whistle and shouted again at the boat traders in English. They were to do exactly as they were fucking well told, do I make myself clear, you wog cunts? Do exactly what I tell you to do or I will kill you. His transformation from a reasonable young man a little out of his depth, appealing to their decency, into a murderous colonial monster had taken about four minutes.

The boat merchants stopped what they were doing when a shot rang out. Then a second. Looked again at the British officer with the smoking pistol in his hand. The third shot. They began hastily to work at the sweeping oars at the stern of their boats. Terrified to get away as quickly as they could. They had seen this English thing at work before. When they began to swear at you, they might well kill you soon after.

The traders did not look back. They had also learnt that by looking back, you invited attention from the British Army, and this usually involved being shot at.

The troops on board the destroyer began laughing and booing.

It was another hour before the ship docked and the troops began to disembark. It was a slow process. Having made their laborious way down the gangplank, the men gathered into unorganised groups along Victoria Dock. Thronging together. Many of them limping. A few carried captured German weapons as well as their own. Most still wore filthy battledress from the fighting on Crete, torn and stained. Many carried packs filled with extra ammunition, stolen loaves of bread, bottles of wine. They were unshaven and dirty-looking. Some of them had superficial wounds and field dressings wrapped around legs and wrists. Small clouds of smoke from those groups that were lucky enough to have cigarettes.

Different units had become intermingled during the evacuation. What remained of the infantry often stood with gunners and engineers. An Australian Bofors crew. Resupply people, drivers. Ordnance. What Manny called the fuckin' blanket counters. Some Royal Marines and Welsh Fusiliers. Jocks from the Black Watch.

On a large flat area that had been used to stack four-gallon tins of petrol, a regimental sergeant major from the 51st Highlanders stood up on the tray of a Chevrolet truck.

An impressive-looking man. Well over six feet tall. Large red moustache. Heavily tattooed arms and hands resting on kilted hips. He raised his chin as he shouted out to the crowd of men.

'Now listen to me, wee laddies,' he bellowed. Fearless.

The great moving throng stopped and fell silent.

'Come here to me now, ye shower of shite. I'll tell ye what we'll do.'

There was a certain respect in his voice even as he bellowed. 'Get into three ranks, for a start. Heels together now and get yer wee chins up. Have some pride in who ye are, now.'

79

The sar'major cleared his throat. 'Hands by your sides. Thumbs along trooser seams. Aye, very good. That's the way.'

He began to assemble the men into their respective military units. It started with their countries of origin: Australians, Brits, Jocks, Indians, South Africans.

When he called out New Zealanders now, some of the 9th Div Australian boys made baaing noises and a broad Queensland accent shouted out, 'How many sheep did you shag last night, Kiwi? You find any in the hills up there? You blokes like to root sheep, don't you?'

Silence descended over the crowd. Some of the New Zealand men gripped their hands into fists.

After a while—it had only been a few seconds but it felt longer—one of the Kiwis spoke up. 'Sheep are easy, mate.' The voice came with that slow, back-country New Zealand drawl. 'What I'd like to know is how you Aussie blokes get on with the kangaroos, bouncing around like that. They any good?'

After another gaping silence, a wave of laughter swept through the Aussies, led by the Queenslander. The 9th Div boys in particular seemed to appreciate the joke.

Tony was woken by the sun coming through the open doorway of a warehouse on the dock at Suda Bay. Screeching gulls and the sound of the ocean washing against the pier. Small waves slapping beneath them. Waterside workers yelling to each other. The Italian hospital ship *Pietro Badoglio* alongside the wharf. The wounded men had been laid out on stretchers and in lines waiting to be carried up the gangplank of the ship.

The freighter pressed against the wharf. Creaking ropes and somewhere the *whoop-whoop* of another vessel. You could smell the sea water. Crushed shellfish. The wind coming up through the pier.

He did not know how long he had been sleeping. It could have been a whole day. Two. He did not even remember coming here from Maleme, let alone the operation.

He looked down at where his left leg had been. Gone now, from the knee down. Remembered being hit by the bullets. How it felt like a madman chopping at his ankle with an axe. Numb from the blows at first. That rapid German machine-gun fire.

The black smoke over the port had grown huge.

He and Roy had been playing cards the morning of the attack.

The JU 52 engines became louder and louder as they approached, he remembered that, and the sky filling with parachutes. Roy dropping his cards and grabbing his rifle.

He saw the impact of his brother's first shot as it hit the German captain. How it spun him in the air. Roy reloading. And how, with the second shot, he hit him in the middle of his chest. His brother was a good shot, no doubt about that. Blew out the German's heart. Dead before he hit the ground.

They stole everything he had and Roy seemed to prize the binoculars above all else. Zeiss. He said he could see for fucking miles with them.

Tony lay back on the stretcher and waited for his turn to be carried onto the transport.

They, him and Roy, had grown up in shearing sheds and slaughterhouses where the men cut out animal hearts on half-dark mornings. Scored and uncooked. Eaten raw.

He thought about the many men who had lost a leg in the first war. Known as Hoppy and scolded to hurry up. Given carved walking sticks, treasured gifts, wet with tears.

Tony lay back and closed his eyes. People telling the one-legged men to bloody hurry up. To rattle their dags. Waiting for them. I don't care how hard you are trying. Just do the fuckin' job, Hoppy, or hop off. On your crutch, mate.

He would be able to ask the bootmaker for a discount now.

Tony barely remembered the rushing retreat through Greece. Just Crete, where he was shot to bits. Roy would be upset. He would worry. But mostly he would begin to berate himself for running away. He should not, but how can you tell someone you love not to do things? Best to be quiet and accept them for who they are.

He thought a lot about David. The others in the section had begun to call him Sister because he did not act like them. They called him Sister because he covered his penis with his hands in the communal showers. Because he said grace, gave thanks before eating food in the mess tents.

He remembered David, Sister, saying to Manny that grace before a meal was an act of humility of self, not of obedience. The consideration of others before yourself, Manny. Also, never to forget that the word itself, humility, came from the Latin humus, which means earth. It is where our food comes from and therefore where we come from. Return to. Who we are. The earth. A humble person is, by definition, a down-to-earth person. It was no wonder Tony loved him.

'Sister,' Manny had replied. 'You are a fucking cunt.'

'Manny.'

Silence. David nodding.

Manny did not know what to say. He waited for another moment before repeating himself. 'Sister, you are a fucking cunt.'

Two Italian stevedores picked up his stretcher and moved him to the entrance of the warehouse. Still in an angle of shade, thankfully, now soon to be taken aboard.

Tony remembered that once David had put his hand on his shoulder. He let it rest there as they talked and began to fall in love.

Tony spoke to him of their father, who had been considered by most as a damaged and pathetic man. And how he had loved him more for that. His failings. He was mad, after all. Incoherent most of the time. Once he said that kindness and decency were the holiest of the ghosts that come tapping at windows on windy nights wanting to be let in. Like memories and cabbage trees. And nobody knew what he was talking about except Tony, it seemed, who was laughing.

He had told David that he often saw mothers hanging out their dead sons' washing on wet days and weeping at the same time. Wooden pegs in their mouths. Who would see such a thing? Mothers hanging out their dead sons' washing?

He had also whispered to David as they kissed, tentatively, that he dreamed of becoming a painter. An artist like Rita Angus. He would never have told anyone else this. It was impossible. Even Roy. Especially Roy.

That same secret seeing was, for Tony, the curved-beaked ibis flying above the Nile's width. The muscular strength of them above the wide river. Roy would have said it's a fuckin' river, Tony. The Nile. Why do you want to paint the thing? If you fall into it you need to be inoculated for a thousand diseases before breakfast.

David said that he believed Tony was an artist now and he had always been so. Smiled when he said that and kissed him back. They had felt the softness and muscularity of the other's lips.

The old people would say: it's not an arm or a leg, when they wanted to say life is bearable. Not to be taken seriously. It seemed funny at the time. Don't worry: it's not an arm or a leg.

It was still another hour before he heard the *slap-slap* of bare feet approaching. Then the sensation of the stretcher rising, lifted by dock workers seemingly oblivious of him, of what they were carrying, as they continued calling out to each other. Speaking among themselves. Strong suntanned arms. Black hair. Bare feet. Sometimes mock outrage and shouted insults as they waited. The most natural laughter. Approaching officials. It was a long time getting up the gangplank.

Once on board, the wounded were laid out on the rear deck. Some care was taken setting them down and often simple prayers were recited for them by the stevedores as they walked off. Everybody knew there was no holy water on the docks.

The badly wounded were mostly silent. Occasional cries of pain. A groan or two and some cursing.

The medics had rigged up rough shade on the exposed deck. An old sail and some tarpaulins. They knew about half of the wounded soldiers would be dead by the next morning. Buried at sea by midday. Best before it got too hot. The smell. Tony's amputated leg seemed heavy and had become hot. It was gone, he knew that.

He was drifting. The morphine lifted the pain away. The unfairness. What a word. Morphine. In the Greek campaign, the white dust had settled on everything as they walked south. Mostly running, backs turned, but they didn't say that. Oracles and philosophers at every bend of the road. The acrobatic whores wanting to make sense of what had happened. Why is a horse a horse and not a duck? Captain Davin asked him that. Aristotle told us why. The him and her of their existence. He would never tell the others of his memories and imaginations being as they were. But what should be.

The morphine had almost completely taken him and in that place between falling asleep and being awake he was again learning to swim in a stream called the Mangawhero. Touching the stony bottom with his toes. How could you be anything else but what you have become?

I am nothing and now I am less than that. I only have one leg.

I will sing a different tune now. I had my leg shot off on Crete. My brother believes I am dead.

Sister had told him he learned to swim in the Huatoki. Wading out, lying back, closing his eyes and allowing the water to take him to the ocean. The rivers, they all began somewhere up the mountain. Te maunga Taranaki. The head. Hua. There were twenty-eight rivers. Each making its own way to the sea.

Those assigned to help the wounded and dying soldiers on board the ship were also prisoners of war. Der Kriegsgefangener, KGs, the Germans called them. They usually came from captured medical staff. Hospital orderlies and medics. Doctors. Older men, often. World War I veterans. Balding and grey haired, they were usually good under fire. These strange, sometimes embarrassing old men. Calm, with a sense of humour born of other times. They were Australians, Punjabis, New Zealanders, Madrassis. Scots and dark-eyed Welshmen.

These same men carried water for the wounded and held them as they urinated and defecated. Wiped up the mess made by those with the most terrible dysentery. They would dry-retch, and say don't worry mate to the men who apologised to them. You can't help it and nor can I. No I cannot. Both laughed at another retch.

No became: I am no better than you. I am you. There is no need to apologise for your shit-covered arse and legs. I will clean you up. You would help me, too, just as I help you. Look away from what I am doing. Think about home.

No became forgiveness. Once a word of exclusion, it became for them at that time just the opposite. Who would have guessed? Most of them had never known such patience for another human being. It was like being a child in church again.

86

Tony heard the heavy steel rattle of the ship's anchor chains. Felt the vessel roll slightly as it let go the dock moorings.

Leaving Suda bound for the port of Monfalcone. The armpit of Europe, the Italian dockers who spoke a little English said. Smells like it too. They were always laughing at something, it seemed.

The rumbling engines beneath the deck plates gathered strength. The ship's horn sounded farewell and they began to ease into deeper water. The tugs let go and the *Pietro Badoglio* turned into the Adriatic.

By the next morning, the amputation site had begun to stink. Tony was holding his breath against the pain. Ragged, stuttering noises as he took a breath and held it again. The stench of his leg rising up at him.

An old bald Australian orderly looked up. A lean man with a lined face, he was wearing a dirty white singlet and a pair of faded khaki shorts. The tattoo of a naked woman on his arm. Her hands behind her ears. Those were the same noises that had kept him awake every night since he came back from the war. Had trouble sleeping. Had trouble eating sometimes too.

Those young men. He had seen and heard them first at Pozières. That bloody triage station at the casualty clearing area. A well-built underground bunker with a sign that said Circular Quay. Darlington. Another with an arrow and Woolloomooloo, mate. The crossbeams were French oak, three foot square. Someone had written I love you Mary with chalk. Beneath that, a badly drawn kangaroo. A boomerang. A kiwi. More arrows in chalk. The walls were covered with their blood.

The Australian medic came over to Tony. Knelt down beside his stretcher and held his shoulder.

'Mate. You all right?' he said softly and leaned over the bandaged stump. Sniffed. Rocked his head back. 'Fuck me.'

Tony looked away. He was ashamed of his rotting leg.

The old medic watched him. 'Sorry, mate.' He patted his shoulder. 'Hold on. I'll get you something.'

It was another five minutes before he returned, carrying a bucket of sea water. A cloth and sponge. Two yellow tablets and some fresh water in a canteen.

'Bit of the daytime snake, mate,' he whispered. 'Go on now. There you are.'

Tony swallowed the morphine tablets. Drank from the canteen the medic had brought him. Nodded thank you and lay back onto his soaked blankets. The pain eased and after a moment, he began to doze.

The Australian lifted Tony's head and turned over the wet pillow. Gently lowered it.

'You're a bloody nuisance, all right,' he whispered to him. 'Fuckin' Kiwis. Sheep shaggers the lot of you.'

Soon he would wash and clean the stump. Drain the stinking pus. He could not change the dressings as they didn't have any fresh bandages. He would rinse the old ones in the bucket of sea water. At least it was clean and the saltiness had some sterilising effect. If they were lucky there would be some sulphur powder when they reached Monfalcone.

Holding up the New Zealander's stump in one hand, he wiped away the blood and serum which had leaked into the hollow he'd made in the canvas of the stretcher. The old medic wept, and would never to his dying day admit he had done so.

•

When they reached the first POW holding camp, the orderlies and medics would continue to wash the cloth bandages until they fell apart. Then they would begin to use toilet paper. Much too valuable to be used for what it was made for. The rolls became bandages. The French toilet paper smelled of lavender or lily of the valley and was quite soft. Probably for the officers' latrines. English paper was much too thin. Several sheets required to make a decent covering for an average wound. American toilet paper was by far the best. It smelt of chlorine and was brown and waterproof. They would only get this after 1942, when the US Air Force began bombing Germany, but US toilet paper was resilient and extremely generous. It was said the Soviets did not provide any. Newspapers or dock leaves would suffice.

After they had been organised into their relevant military units and countries of origin, Roy heard someone talking about the soldier he knew as Otago.

Apparently Otago had gone hunting Germans after his little brother was killed that first morning. He seemed to have no ability to stop. Became a complete fucking lunatic, they said. Absolutely terrifying.

It was estimated that he had shot dead seventy-three of them before he was evacuated. Took part in the bayonet charge at 42nd Street with the 28th Battalion. When he had first found his little brother he held his hand and said, come on, Jim. Get up. That was his name, Jim. He gave him a drink of water but it was no use. It just ran out of both sides of his mouth. No bubbles. The water was pink from all the blood. And his eyes, they were not blinking. Come on, Jim, get up, he said again. It took him a bit to wake up to his brother being dead. Then, when he did, he went overboard.

He was twice mentioned in dispatches and cited for the VC. They said it was for all those Germans he killed. The true total they did not want to know. The citation said twenty-six. He was well gone in the head by then. It was three times that. At least.

The bloodthirsty bastard. Mad as a cut snake, as the Aussies would say, for a while there. But they sent him back to New Zealand for a rest and he come right after a year or two.

The train carrying Tony and the other amputees left the Monfalcone Central Goods Station at 1700hrs, destination Upper Silesia. A work camp near Myslowitz. A POW enclosure for both officers and ORs. There was a coalmine there. An iron factory. Railway lines to Kracow and Ostrava der Oder. Two clearing houses. One for Austrian and Rumanian Jews. The other for any Slovakian or Polish deportees. A large repair workshop for artillery and tanks returned from the Russian front. White signs with black arrows that read: *Der Ostfront*. Someone had painted a rough skull and crossbones below the sign with black-and-white paint. It was meant to be funny but it was not.

German steel mills were often built close to their coalmines. Practical and commercially sound. Lower transport costs. What comes next? Albert Speer, the handsome Nazi armaments minister, asked and smiled. And it was then the angels of Wall Street could be heard singing minimise overheads while John Pierpont Morgan squeezed the pimples on his large red nose and exclaimed, there is virtually no cost except that of keeping them alive. If they die they die; there are plenty more in the East. Like slaves. Profit margins exploded. The Reich had imprisoned over three million people by then.

A platform worker said they were leaving the armpit of Europe and going to its arsehole. Myslowitz.

As the train gathered speed, Tony could see the plume of his breath. High-country horses breathing on cold mornings.

The Polish night was freezing and as they travelled across Slovenia, wind blasted between the gaps in the carriage boards. Through high narrow windows covered in barbed wire. Inside the carriages, straw had been spread out between the stretchers. Two latrine buckets. There was no stove for heating.

The carriage of war amputees did the best they could. They covered themselves in what blankets and greatcoats they had and, if they could, held each other for warmth. Awkwardly pushed the stretchers together, thinking nothing of the intimacy. Close and somehow more dear, these maimed men with stumps for arms, stumps for legs. They were just trying to stay alive. Holding each other. One night at a time will do. Shivering as they breathed and saying please and it is all right.

Occasionally they passed dimmed lights and heard the rattle of bells in the dark. Muted steam whistles. The American bombers had been coming from England in the daylight. The enormous and terrifying silver Boeing B-17s. The RAF Lancaster bombers came after dark.

The damned English, the railway man said, they like to fuck you in the dark. Remain unknown. Americans prefer the daylight with eyes open, looking into your face when they fuck you with their silver bombers. They like to see their explosions.

•

After about four hours' travel, the train veered off the main line, slowed and slid to a stop in a rail siding. Steam hissing.

Metal doors clanging and sliding open. Tony would come to learn of the German obsession with regular cleaning. A welter of German voices marching towards them. Barking Alsatians and humming generators that powered searchlights along a platform.

'Juden.'

Tony saw four skeletal men dressed in striped uniforms climb into the wagon. One of them carried a wide shovel. The other three held stable brooms.

He watched as they began to shovel and sweep the soiled straw towards the door. They did not speak as they worked around the stretchers. They did not look at the wounded POWs. The only noise coming from them was their use of the shovel and brooms.

Long strands of straw matted with filth blew away from the edge of the carriage as the wind took them. The two overflowing latrine buckets were carried to the entrance. One of the skinny men in striped clothing placed the buckets on the edge and jumped out of the wagon and these foul buckets were carefully lifted out, one at a time. Tony saw that the man who had jumped out of the carriage was holding his breath as he lowered the bucket to the ground.

Once the carriage had been swept clean, carbolic acid was splashed onto the floorboards where the latrine buckets had been. Armfuls of clean straw thrown in and spread between the stretchers.

Tony heard another order being yelled from the platform.

'Juden hier.'

The men in striped uniforms stopped immediately and ran towards the command. They were still carrying their brooms and

94

shovels as they ran. Stood in a line, bent their heads forward and removed their caps.

Occasional blasts of hot steam came from beneath the engine onto the black stones of the tracks. Water dripping as the brake valves vented. He could hear how the train's boiler had maintained its working pressure, ready to resume its journey at a moment's notice.

Two rinsed latrine buckets were thrown into the carriages by a Wehrmacht soldier as he slid the carriage door shut. Another shout and the stationmaster's whistle. Stand away. The fireman rang the bell.

The train lurched forward. A final all-clear shout from the engine driver. Gouts of black smoke coughed from the smokestack, oiled gears rotated almost in anticipation, and they began to move. The trucks banged, jolted right and right again and within a few minutes had rejoined the main north rail line.

The train began gathering speed and soon they had settled into the rhythm of travel. Every thirty seconds or so, the clicking across the joining plates of the rail.

Outside, the Polish night was rushing by and the wounded prisoners were lying quite still on their stretchers. No one spoke much but some of them were holding hands. Tony could hear nothing but the sound of travel, the clicking steel rails and the whimpering of the wounded men. Eventually, he too fell asleep.

The day broke with weak sunlight coming through the high carriage window. Quivering wet lines against the endless sky.

Tony saw thin men in striped uniforms dancing in the light between the strands of barbed wire. Wasn't that the most unusual thing? He blinked and tried not to see what he was seeing. He could not speak of such things. Fuck my sight. Tony continued watching this window, this matapihi to the world until there were no longer any dancers in it. Just grey and pearl light moving as they moved. Cloudy skies. Closed his eyes.

It was merely vanity. These visions. These thoughts. Hah. Roy said once, don't tell anyone what you see. They will lock you up in a mental home.

He had replied that he did not summon them. And sometimes it seemed that every precious thing in him had become vile. That such understanding was an ancient thing. The opposite was also true. Everything considered vile and abhorrent was also the most precious within him. To be treasured. And that it was all right to see yourself in another. You could become infinitely more capable of forgiving yourself if you knew you were indeed the other person. Some have always known this. Many simply run around in circles instead.

Roy had stared at him for a bit and repeated, 'Do not tell anyone else this shit. Jesus. I don't want to know.'

The morning their mother left, Roy lay down on the bed beside him and held his hand. And, like that, they watched as the light began coming through the bedroom window. Cast shapes on the wall. Ridgelines and the mountains. With the wind, shadows and sunlight, the mountain began to dance. Moving its hips. Ruapehu was moving her hips.

Tony did not say that to Roy. He simply held his brother's hand tighter in their silence.

Their mother closed the front door behind her. They listened to the way she walked. Forever moving around the familiar. Everyone has a certain way of walking.

She would have had her green church hat on and would be

holding the brown cardboard suitcase with vinyl corners that bumped against the door. They heard her hush the dog, who wanted to follow her. Told him to stay. To stay there.

Later, Roy would say she had fucked off and that was that. No good sooking about it. Can't blame her really. But he was still holding Tony's hand.

Their father was away out the back clearing bush when she took off. She had family in New Plymouth. An auntie. Went on to Australia after that, they heard. Bondi Junction.

Left them, but who could blame her? Her husband was a pathetic wreck. He wet his pants in church. All the time. Talked nonsense. The boys, she said, were old enough to look after themselves now. So she took off. Like a bird, Tony would say.

He had read somewhere that a thousand years ago Minoan women, Cretan women, somersaulted above the horns of charging bulls. It was on Crete. Those women. Who would do these things? Did they have in mind the betrayal of Ariadne? She was, after all, not the first Minoan woman abandoned on Naxos. Their treacherous reward for such love. The destruction of themselves with Bacchus.

Trying to understand, he told Roy the story. Roy said Theseus sounded like a prick anyway.

'Theseus?'

'He was the one who fucked off, wasn't he? And Bacchus was just a hopeless pisshead like Dad.'

97

Roy waited with his section at the railyard near the Alexandria docks. After the confusion of the evacuation, it was good to be back as a unit again. Reunited with the Taranaki men.

The gunner, Ken Corbett, was sitting on an empty ration box. He had his ankles crossed and was cleaning the Bren. The muzzle resting in the crook of his arm. The rear and trigger assemblies in his lap.

Peter Clarkson, next to him as usual. His number two. Peter was leaning forward, also sitting on a ration box and blowing away any sand which may have accumulated in the tops of the curved Bren magazines. He carried sixteen: ten more than the recommended number. Filled with .303 ball. Thirty rounds per magazine. A total of 480 rounds with another thirty in the magazine on the gun itself. Making a total of 510. Every fifth a tracer round. Thirty pounds more. A cement sack of loaded magazines. Beyond any price, any weight when you needed them in a fight. That firepower: 510 rounds is a lot.

Recognising this, the others in his section made sure he carried almost no extra food or water. They shared what they had with him. Urenui Bill Reid also made sure Peter was looked after. He had recently become the cook for the platoon. Displaced the other useless bastard. Bert Sutton, Jesus. He was blind as a welder's bitch, Urenui said. Couldn't tell an egg from his cock. Thought rewena was a place. Rewena was a bread his grandmother taught him to make. He said the bug from potato water was the key.

Alongside them and sitting on a block of ancient white stone, Manny Jones was speaking to himself in a low murmur. Most of the other men in the section ignored him.

He was looking down as he spoke. Elbows on his knees. He had once told them that all old lags hesitate at the entrance of any door. They can't help it, and that's how you know if they been inside or not. He was talking again. Don't let your mouth be seen, especially when it's talking like a duck walking. Quack-quack the guitar-playing cunt, he would say. He used a lot of convict slang and nonsense words and was known generally to be a terrible man.

Another rifleman, Gerry Campbell, was rolling cigarettes and carefully laying them in rows into the red Kauri tobacco tin he had carried since Whanganui. For later. The tobacco and the cigarette papers were both English. Sent from the BTE Stores near the Cairo docks to the NAAFI at El Maadi camp. Taken on the Greek campaign. Then Crete, then back to Libya. Egypt. Wheatstraw papers and Old Holborn rolling tobacco. He shaped each of the cigarettes with care and licked the gummed edge with the wet tip of his tongue.

Young David Brookes was sitting alongside Gerry. His back against a low mudbrick wall. Knees up, he was reading the *ANZAC Times*.

Next to him big Bert Sutton, the ex-section cook, was dozing, lying on his back. Legs splayed apart. His pack pushed under his head as a rough pillow. Helmet tipped to cover his eyes. Rifle by his side. The muzzle in his armpit.

His fingers, together on his chest, rising and falling as Roy watched them.

The POW train continued through the Polish night towards the camps at Myslowitz.

Tony had slept in only fleeting moments, it seemed. Waking and sleeping and waking again, like all wounded men do. The further north they went, the darker it seemed to become. He was lying there with not much to think about except his missing leg and the pain. The old Australian medic on the ship giving him what he called the daytime snake. It began to rain heavily, hitting the side of the carriage so loud you couldn't think.

It had rained like this only once in the home valley. That was when Roy became trapped underwater in the flooded Mangawhero Creek. They were only kids.

'How did you find me?' Roy had asked him later. 'How?'

'I heard you.'

'How could you hear me? I was under the bloody water. Trapped. Couldn't see a thing.'

'In my heart.'

'In your heart, you heard me?'

'Yep.'

'Fuck off. Heard me. Don't tell anyone else that.'

They were only thirteen years old and it had been raining for the entire week on the bush farm. Early spring 1933. Downpours were common in the high country, but this rain had become much worse. Whole hillsides were slipping away. Fence lines destroyed and stock drowned. The entire valley was in flood.

That morning Roy had insisted that they check a fur possum line in the bush on the other side of the creek. The traps had been set out up a steep scrubby ridge their father had named Messines. Soldiers coming home from the war often did things like that. Name parts of their home after places they had been when they were away. Spion Kop Hill. Messines Way. Somme Parade. As if they wanted to make sense of something they'd lived through, somehow.

Their father was always drunk, it seemed. Slurring his words and saying things he should not. It was awful and mostly they did not want to be anywhere near him.

We should have the 12th of November, he said. Not the 25th of April, that is Gallipoli and we share that with the bloody Australians. We should have the 12th of November, Bellevue Ridge Day, 846 New Zealand boys killed there. In four hours on that morning in 1917. That's over fifty rugby teams. The bloody Bellevue Spur near Messines. Place called Passchendaele. Over fifty rugby teams, can you believe it? In four hours. All those boys. None of them over twenty-five. No one hardly even remembered them. Means a good view in French, Bellevue. Two shearing runs. He said it took him longer than four hours to walk down to the general store on the main road.

He was always saying really stupid things like that, and then there was the time they heard him asking the sky if it had ever seen a woman weeping as she hangs out the washing on a wet day?

That's where he would disappear to every 12th of November. Up on the bloody Messines Ridge, along the Bellevue Spur. Talking shit. Making no sense at all. Roy called him a fucking embarrassment most of the time.

Tony had told him that with all the rain, the creek would be dangerous. Had he not seen the slips? The flooded tracks in the valley? The cliff tops were breaking away along the high edges.

'Not to worry,' Roy said. 'I have to check the traps.'

Tony looked at him for a bit before he nodded. He was loyal to his brother above all things.

Early the next morning, they slipped quietly out of the family house. The old house dog, Sam, emerged from the hayshed where he had been sleeping. Blinking as he ran, unquestioning, behind the boys. A light misty rain falling, Sam kept shaking the rain off himself right to the tip of his tail as he followed them. Almost in disapproval.

'Fuck off then, Sam. Go on,' Roy stopped and said to the old dog, 'if you don't like it.'

Sam just looked away and shook himself again. Sat. Continued to look away from Roy. When the boys turned and kept walking, Sam followed.

The Mangawhero was filled with raging brown water. The footbridge still intact, but only just. Ankle-deep water flowing over it.

The boys and old Sam quickly crossed the bridge and

immediately began climbing the scrub-covered spur opposite. With Sam scrambling up behind them and using exposed tree roots as hand- and footholds, they were soon onto the main north south ridge of the rising country.

They continued to follow the ridge further into the old untouched bush. Mist rolling down. The larger trees sheltered them. Wild and isolated, a perfect place to set out their trap lines.

Roy stopped when he came to the first of the traps. It was still primed but the lure was gone. The flat plate they called the tongue of the trap was clean. Untripped. Slick. The rain had become heavier again. He looked up at it streaming through the trees.

The trap had been laid in the lee of an ancient fallen tree. Best traps were always set a little sheltered from view. He pushed a stick into the trap and the metal jaws snapped shut on the wood.

The boys and the old dog continued to climb. The heavy rain not letting up. All the traps were the same, washed clean of lure by the rainstorm.

'We had better get back, mate,' Tony said. They had seen all but three of the traps. 'Enough, Roy.'

The rain still came at them through the swaying trees. The smell of mud getting stronger. Exposed ferns. Exposed rocks. Rivulets turning into body-thick torrents flowing and spilling off the sides of the ridge. A larger ponga tree tilted and fell. The water continued gushing over it.

Roy nodded. 'All right then.' This rainstorm was exceptional. 'Come on.' He turned downhill. Sam ran ahead, his tail going in circles as a balance.

When they reached the footbridge over the Mangawhero, it had been completely washed away. The water was at least six feet above where it usually was. Maybe ten. The brown flood rushing by with a strength they had never seen before. A drowned cow came past them, legs in the air, circling and bumping into exposed rocks.

Roy had not told Tony that he had promised their father to open the gates of the pig pens on the flats at the back of the house. If he did not, and the river kept rising, the sows and all their new piglets would drown. If the pigs were set free, their father assured him, they would swim to higher ground. Something to see, a sow swimming and all her piglets behind her. Little heads up and snouts like snorkels. Make you laugh. In the rain, a line of pigs swimming in the flood. Pigs are good swimmers, like ducks. He confessed to his father that he had never seen a pig swim.

Roy stood at the water's edge and studied the flooded creek. The footbridge gone, tangled and caught up against the bank further downstream amid a circling accumulation of strainer posts and battens with barbed wire still attached. The fast-rising water. The dead cow had disappeared over a newly made waterfall. Its hooves had left scrape marks along the clay bank on the far side.

'Roy,' Tony shouted through the rain. 'It's too deep, mate. We should wait.'

The rain had become white in its intensity. A large tree passed by them now in the rushing flood, one sunken end catching and dragging along the bottom. The top branches and foliage almost nodding as they were swept past in the hurtling, smashing brown river water.

Roy sat down on the wet grass and took off his boots. He had promised their father they would let the pigs out. Tied the laces together and hung them around his neck. Took off his jacket, knotted it around his waist. Walked to the water's edge. He was barefoot. They would never break a promise to their father.

'Roy,' Tony said, 'don't go.'

'See you on the other side, mate.' Roy smiled and dived into the flooding water. He disappeared almost immediately. Torn away by the current.

Tony stepped forward. Put his hands on his head. Staring at the flood, searching for his brother.

It was at least another thirty seconds before Roy burst through to the surface. Mouth wide open, heaving big breaths. The boots around his neck were gone. The force of the water had torn him downstream and he was desperately trying to get hold of something to keep himself afloat.

Then, just as Tony wiped the rainwater from his eyes, his brother was gone again.

He did not hesitate. Ran down to the edge of the water. Pulled off his boots, his oilskin coat, woollen jumper and flannel shirt. Stripped off his trousers and underpants, leaving just a black cotton singlet. Bare-arsed and bare-footed, he glanced back to orientate himself. Noting the place where he went into the water. Sam, the old dog who had loyally followed them, sat on the bank and barked alarm at him. Lifting and replacing his paws in the same place. Waiting for him despite his stupidity.

Tony dived in. He allowed the current to pull him under and take him downstream.

He found his brother. Roy. Trapped underwater. Naked. The water had stripped his clothes from him, his boots from around his neck. He was drowning. Pressed against the clay bank and caught up among some fallen tree branches. Unconscious. Becoming limp.

Tony managed to get his arms around his chest and held him as tight as he could as he kicked them both towards the light.

In Alexandria the remnants of the 22nd Battalion were waiting for any transport to take them to Cairo and their camp at El Maadi.

It was another hour before the British Military Administration appropriated fifty-eight uncovered wagons from the Alexandria Rail Authority to transport the troops. Two steam locomotives had also been commandeered from the ARA and assigned to them.

It was a four-hour trip to El Maadi and Roy could see that they would be exposed to the sun all that time. There was no cover at all in the rail wagons. They were told to get in or they could bloody well walk. Someone else will take your place. Shade or no shade, please your fuckin' self.

The Taranaki boys immediately scrambled in. The Egyptian sun was merciless, blazing down on them and turning the metal-encased wagons into open-air ovens. Almost too hot to touch with bare skin.

They did not hesitate and got to work making shade, using tents and canvas ground sheets propped up with rifles with fixed and sheathed bayonets. Tied off at each of the corners with toggle ropes. Left about an eighteen-inch gap around the sides for fresh air. It had taken them ten minutes and once it was made secure with a few more ropes, they could begin to relax.

Beneath the shade they spread out their remaining groundsheets and blankets on the steel floor of the wagon. Some of the men made headrests from their packs, took off their boots and lay down to sleep. Kept their rifles close.

The locomotive's boiler was building steam. Black smoke puffing up from the fire stack. Rotating gears. Valves hissing and one or two muted steam whistles. After a few more moments, the brake was released and they eased away from the yards. Small jolts and metallic bangs. Familiar sounds, familiar movements. Clouds of smoke and steam blowing over them. Increasing speed.

After they had been travelling for ten minutes or so, Roy made his way to the edge of the wagon and stood up from under the canvas. The train was gathering speed, the sun-hot steel under his forearms. His black hair being blown about as he leaned forward to see where they were.

They were passing through the outer city suburbs of Alexandria, the workers' dwellings, shacks and narrow streets. Several mosques. Frangipani trees growing along chain-link fences. Great splashes of red and white. Children playing and occasionally an overloaded donkey being driven along an unpaved street. Dust everywhere.

As they reached the outer limits of the city, the land changed to flat, cultivated fields and stretches of market gardens broken by lines of date palms and the occasional well. Orchards of lemons and oranges. Irrigation ditches. Water channels made of earth.

Continuing in a northwest direction they soon came to and crossed the flat Nile Delta at the edges of the Nitrian Desert. Roy felt the hot winds coming off it. He knew these winds were unpredictable and could bring destructive sandstorms. Stop any desert travellers in their tracks. Dan Davin, the Regimental Intelligence Officer, had told them they were known as Khamsin in Egypt. In Tunisia, it was the Ghibli.

Roy had grown up in the cold, high country of the Central North Island of New Zealand. Never known hot wind. He remembered the 1933 storm and how the entire valley had flooded. Never forgot how he had almost drowned in the swollen Mangawhero. Tony had somehow found him underwater, trapped among those tree branches.

The pigs had not drowned. They swam to higher ground. Their father said they were lucky. The force of the water must have broken open the catches.

After a while Roy ducked back under the canvas cover and found a place to lie down among the other soldiers in his section. It was another three hours to the NZEF camp at El Maadi.

Tony was also travelling by train that day. He was in a much colder place. The train to Myslowitz had taken another full day and night to reach the POW camp. It was dark, and snowing.

They slowed and came to a clanging, shunting stop. The boiler venting steam and powering down. After a few minutes, the carriage doors slid open and from his stretcher Tony could see the falling snow was coming at an angle across the doorway. Black pine trees and a row of yellow lights above a black-and-white sign: Stalag IIIAC. Barking dogs approaching them and then the voice of somebody who sounded like they were in command.

English spoken badly in a heavily accented voice was coming from behind the lights. Loud, clear. To Tony's ear, the sentences were strangely jumbled and the W sounds were pronounced as V.

'Allied wounded. Also, you are prisoners of war. You people are now disembarked being here. They are taking you to the barracks trucks, all men. Prisoners also, yes. Jawohl.'

The German officer stepped back and spoke irritably to someone behind him. His English was failing him.

After a few moments of silence, another voice out of the darkness.

'My name is Walter Schmitt.' A tall, heavily built German NCO stepped forward into the light. Regulation greatcoat and square helmet. Mauser carbine by his side. 'My rank is Feldwebel. That is sergeant in your language. Jesus, you Tommy bastards stink. I can smell you from here.'

He climbed up into the carriage. 'Raus, Kameraden,' he said, and gave a small chuckle. His considerable bulk standing in the light of the doorway. 'I am forbidden to help you fucking ugly foreign swine. You are beneath me,' he said. 'Do you understand?'

His English was good. He continued speaking and, like all good and natural leaders, he made them laugh as he began to help them. Everything he said he was forbidden to do he was doing, it seemed. Every insult denied.

'Come on now, we have to get out, you smelly bastards. Out. I am not helping you. That is verboten. You will soon learn it means forbidden.' His rifle now slung over his shoulder. He picked up one end of a stretcher by himself and began to help carry it towards the door.

The Taranaki Company was resting in the Wadi Degla en route from Helwan. The acting OC, Major Harris, was consulting his map and all coordinates. A prismatic compass beside him. A protractor, ruler and pencil. After another moment he nodded. Made a cross and a circle on the map. An exclamation mark.

They had reached the location they were supposed to be in. It was very difficult to be exact in the desert but the nearby high point was known as Yanaam Ridge or Hill 114. The ground features corresponded with what the major could see on the map.

Since their evacuation from Crete, their platoon had lost Lieutenant Ross, seconded to Freyberg's staff HQ in Cairo. The platoon sergeant had been killed. The original section commanders had also been either killed or captured. There had been no replacements and Roy had been promoted to lance sergeant and placed in temporary command of what remained of their platoon.

The shortage of experienced officers and NCOs was a severe problem and Major Harris had temporary command of the company until Major McFarland, who had been wounded on

Crete, returned from a Cairo hospital. Harris ordered them to dig in along the leading slope of the Yanaam Ridgeline.

Along with the other platoon and section leaders, Roy was summoned to company HQ and Major Harris for an orders group. They were instructed to form a series of defensive positions in locations designated by brigade.

To demonstrate what he meant, Harris drew several rough open-sided squares on the map. Double-checked the locations by consulting earlier compass bearings; looked at his orders and at the ground itself. Ran a protractor over the map while orientating his field compass on it. Cleared his throat.

These defensive and holding positions were to be known as boxes. The Taranaki Company was to occupy the left flank and to await further instructions. Theirs was to be the Kaponga Box.

Major Harris confirmed the naming order from brigade and they were dismissed.

The soldiers of the Taranaki Company set about their work as soon as they could. They dug a series of tank traps. Constructed interlocking bunkers and fire trenches. Secured all lines of communication and strongly fortified any trenches to their HQ position. Laid anti-tank and anti-personnel mines to protect their eastern flank.

Of greater immediate concern was the fact that they only received one resupply from brigade. It came in the form of two Bedford MW trucks, escorted by a Marmon armoured car from the Royal Dragoon Guards. They drove up to their position on Yanaam Ridge. Unloaded four hundred rolls of concertina barbed wire and twelve stacks of iron fence pickets. Several boxes of ammunition. Rations and several jerrycans of water.

•

On the fourth night they heard the sounds of strange vehicles approaching. This was completely unlike the noises made by the British vehicles. Raised voices. Yelling: insults exchanged.

The Kiwi soldiers loaded their weapons and watched the erratic swaying of the approaching headlights. Heard the engine noises and the cursing between the drivers. High revving truck engines in the clear air. Horns were even sounded. These inexperienced drivers using the clutch as a brake. Lights began to flick on and off. A convoy of Lancia trucks drove up and stopped. Angry young men shouting insults to each other in Italian. The engines still running. Headlights on high beam. Each of the trucks' doors bore the green, white and red insignia of the Royal Italian Army. The red cross and golden crown.

A water resupply convoy had blundered into their position. Some of the Kiwi soldiers began to laugh.

The New Zealanders would eventually discover the Italians had been dispatched from Benghazi the previous afternoon to resupply an Afrika Korps Panzergrenadier regiment. They were ordered to turn off their headlights to avoid the RAF but had taken several wrong turns. Unable to navigate by the stars, they said to hell with the English air force, we will appeal to God for guidance, and turned on their lights to try to see where they were going. And, like many lost people, they just kept going. Hoping for the best.

Two large New Zealand soldiers approached the convoy and pointed their rifles at them, bayonets a few feet from their throats. They began to laugh again at the terror this provoked in the Italian boys, barely teenagers, who surrendered immediately with tear-filled eyes. Some spoke broken English. 'We hate Mussolini and Clara Petacci is a whore,' they said.

They clearly believed that two New Zealand soldiers were cannibals who were laughing at the prospect of eating them. They did not want to be eaten. They were Catholics.

Once the New Zealanders understood this, one of them began licking his lips and rubbing his belly. The increasingly horrified reactions provoked even more laughter.

The leader of the Italian convoy, an older man with black moustaches and a beard tied up with string, got out of the rear vehicle and began to yell at the youngsters under his command. Waved a map at them. Pointed to his ear and made circles with his forefinger.

Another New Zealand soldier approached. 'Shut up, man,' he said and hit him in the face with the butt of his rifle.

The NCO fell to the ground, horrified. He held his broken nose in his hands and curled into a foetal position. Eyes closed, the map abandoned.

The Kiwis took over the water trucks and opened the taps at the rear of each of the vehicles. Water began gushing and the thirsty soldiers drank as much as they could, then filled their canteens.

The Italian convoy was part of a newly formed ordnance company. The youngsters had been taken mainly from country villages. Some of them did not even know they were at war. They just wanted to see their mothers again. Most had not even begun shaving.

The Italian boys eagerly shared their cigarettes and what food they had with their captors. They said their canned meat was tinned dog and made barking sounds as they opened it. Some of them giggling so much at the barking they could barely stop. Like the children they were.

The Italian NCO with the broken nose was chained to the

bumper of one of the trucks while the teenage drivers were taken to a barbed wire enclosure behind company HQ.

The Company Quarter Master Sergeant immediately shouted that, by morning, they would be exposed to both the sun and wind and any dust storms. And the rest of the night they were to dig in and behave themselves. He spoke in English and said he did not give a fuck if they understood him or not. He told them if they misbehaved, they would be killed.

The CQMS was in his late thirties, a regular soldier from before the war. Folded tattooed arms and wearing a British steel helmet. He wore three chevrons and a crown on his arm and he told the Italian boys that they would be the first ones he would kill if any Germans attacked. 'It won't be any of your wog lot attacking, as they are too busy fucking each other in the arse and surrendering.'

'Jesus.' Someone had yelled out from the dark nearby. 'Don't say that shit, staff. Jesus, man.'

The CQMS guessed it was coming from near Lance Sergeant Roy Mitchell's section. Must be that queer. Sister. In the dim light coming from the truck headlights, the young prisoners watched the older NCO. A private soldier yelling at a senior non-commissioned officer, essentially telling him he was a fool. Unthinkable. In Mussolini's Regio Esercito, any NCO could physically punish a private soldier for showing such disrespect. They would still hit their soldiers with their fists. Whip them with riding crops. They did these things and men stood still as they did it.

Once Roy's section had filled their canteens, they returned to their slit trenches and sangars. Took turns sleeping as they could as they waited through the night. The soldiers would yell out to each other in the dark. Some of the boys began to voice their disapproval of their defensive box being named Kaponga.

'Not much happens in Kaponga.' It was Ken Corbett. 'All you can hear are pine trees growing and cows shitting. The fuckin' wind coming off the mountain would freeze the balls off a goat.'

A moment of silence before Peter Clarkson called out. 'What about calling it the Midhirst Box?'

'Fuck Midhirst.'

'Or Stratford? The Stratford Box.'

'Why would you keep a goat in Kaponga anyway?'

Someone else. 'What about the Ohura Box. Coalmine there. Black coal. Bastard of a place, don't you worry about that. Rains all the time.'

'A Kaponga goat with frozen balls?'

Sister began to laugh. Called them priceless.

Manny said, 'Fuck up, Sister.'

The wounded prisoners of war were encouraged to assist in their own recovery. The Red Cross sent braille kits, food parcels and prosthetic limbs for the blind men, who were put to work untangling Kreigsmarine ropes. They received the food parcels, minus the chocolate and cigarettes. The prosthetic arms and legs were confiscated by the SS. If they complained they were told most KG amputees had to do without. Russian prisoners were being used in medical experiments or starved to death.

Walter Schmitt told Tony of the courses being offered by the POW officers in the camp alongside theirs.

'What? I just want to stay alive, Walter.'

He had begun to wash the stump of his leg with white vinegar mixed with water. This was to toughen the skin and scar tissue around the amputation. The German surgeon had done a good job: the flaps of skin were overlapped and sewn where the rest of his leg used to be; small rubber drains had also been inserted.

It was Walter Schmitt who was the first to say to Tony that he had an ability. A calling.

He had first seen Tony's fingers on the perforated stainless steel table that the crippled prisoners of war had been allocated to untangle Kreigsmarine ropes. Watched them.

Tony's fingers, like all the prisoners', were covered in tar and kerosene but he had begun sketching with them. Something would appear on the metal face of the table. The Madonna. A horse. A falling angel. The other prisoners ignored him.

When Walter asked Tony about one of these sketches, he rubbed it out and said, nothing, I'm sorry.

'You,' Walter said and nodded. The prisoner had used the first two fingers and thumb of his right hand when he drew the Madonna. The other two fingers tucked back into his palm. Like the son of a whore. Like the Grand Inquisitor of the Brothers Karamazov. Like Jesus of the Russian icons. 'You have an ability, New Zealand.'

'I do?'

'Perhaps,' Walter said. 'Have you heard of Rilke? How the world is trying to make us all invisible?'

Tony was hiding his hands in the tangled mass of black ropes. 'No.'

'Dostoevsky? Kandinsky?'

'No.'

'What happened to your twin sister, Tony? At birth.'

'What?'

'Jung. I prefer him to Freud, don't you?'

'I don't know who Jung is.'

Walter was silent then for a few moments before he spoke again. 'Were they proud of you where you came from? Having this ability? Your people?'

Tony said nothing. He smiled and continued hiding his hands in the tar-covered ropes on the sorting table.

'Your mother?'

'Our mother walked out when we were young. And when I tried to draw things or untangle things in my mouth, I was told to pull my head in. How many sheep can I shear in a day, or crutch, or if I could put up a fence or work a team of good dogs or break in a horse. Did I keep working even when completely worn out? Could I swim a horse and a pony across the river, and fight and play rugby?'

'They asked you that?'

'Of course not.' Tony laughed.

'Did you ever say you wanted to paint?'

'How do you know this?'

'It's obvious. Did you tell your people?'

'No. No, they would simply tell me to grow up or ask who will milk the cows tomorrow morning. Our father had not recovered from the first war and when Mum walked out he took to his bed and never left it.'

Walter stared at him for a bit. 'But I am not the only one who thinks this? Am I, Tony? Your ability?'

Tony shook his head and turned away. He was thinking again about David. Sister. How his own face often transformed into David's face in the mirror. His brown eyes and beloved smile. How he would sometimes even recognise David's smell as his own smell.

But that was impossible.

There was no shade for the 22nd Battalion in their positions on the Yanaam Ridge. The camouflage nets they had spread over the slit trenches gave little relief from the sun, just seemed to attract more flies. When they opened the cans of bully beef there were so many flies that they would often drown in the liquid fat and float there like swollen black raisins.

The soldiers were told to ensure no weapons were left out uncovered in the middle of the day. The metal parts of a rifle or machine gun would become too hot to handle. A spanner left in the sun would burn your hand if you picked it up. You could cook eggs on a shovel. On the mudguard of a tank, if you oiled it first.

They sat, dappled beneath camouflage nets and the canvas tent sheets, and waited. Waited for orders from command. Drank what water they had and waited. Sometimes they would try to sleep, but were constantly disturbed by the flies and the heat and other men moving about and shouting orders near them.

Some cheeky South Island bastard from an artillery battery attached to the 22nd had described the patch of desert they were defending as the longest stretch of fuck-all they had ever seen; something like a politician's smile, he said.

The New Zealanders did not know the ancient ridge they were on was where generations of travelling Bedouin had slept. It was where the old men of the tribe would give their camels the last of the water before crossing to the coast the following day.

An outcrop of broken yellow sandstone marked the summit of the ridge from where Roy looked out over the desert to the blue water of the Mediterranean. On the coast, palm trees marking the village of El Alhamajim. The white buildings of the Ottoman refuelling depot on the edge of town. Shimmering in the heat on the rail line to Cairo.

For over two thousand years El Alhamajim was known as a place of clean water and good food. Fresh vegetables and fruit. Surrounding the town, there were neat rows of orange trees and date palms. Lemon trees. Grapevines.

Doves lived in the eaves of the minaret in the town centre. They exploded in white clouds from the tower when the muezzin gave the call to prayer. You could set your watch by it. Five times a day, every day, the doves. That is how the town got its name. El Alhamajim. The doves. The 8th Army artillery would later destroy the coastal township entirely.

'The Theory of Art. Painting and Drawing Classes. 1A. Modernist Perspective in the Stalag.'

Captain Harry Whitten was running the art course at the OR's enclosure. Other Ranks. Some of the Cambridge old boys, in particular, seemed pleased with this democratic gesture while Captain Whitten, smiling, wondered indulgently if any of these fools would even know what art was. With their stupefied agricultural New Zealand faces and bad teeth. Few if any would come to his classes, and thank God. They would be more interested in carpentry and metalwork and welding. Farming techniques. Would become electricians after the war if they had any brains.

But his standing among the ex-Cambridge officers had been enhanced by his seeming willingness to teach the ordinary men. Communists, the bloody lot of them, but ingratiating himself with those who ranked above him was the most natural of actions for him.

Harry Whitten had chosen to become an artist when he was at Harrow. It had seemed like a wonderful excuse to be lazy and drunk all the time. The indulgent and dissolute artist, suffering with the exquisite pain of creation. And at first it was perfect because he knew that, in essence, that was who he was. A lazy drunkard. He just needed a mask to wear.

The problem that arose for Harry was that the art chose him back. He considered this deeply unfair. Like falling in love with a whore.

Before the war, he was known in the London newspapers as a tragically handsome and dissolute enfant terrible in Knightsbridge. Counted Evelyn Waugh among his circle. A friend of the Prince of Wales; had been invited to shooting weekends at Balmoral. Could speak French quite fluently. Very passable Italian. Urdu, of course, and Hindi. Some Arabic. Related on his mother's side to Wakefield of the New Zealand Company, who had all but civilised the damn place. Created a tiny Britain at the bottom of the world. Made the acquaintance, at the Slade, of Peter McIntyre, who would go on to become the official war artist for the 2NZEF. And through him, the writer John Mulgan. Hence his fondness for the agriculturals.

When war broke out he had immediately joined the Artists Rifles and would sometimes tell the story that Hitler rescued him from drinking himself to death. Laugh in what he considered an ironic way. Adopt a slightly tragic air and look away into the distance, pretending he knew of some greater truth. He soon transferred to the 1st Battalion of a Welsh Fusilier regiment, like Robert Graves. Perhaps he could also become a poet?

The military high command would eventually send Mulgan back to Greece with the SOE. His spoken Greek was perfect. His bravery known and outstanding. Reckless. This man who said he was beginning to know what it meant to appreciate the country of his birth. Killed himself in Cairo with fifteen yellow morphine tablets, washed down with a glass of Black and White whisky. Alone in the Ibis Hotel. Room 28. Aware at last, someone said, that a man alone does not stand a chance.

Mulgan's Latin was beyond excellent. First water, they would say. Both high and spoken. Far superior to the English boys. But as for the common man? Well, there was a lot to be desired about them, wasn't there? Their only saving grace, of course, that the Australians were worse.

It was mid-morning when Roy noticed a cutdown truck, four-ton Ford, approaching their location on the Yanaam Ridge from the south. The direction of Army Group 8 and 5th Brigade HQ.

A LRDG vehicle, modified and painted to resemble the colours of the desert. Almost invisible except for some pale dust rising behind it. An occasional flash of reflected light. The vehicle stopped at the first of the forward sentry posts and was immediately waved on. It slowed, changed gear and continued climbing towards them.

The truck turned right at the first rise, travelled another hundred yards towards them and stopped outside the heavily sandbagged entrance to company HQ. The driver got out, spat and took four large mailbags from the rear of the vehicle. Walked over to the HQ entrance and threw them in.

A sentry had been assigned there. He looked up and raised his hand to the postman. 'Len.'

'You blokes are a bit fuckin' popular, all right,' Len said. 'I don't know.' The expression on his face did not change as he spoke. 'Four. Four fucking bags.' They all knew he probably said this to every unit he took the mail to.

His name was Len Billings and he was wearing a World War I service cap on the back of his head. At forty-two he was considered an old man by the younger men in the battalion.

Len often called the First World War 'the first show'. Said he was a Lower Hutt boy and that was why he joined up for the second show. No brains in Lower Hutt, see. Bad as the Southlanders or even Auckland. No brains at all in Auckland. Len rarely told the truth. 'Once you have seen it there is no unseeing it,' he said. 'Like that first elephant.'

In spite of the length of his service, he was still only a lance corporal because it was known he had once gone mad after smoking hashish in Alexandria. A Kom Bakir knocking shop and he believed he was transformed into a desert wolf from the Atlas Mountains in Maghreb. Began howling at the sky. The moon. Arrested by the military police running naked through the streets later that night. Got sixty days in lockup. The screws were bastards and would often bark as they passed his cell. Some of them would howl. And laugh.

You see, he said, none of this ever happened in Taihape. Or in Raetihi when you were trying to catch a reluctant horse on a wet winter morning in the dark, on the Parapara, or whistling up old dogs who knew better than you. Milking cows who would kick and shit and piss on you.

That is why so many of them went back. Couldn't bloody wait, some of them. They could feel their hearts beating at the ends of their fingertips again. Knew what mates were thinking without a word being said. Would die for them. Better than going to church, some said, and seeing Jesus up there on the cross.

Major Harris and his 2IC, Captain Kereama, came out of the

command bunker to speak to the mailman. They had heard the four heavy bags thudding in the entrance and Billings informing the sentry what popular bastards they were, and that he knew his mother, who had once worked at the Manutahi Hotel. The Onebird.

The major raised himself up and cleared his throat. His mouth immediately tightening with disapproval at what he saw. 'Do you have any orders from brigade to go with the mail, lance corporal?' he said, and looked the soldier up and down. The unshaven and slovenly creature disgracing the black-and-white shoulder flashes in his epaulets.

Len blinked at the major, taken aback by the sudden appearance of two officers. Shook his head. 'I'm sorry sir. No, sir. No orders.'

'Are you sure?' the major snapped. 'We have been waiting for a week. And stand to attention when you address an officer. Come on, now. For God's sake.'

'Sir.' Len shook himself. 'Sorry sir.'

He had dealt with officers like this before. They had usually gone to boarding schools that had houses and rowing clubs. Cunts for the most part, and best not fucked around with too much. Just do as you are told quick as you can.

He was staring straight ahead. However, the fly buttons of his trousers were undone. They gaped open and his army-issue braces were hanging down behind him. The wind coming out of the desert made them sway a little bit.

'Your braces, lance corporal,' the major said.

'Often the way with the dysentery, sir.' Billings looking above the officer's head, continuing to stand to attention. 'Easier not to put them back over your shoulders if you don't have to, boss. Let

128

them dangle, sir. If you know what I mean.'

Major Harris looked away from Billings. CSM McCready, the company's senior NCO, had followed the OC and the 2IC up the steps from the command bunker. He stood quietly to one side. Hands behind his back. A pace stick tucked under his arm.

'Mother' McCready had served with Billings in the first war and had enjoyed the man's company. His rude sense of humour. He had heard good things about him during the push on the Marne. Now he nodded to Major Harris and inclined his head slightly towards Billings. Perhaps, as the senior officer, he could hear the old soldier out. Humour him a little. It would be good for morale. The younger men in the company would hear about it and respect him more. He made a face of reassurance. It would be all right.

'Go on,' the major said.

'Well, sometimes that's all it takes, sir.' Billings nodded, still looking straight ahead. 'By the time you get the braces off...well, it's too late then, sir. With this gyppo guts I got, you could squirt shit through the eye of a needle at a hundred yards. Like a hose it is. Your arsehole feels like it's on fire, sir.'

Billings laughed. He was aware of acting a little stupidly. A deliberate self-effacement intended as an insult to the powerful. Saying thank you, sir, and speaking slowly as if your words were gifts.

A moment of silence as the group took in the lance corporal's most graphic description of the effects of dysentery. Mother knew exactly what Len had just done. Thought, he must stop now.

He did not. 'At least, sir,' Billings continued—slightly breathless and pretending to be delighted that the officer had even asked for his thoughts—'my fucking cock's not hanging out.'

The CSM looked at his moving feet. Coughed and cleared his throat. 'Do up your trouser buttons, will you, lance corporal,' he said softly.

The colour seemed to drain from the major's desert-tanned face. He did not say anything but his nostrils had flared.

'Sar'major,' Billings replied. He pulled his braces up and over his shoulders, began to button his trousers.

Len was known to bring meat pies out to the troops when they were under heavy fire. He would be there in the worst of times. The pies were usually a bit squashed and sometimes cold. But most of them said they had not tasted better. He would give them to the soldiers and simply say: here. Sometimes he knew of their family and would ask after them. How is your mother doing with Dad gone? Your sister? Who is milking the cows? You can always shut up the seven-acre paddock for hay this summer if you have to. Up along Smart Road. Inglewood and Kaimata have some good hay paddocks as well. Grow green swedes or kale for a winter crop. Chou moellier. Turnips.

After a while Major Harris coughed. 'No orders? Are you sure, man?'

Lance Corporal Billings shook his head. 'Just the mail, sir. That's all I brought. There was nothing else.' He nodded at the four mailbags lying in the bottom of the trench.

All the bloody way from home to here. The North African desert. And now all the major could do is ask the postman about further orders from brigade. He had told him three times now. There was not. There was just the mail.

'Nothing?'

'No, sir.' Four. 'They were buggering around a bit this morning at HQ so I thought I might as well take what I can out

130

for the boy-wah-wahs. They'll be at the bit, y'know, wanting news from home. Means a lot to them on the front line. Y'follow? Good and bad. Don't stand in their way.'

'Yes, yes.' Major Harris interrupted him. 'And try not to use such vulgar language when you are reporting to me, lance corporal, will you? Do I have to tell you again? Refer to the other ranks as the men. Boy-wahs. Goodness me.'

The 2IC, Captain Kereama, had remained diplomatically silent throughout; he cleared his throat, hummed something his grandmother used to hum and stared at his boots. Hands behind his back. Mother was doing the same.

Billings smiled, cross-eyed, at Major Harris. Most of his front teeth were missing. The others, black and rotting. A putrid breath. He wanted to ask the major, how was the occupation of German Samoa during the war? Sitting on your fat white arse under a palm tree with a cold German beer, while we were over there? You bludging, red-faced fucking officer, you. How dare you even speak to me?

But he did not say that. He just kept smiling and said, 'Yes, sir. I will never refer to them as the boy-wahs again from now on, sir.'

'And no orders, you say?' This man. It was the fifth time.

'No orders, sir.' Len replied. The officer had become like a child, hoping the answer would be different if he just kept asking the same question. 'No orders. Sir.'

Major Harris turned to the 2IC and they exchanged grim-faced nods. Bent and disappeared behind the khaki blanket that served as a door to the HQ bunker.

Mother stared at Billings for a while. Nodded and held up an open palm. Four fingers and a thumb. Confirming that, indeed,

Major Harris had asked five times for something to be different than what it was. He looked at Billings.

'At least your cock was not hanging out, eh, Len?' he said. Smiled, shook his head. 'You fucking clown.' Followed the officers into the HQ bunker.

When they were gone, Len sat down on the running board of the truck and rolled a smoke.

Whispered something as he cupped his hands around the match and lit the cigarette. Picked a shred of tobacco off his bottom lip. Almost smiled.

He waved to the various assembled section leaders who had been waiting for the mail distribution. 'Mail for the boy-wahs,' he called out to them as they scrambled forward.

Roy returned to his section with the mail and they began sorting through the letters. The parcels addressed to them. It was the first mail they had received for ten months and the only sound for a while was the tearing open of letters and parcels. Then there was silence.

Roy watched them. The men in his section. They soon became engrossed in reading any news from home. Soft laughter as some of the young men recognised beloved handwriting. Read of a wedding or a birth in the district. The weather on the farm. How they were missed and loved, but no one went on about that too much as it just made it worse. How a younger brother had lost a tooth or Dad was working longer at the factory these days. Inglewood had won the senior colts rugby competition again. The Tukapa club might do all right against Old Boys this year. Sally, that good black-and-white bitch, whelped to a springer spaniel owned by the Wilsons. Dianne asked after you at a dance in the

Memorial Hall on Rata Road.

Manny had received no mail.

He sat alone and slightly apart from the other soldiers. Sometimes he smiled if one of them looked up and caught his eye. Shrugged that he did not give a fuck about such things.

After a while, he decided he would brew up. He walked a little way off and poured a small amount of petrol into a sand hollow, size of a nest, set it alight and placed the Benghazi over it. The water soon boiled in the jacket encasing the central flue. The soldier's simple adaptation for the war in the desert.

There was sugar and powdered milk for those that wanted it. Most drank their tea black and gave the powdered milk to the local Arab kids. Manny called them little wog cunts and asked if he could fuck their mothers.

The water boiled. Manny retrieved the burner from the petrol flames using a pair of pliers and emptied it into the large teapot the section carried. As he carried the teapot back to the section, a hot easterly wind came out and across the desert. The soldiers had become used to this wind in the afternoon and barely noticed it.

He poured the tea into several enamel mugs. Carried them back to the boys and placed a mug beside each of them. Sat on an ammunition box and sipped his tea. Watched them.

Peter Clarkson had received a parcel. He was holding a small, dark brown jar in his hands, staring at it. The paper wrapping at his feet. He unscrewed the lid and sniffed. Shook his head.

'What is it, Pete?' Ken Corbett, watching him.

'My grandmother sent it. She comes from Tarata.'

'Yeah. What is it?'

'She calls it the stuff. Puts it on the cows' teats after calving.

And every morning at milking. Reckons it stops them getting mastitis. Healthy teats are important, she said.'

'Why did she send it to you?' Manny asked and sipped his tea. 'Trouble with your teats?'

'What?' Peter frowned.

Manny had not finished. 'You can put it on your cock, though. When you bat out the innings tonight.'

He believed his crudity was the funniest thing. Nobody else seemed amused, but he didn't care. Insisted that he would say what he wanted. He had frequently shared with them the many terms he had for masturbation. Strangling the chicken behind the shed and batting out the innings were his favourites. Sometimes it was dancing in Sydney or catching a schnapper.

'Desert sores,' Peter said. 'I told her all the boys were getting desert sores. She sent me this. Morning and night, she wrote.'

'Like you, Sister.' Manny looked over at David Brookes, who tried, as usual, to ignore him. He was reading a letter from his mother. The mug of tea Manny had placed beside him forgotten.

At Peter's mention of desert sores, most of the men began examining their hands and shins. Looking for signs of ulceration. Undue redness.

Without any fresh food, unable to wash properly, they would see the smallest scratches lead to infections and skin ulcers that quickly festered. The constant flies and lack of water only made matters worse.

'What's in it?' Bert asked.

Peter was still looking at the small jar in his hands.

'Kawakawa leaves, I think,' he said. 'Mutton fat. Stockholm tar. White pepper. For purchase, she wrote. I don't even know what that means. Mostly kawakawa, though.'

134

Everyone was silent as they inspected themselves. After a while Manny spoke up again, 'Kawakawa for the skin. Koromiko for the guts,' he said. 'The shits.'

Urenui Bill, the cook spoke up. 'My auntie used to have the store out the back of Ohura,' he said. 'Gave away the kawakawa and the koromiko to anyone who asked.'

'Did she?' Peter said, pleased to change the subject.

'She did. Told us once how a rough old cow cocky from the back blocks comes into the shop one day and asks her if she had any remedies for the runs, y'know? The *torohi*. My auntie was an old moko kauae and he thought she might not understand the pakeha word: diarrhoea. Hah.'

They fell silent watching him. They knew only too well about diarrhoea. Dysentery was endemic throughout the 8th Army in the desert. Everybody had it, from the generals down.

'Anyway, she says have you tried the koromiko? Offered him some. She would tie the branches together and hang them from the rafters in the store. At the counter, y'know?'

All the section was quiet. Watched him as he spoke about his grandmother.

'But this old bugger would not try the koromiko. No, he would not. He said he wanted to buy a cure from Britain. A civilised place. Not your fuckin' mumbo jumbo Maori shit. Y'know? That's what he said.'

The boys were looking at Bill telling his story.

'And so my auntie goes quiet and just looks at this silly old man. He had deeply insulted her to her face and did not even know he had. But she did not show it. Just smiled at him. Typical bloody Ngati Tama. Just before they kill you with an axe, they will smile at you.'

135

Peter was passing the ointment around the rest of the men. They each dipped a finger in the black ooze, sniffed it and rubbed it gently onto their ulcers and sores.

'What happened?'

'She gave him a newspaper and said try this, then. For your *torohi*.'

There was silence while they thought about what Bill had just said and then the laughter swept around the men.

Amid their laughter, the sound of artillery. The shelling was miles away and of no possible danger to them. They stopped laughing. That distant, sharp sky whistle of the German 88s and crumping fire. It was coming from the direction of Tobruk. The poor bloody 9th. The Aussies were copping it again.

Harry Whitten was not surprised when only two of the colonial prisoners were wheeled in. Private soldiers, both. A cripple and a lunatic by the look, uneducated country types. Similar to the Irish. He stood before them. Smiled, scratched behind his ear, yawned and excused himself.

'My name is Captain Whitten.' He paused. Studied the two men sitting in their wheelchairs before him. One of them had begun to whimper. He was drooling, groping down into the front of his trousers and then smelling his fingers.

'You do not have to call me sir or address me by my rank in the classroom. Otherwise, you will be required to do so. It would be appropriate also for you to try to salute me when I am wearing my officer's cap in public.' He smiled at them both. 'I am related on my mother's side to Wakefield of the New Zealand Company; I am sure you have heard of him. So I dare say we'll get along splendidly. Names, please?'

The boy with one leg had not taken his eyes from him. 'My name is Tony Mitchell, sir.'

'Yes, good.'

The other whimpering fellow had no idea what was going on at all. His name was Maurice Bell and he had been terribly affected by the Stukas in Greece. Taking fright at the smallest noise and screaming at the top of his lungs. Fuck me drunk, most of his comrades said when he started screaming, the poor bastard has started again. They called him Ding.

Whitten regarded them both. The madman and the one-legged stoic.

'Has anyone here heard of the modernist Spaniard Picasso?' he asked. Looked at the ceiling, not expecting an answer. Holding his hands behind his back.

One of the New Zealanders was speaking. God, he hated that stupid accent.

'Guernica,' the man named Tony said. He nodded towards Bell on his left. 'Guernica is sitting beside me.'

It was known that a large bomb fragment had taken Bell's friend's head off. Tom Goodenough. They had known each other since primary school. Grown up together in Horopito on the high central plateau of the North Island. Both their fathers had worked for the New Zealand Railways.

The Stukas had devices fitted that emitted high-pitched screaming sounds as they dived. The Trumpets of Jericho. When Maurice started to scream, he screamed just like the Stukas did. The sound blocked everything else out. Difficult to forget. Tom's entire head had disappeared in the blink of an eye and he had walked about in circles for a moment just like a chook killed with an axe. Flapping his arms like wings.

They brought Ding to the art class in a straitjacket. His screaming and howling had become a constant nightmare.

He did not come to any more classes after the first one. He

138

was sent to another camp in Central Poland called Majdanek, where, the guards said, he would be looked after.

Tony would always remember that Maurice almost seemed relieved to go. He knew what he was, what he had become and he hated being such a burden on his mates.

He had nodded and winked at Tony as he was loaded onto a truck. It'll be all right now. Say no more.

The German attack on the Yanaam Ridge came the following morning. Leading elements of Rommel's 15th Panzer Regiment came up out of the desert to attack the New Zealand positions from the east. The blinding sun behind them. They had travelled all night to arrive at dawn.

Five pale yellow Daimler-Benz Mark 4 panzers coming up at them from the dry wadi below the ridge. Their twelve-cylinder petrol motors almost screaming at full power. Plumes of black exhaust pumping into the desert air. The panzers firing as they came at them. Machine guns hammering. Their main guns, the 75 mms.

Clouds of dust and smoke rising into the air, the New Zealanders mostly firing blindly at the noise of the German assault. Tracers floated up and gunfire exploded against the rocks and sandbags of their slit trenches. Sprays of sand and bullet spatter. Larger explosions from the tanks' guns.

They could barely see a thing. 'We have to go,' Roy yelled. 'Get back to the reserve lines.'

The men of the Taranaki section obeyed him immediately.

Rose as one out of their slit trenches. Began falling back.

When they reached the next line of defensive foxholes, they scrambled into them and waited. 'Let the tanks come on,' Roy yelled. 'Pass through us. We can deal with their infantry coming behind them.'

He knew there was an old Italian tank trap hidden in the wadi behind the ridge. It would stop them.

The panzers were churning up clouds of dust as they advanced upon the ridge. Behind them, the 90th Afrika Panzergrenadiers. The mechanised infantry.

The New Zealand soldiers watched as tanks drove through their lines and disappeared into the tank trap. They could not scale the leading edge. Rocked back and forth. Tried to reverse and collided with each other.

The Panzergrenadiers were jogging forward in their battle order towards the stranded tanks. Machine-gun crews on their flanks had taken cover and were laying down fire for the grenadiers, who were also firing their rifles as they advanced at the run.

The Germans wore sand-coloured webbing. Shorts and tunics. Lace-up desert boots. Some wore peaked caps and others the familiar square shape of their steel helmet. They had also been painted brownish yellow, the colour of the desert. No longer the beasts of burden they jokingly called themselves. Pack animals. Foot sloggers. The Landsers.

Their commander, a young lieutenant, had positioned himself in the centre of his men. A young fool. He was calling to them to attack.

Running faster, they began charging, directly towards the New Zealand line. Yelling as they came.

'Ken,' Roy yelled out.

'Roy?'

'You got that Bren ready?'

'Roy.'

'Shoot the bloke running in the middle first. He'll probably be their boss. If there's a radio next to him, take him out too. Look for an aerial.'

'Righto mate.'

The Bren gun began firing, followed by the .303 rifles. The New Zealanders had begun throwing hand grenades.

They saw the leading Germans of the Panzergrenadiers fall. Screaming. Explosions. The spraying of sand and dust. Charging soldiers being shot to bits.

Brigade had watched the attack on Yanaam Ridge unfold and the 2/12 Australian Field Battery was ordered to lay down supporting fire for the Kiwi 22nd Battalion.

They requested the order of guns guns guns. The most extreme of orders.

The waiting Australian gunners did not hesitate. Knowing it must be desperately needed, they turned and immediately swung into action. Settled into the quickening rhythm. Walking back with the recoil and throwing away the ejected shells in one motion. Swabbing and reloading the smoking barrels. Steadily lifting their rate of fire until they reached maximum. That almost mythical rate of achieving guns guns guns. Firing their 25-pounders. Taking deep breaths as they did so. Shrouded in smoke and dust, firing as they breathed.

The panzers were being destroyed now, trapped in the deep hollow. Black smoke engulfed them, clouds of burning oil and orange flames. Exploding turrets and pieces of hatch hurtling into the air as the ammunition cooked off.

Roy's company was ordered to fall back once again and swing around towards the rail line that led to Cairo. Some of the Auckland 21st Battalion had also taken up defensive positions along the railway line itself. Three other platoons and an HQ section had gathered in a shallow wadi nearby.

They had to cross an open area of about a mile before they reached the rail line. This was their part in what Montgomery had called Operation Lightfoot.

The mile of exposed ground they had to cross was bordered with barbed wire and a sign displaying a drawing of skull and crossbones. A known minefield, it had been liberally sown with both anti-tank and anti-personnel mines.

'Oh Jesus,' someone said. 'This doesn't look too fuckin' good.'

'The orders are we have to get to the railway line as soon as possible,' Roy yelled out to them. 'When we go, boys, we go. And keep fucking going no matter what.' He looked at his watch. One hour until sunset. 'Make yourselves comfortable. We wait for another hour.'

They lay in the sand and waited. Most of them tried to sleep. Some cleaned their weapons. When the sun began to go down, they stood and pushed the barbed wire aside.

'Now we run,' Roy called out.

They began to trot across the minefield. To their right flank, an explosion. Someone from 12 Platoon immediately stepped on one of the mines and was blown into pieces. Two of his friends stopped and tried to help him. He died within seconds and they had to leave him. 'Come on, boys, we have to keep going,' Roy called, and made a sweeping gesture with his hand. Encouraging them. 'You are still alive now, come on.' They left their mate and continued running. One of them crying as he ran. More explosions. More Kiwis blown apart.

Roy could hear the sounds of the soldiers running in the sand. The rattling of their equipment, their heavy breathing. Wheezing. Coughing and spitting. Some cursing. Their boots sliding in the soft sand.

After a while, they seemed to have got through the first band of mines. More sounds of weeping from someone. Low cursing, telling him to fuck up. That would be Manny. Sister was silent as he ran. He was not weeping with fear.

It was another five minutes or so before the running soldiers began to speak to each other. Breathless, snatches of conversation. Quite odd, sometimes it was as if they were almost somewhere else. Ken Corbett yelled to his old friend Peter Clarkson, alongside him. 'They reckon old Freyberg has been wounded twelve times.'

'Twelve?'

'Covered in scars, the old bastard. Got the VC and DSC two times. Must be doing something right.'

Peter coughed. 'What would you fuckin' know, Corbett? All you ever did before the war was make cheese.'

Running in the soft sand, yet so near his old mate that sometimes their hips touched.

'And go to the races,' someone else yelled. 'You lazy bastard.'

'I know he's building a swimming pool at Maadi Camp,' Sister called out from the left flank.

'Fuck up, Sister,' Manny said.

Peter looked away. Everyone was laughing. 'I can't see a fuckin' thing in this dark.'

They were gasping as they spoke. Running in the sand.

Another explosion and a bright orange flash as a mine exploded. The screaming man in the dark. Another friend. Another bloke they knew.

'Keep running, you men.'

'What?'

'Just bloody keep going.'

They must have come into the next band of mines. That's how the Germans did it. Laid their mines in bands and often mapped them.

'Okato might beat Inglewood in the Senior A this year.'

More explosions and more screaming, terribly wounded young men. Reinforcements from the mechanised were firing their machine guns in support of them.

'What the hell are you talking about?'

'The Senior A's. Taranaki rugby competition.'

It was dark in the minefield and Very flares were being fired. Directional mostly. A parachute illumination flare hung in the sky. Strange swaying white light rocking back and forth on the infantry running through the mine field. They were almost at the rail line.

'Okato have all their good boys overseas. Here with us.'

'Keep going, boys. Keep running.'

'They all do. Only kids and old men playing now. Inglewood have some good youngsters coming through. Inglewood will win.'

'Keep running, boys. Go. Go on now.' The flare died and the night returned to a certain darkness.

'Ingle-mud,' someone called Virgil Matoe yelled out from their left flank. The Matoes were Clifton people. Northern Taranaki. Motunui in their bones.

'Clifton has no hope,' an Inglewood supporter yelled back.

'Ingle-mud,' Virgil repeated and laughed. 'That's all you need to say.'

When they reached the rail line, they pushed through the barbed wire and lay down on the track at the bottom of a slope. At the top of the slope, the rail line direct to Cairo.

'I wish I was back in that knocking shop in Clot Bey Street,' Manny panted. 'I left my heart there.'

'That wasn't your heart, Manny,' someone replied. 'You filthy bastard.'

The exhausted soldiers were spreading out along the sandy ground. Lying down and trying not to think about what they had just run through, the explosions, the screaming, running through a mile of a German minefield. Instead, like Manny, they tried thinking about something else from before they came up here.

'Are you there, boys?' Roy yelled out. 'Call back.'

The donkey had stopped outside the brothel at eighty-six on Clot Bey Street. Wagh El Birket in the Cairo brothel district. Three other gharries were tied to the iron fence railings of the well-known eighty-six. Smaller palm trees in large waist-high pots decorated the front entrance.

It was mid-afternoon and Roy could see heat waves rising from an open-air market at the end of the street. It was filled with crowds of people. The smells of frying fish and fresh bread being cooked. Sandalwood. Chicken frying in hot oil, garlic and chilli. Beer. American piano jazz playing on a gramophone. Fluted columns, iron rails and alcoves. Striped shade porticos. Someone was calling out lewd invitations in a heavily accented English. It was well known as the brothel district. Such open invitations were common.

Sitting amid several frangipani in the front yard of the Clot Bey brothel, two bare-breasted women were holding hands and sharing a hookah pipe. Hair covered, but otherwise naked from their necks down to their wide hips. Their hands decorated with henna flowers. Painted brown floral patterns representing the gardens of Allah. Wrists and forearms heavily bangled. The bangles slid and rattled as they smoked. Their nipples painted red. Areolae, turquoise. A sun rising from each umbilicus.

Roy saw them stand and kiss. Hug each other. The older of the two stepped away and turned to them.

'Helloo, Keewee boys. Look at my beautiful tits.' She bent forward and shook her shoulders at them, her breasts rolling from side to side.

'Hello,' Roy said. 'Hello.'

'Salam alaykum. Welcome. It is five Egyptian pounds to come inside.' She had gold front teeth. 'I will suck your cock off for seven.'

Manny lifted his hands above his head and interlaced his fingers. 'Oh,' he said. 'My baby Jesus.'

The younger New Zealand soldiers laughed and looked at each other. They had never heard such incredibly outlandish things, such crude things, said before by a woman. A man, even. No. Jesus. Suck your cock off for seven pounds.

Manny stepped forward and smiled at the woman with the golden teeth. 'I was wondering if you would consider marrying me?' he asked.

She looked at him and laughed. She had been asked this many times.

'Yes, I will marry you,' she said. 'Of course I will marry you. Now, if you wish. Do you have any money to pay me first?'

'Yes,' Manny replied. 'I am very, very rich.'

'How rich?'

'My father owns the entire South Island of New Zealand. It's enormous. Like my cock.'

She laughed, winked and bumped his hip with her hip. Her hand held out. Palm up. Lips pursed. Forefinger beckoning.

'Please come into our house and marry me. You are most welcome. Salam. But give me some money first, please.'

Manny smiled, nodded and put his arm around her. 'It's in my pocket,' he said. 'Can you feel it?'

She shook her head as she placed her hand in his pocket, walking, through the front door of the brothel.

'I can feel your cock,' she said, squeezed and laughed. 'Not your money.'

A terrible noise reached them from the marketplace down the street. They all stopped and looked towards it. The harsh sounds of breaking glass and yells and drunken men fighting. At first, it was like the crowds of supporters at football games. But the savagery was increasing. The intensity of the shouts. Roy walked over to a verandah rail and saw that a crowd of laughing Australian soldiers had gathered below a toilet in the middle of the market square. It was a well-known toilet at the crossroads of the most infamous streets in Cairo, the Bey and Albert, and there was a naked man standing on the roof.

The naked man was wearing an Australian slouch hat with a 9th Division patch on it. A pair of desert boots on his feet. That was all. The skin where his shorts had been was starkly white, unburnt by the desert sun. The rest of him was tanned deep brown.

He was lurching about on the roof as he danced, his uncircumcised penis lolling amid the exuberant red pubic hair. He was holding a rolled-up newspaper in one hand. A box of matches in the other. He suddenly bent forward. Reached up between his legs and pushed one end of the newspaper into his anus. Began striking matches and touching flames to the pages. After several staggering attempts, he managed to get the newspaper alight.

The flames took hold and he began dancing again. Arms and legs flailing, he was singing at the top of his voice on the roof of the brothel toilet. Waltzing Matilda.

More Australians began emerging from the bars and brothels along Clot Bey Street. It was probably the terrible singing of the old song that drew them. They saw their drunken young comrade on top of the public toilet. Making a fool of himself trying to sing, flames coming from the burning newspapers pushed up his jacksie. They began to laugh and shout encouragement. Who is he? A politician, someone answered. Great roars of laughter erupted and continued to punctuate the cheers. They began throwing beer at the dancing Australian. Someone yelled, he must barrack for Collingwood. The bloke's a gorilla. Another said, no no no, he is South Melbourne. Look at the colour of his balls. A blood-stained angel dancing on a toilet roof.

They continued cheering and laughing at him. As if, just for a minute, they were back at Punt Road Oval or Albert Street, barracking for their team.

A piously dressed Arab man was hurrying down the street. Rushing towards the noise and uproar. A bookseller of Islamic poetry and novels, he was returning from the midday prayers at his local mosque to his small shop near the square. An exquisitely crocheted skullcap on his head. The beautiful taqiyah, from his grandmother. A kiss with each stitch, she would say. Your lips are now at the ear of the Prophet.

He began calling out in Arabic for them to please stop what they were doing. He tried to show respect towards the visiting soldiers. But they must understand that this was deeply offensive behaviour.

He reached the public square, pushed his way through the crowd gathered at the toilet. Stared for a moment at the young fool on the roof. Picked up a chair from an outdoor café and swung it up at the naked Australian. Threw it at him. Knocked him off the roof.

Silence from the mob of gathered 9th Division soldiers. They stopped laughing. Someone in the crowd said, 'Settle down, mate.'

The pious Arab turned to the group of soldiers. 'Are these actions holy actions?' he asked.

The soldiers stared at him.

'Would Muhammad, our Prophet, peace and blessings be upon Him, approve of this dancing naked on the toilet roof?'

The crowd of drunken soldiers remained silent.

'Please, Australia,' he pleaded. 'Is this normal behaviour? Are we not human?'

Another moment of silence and then, almost as one, the soldiers attacked him. Punching and kicking and yelling insults at him. His faith, the Prophet and the country they were in.

More Egyptian men came running towards the distressed cries of the bookseller. Someone else was cursing loudly in Arabic and urging them forward. Flames were coming from the windows of a ground-floor bar. Yellow beer signs turning black.

The rattling sirens and ladder trucks of the Cairo fire brigade arrived amid the chaos of the street—someone must have called the military and civilian authorities—and a unit of British redcaps drove in just ahead of the fire brigade. Leaping out of the vehicles with truncheons in hand, the military police began attacking the throngs of brawling men. They adopted an old and proven tactic to subdue protesters. They began attacking whoever was in front of them with their fists and truncheons. Destroying them. Walking forward as they did so. Calling out in unison.

Behind them a British sergeant major, marching back and forth, yelling out commands. 'One.' Pointing with a pace stick at something to his front. 'Two three. Cover your legs in attack mode, Johnston.' Correcting small things. 'Walk forward, you men. Listen to me. Walk forward. One. Two-three. One. Stand still. Wait. Walk forward on my command.'

Thus, with calm and firm directives, as the firemen hosed the crowd, he exerted an ancient British control in a broad Geordie accent.

'Bloody Australians,' he whispered and could not help grinning. 'Unsettled types.' Shook his head and looked around. One of the redcaps under his command had dragged a soaking-wet red-haired boy towards him. The dancing Australian soldier whose performance had started the entire bloody riot.

He looked at him. The Australian. The red-haired boy looking a bit dejected. He sat on the ground, one hand out to support his weight. He looked like the wounded Gaul. Knocked off the toilet roof by the outraged bookseller. The soaked and blackened *Cairo Times* still hanging from his rear, a sodden black tail between his legs as he sat and stared at the ground.

The redcaps sergeant major smiled and shook his head. A terrible pockmarked face he had. 'If I told thi' mother lad,' he said.

The young soldier looked back at him, and brightened. 'Tell her, mate,' he said. 'She won't fuckin' mind.' Coughed. 'Jesus, what happened?'

Another brawl erupted along the street. Cursing and yells. The smashing of windows. And then more windows. The Australians were proving to be difficult men to control.

'Get that bloody gharry driver,' Roy said. 'Fuck this. We're getting back to camp.'

'Where's Manny?' someone asked.

'He followed the girl with the golden teeth inside.'

'Get him. We have to go.'

'Is Sister here? Brookesy? Did he come down here? We better get him too.'

'He would never come to a place like this, mate.'

After the first lesson Harry Whitten asked Tony if he had studied. Added: formally?

This question. His tentative smirking at the answer. Holding his earlobe.

'No,' Tony whispered.

Whitten was staring at what Tony had just painted. An untaught amateur. The English captain closed his eyes and smiled his hatred. A true autodidact. A crippled New Zealander, for God's sake. A one-legged brute with his rustic fingers. It should have been an axe he was holding, or a shovel. A box of Silver Fern matches to set fire to their world. They were, after all, a very simple people. Peasants, essentially. Most of them were unable to read and write, let alone paint.

The New Zealander was speaking. That accent.

'Someone told me Wakefield was not a good man,' Tony said. 'That he had once stolen a child. Raped her when she was only fifteen in order to marry her for the money her father would give him.'

Harry stared at Tony, the New Zealander who painted

naturally like Van Gogh, and resisted the urge to put his fingers in his ears.

Walter got him a place to paint soon after that. To be an artist: 'Like you said you were when you were joking. Telling me the truth when you thought you were lying to my face, New Zealander,' he said. 'Being a smartarse to cover up for your pathetic terror. So now. There you are. No excuses with your one leg. Work. Paint. I will get you what you need.'

He put Tony at the end of a barrack block. Partitioned it off with a blanket, thereby forming an annexe of sorts. Had a plywood door installed later by the camp carpenters. There was an easel near the rear window. A sofa and a chair.

He had managed to get some hair from the tail of a draughthorse to make a proper artist's paintbrush for Tony. A Wehrmacht horse transport unit had passed through on the way to Rumania and Walter had traded some cigars for the horse hair. The drivers thought he was mad.

He trimmed the strands to fit into the heel of what would be Tony's first paintbrush. The ferrule was made from a beer-bottle cap and crimped with regulation Heer wirecutters. The handle was made from a pencil split and cut to size, the graphite core removed.

Tony could not meet his eyes. He was looking at the paintbrush Walter had given him.

'So,' Walter said, waiting for more to be said. He closed his eyes, smiled at the silence.

'Walter.'

'There you are, Kiwi. Now you can paint.'

After the defeat of Rommel and the Afrika Korps at El Alamein, the 2 NZEF moved on to the invasion of Sicily and mainland Italy. The spearhead of Montgomery's 8th Army had landed at Taranto and were advancing up the left flank of the Italian Penninsula towards Monte Cassino and the Gustav Line.

'That Montgomery is a pommy cunt of the highest order.' Manny said. 'No worries, mate.'

'Monty?'

'All those fucking hat badges he wears. Have you seen how he holds his elbows behind his back?'

'What?'

'Like a mental case, the cunt.' That was when Manny first saw him. Montgomery, the revered general who was, as he said, holding each of his elbows behind his back as he addressed them. Like a fuckin' chemistry teacher, Manny said.

Roy's company had gathered and were in a group about two hundred yards away from the crowd of men surrounding General Montgomery. He was standing on the flat bed of a Commer truck.

'Cut it out, Manny,' Bert said.

'And that bloke comes out the other week,' Manny continued. 'Churchill, the fat prick.'

'What?'

Manny laughed. 'Saying Alamein was not the end or the beginning of the end but the end of the beginning. Confused the fuck out of everyone. He's pissed out of his brains most of the time. No idea what he'll say next.'

'Churchill?'

'Yes, fucking Churchill. Walking about the show with his dancing shoes on like the lunatic he is. Wearing a topi helmet like he owned the world. An overfed pink baby with a fucking fat cigar,' Manny said.

A silence descended on the section. After a while Bert Sutton, the big fool, spoke up. 'He's all right.'

They all looked at him. Bert, the socialist.

'We could do worse.'

Bert had flour on his hands. He had taken back cooking duties as Urenui had received a minor wound and was at a Red Cross Station in the rear echelon. Some shrapnel from a mortar in his backside. Nothing too serious, but he needed stitching up.

Bert was attempting to make biscuits using oatmeal, sultanas, sugar and some desiccated coconut he had stolen from the Indian Army stores depot at Serrano. He had also lifted a four-gallon tin of molasses and twelve desk telephones. The telephones were of no use at all to a frontline infantry unit. Black bakelite. Telephones with cords. Heavy to carry. They were usually only allocated to static divisional HQs with secure communication lines.

'Why did you steal the phones, Bert?' Manny asked. 'We can't fuckin' eat telephones.'

Bert looked at Manny blankly. 'Buggered if I know, really. They were there, so I stole them.'

'Because he could,' Ken said. 'The socialist cunt.'

Manny found this hilarious. He would laugh for days about it. The socialist cunt who stole the phones because he could. Why not?

Before any major battle, the Kiwi infantry boys would put everything of value they owned into the middle. It was what they called the kitty. Stolen things were all right too.

It was accepted that the married men kept their wedding rings and, if needed for the battle, watches. The rest went into the middle.

When the fight was done, those who came back would share what was left with those who were still alive. Their mates' things. Their brothers' things.

They would keep all the money and food. Share it out. It was understood before the battle that this would happen.

Any personal gear like photographs of loved ones and personal keepsakes were usually sent back to div HQ, along with the casualty lists. Mostly wallets, diaries, copies of the New Testament. Those personal things would mean more to their families back home. Anyway. Send them back to where they will be treasured. Worshipped, even. Sometimes they kept the watches.

They often held on to the wounded's gear for safekeeping. Give it to them when they got back, they said. And they would. It became like a superstition for them. As long as they had his gear, the wounded bloke would be coming back.

When he died, they divided up his stuff with those left alive. They all knew this.

In Stalag IIIAC, Tony was painting almost constantly. When he finished one work, he hid it in the walls or beneath the floorboards of the barracks block and immediately began another.

Walter Schmitt told him to read Goethe.

Tony said nothing. Looked at him.

Walter said that when the war ended, he would take all the paintings from the walls and beneath the floor and use them to start another revolution.

'Everybody,' Walter said. 'Not only the wealthy. Everybody.'

'You must not help me if it puts you in any danger,' Tony said.

Walter laughed. 'I am a terrible coward, Tony. And I would never assist any enemy to our glorious Reich. How could I?'

'You do it every day, Walter. Over and over again. Every day.'

Tony would hear the story of how, as a young man, Walter had been a philosophy student at the Humboldt University of Berlin. That was until August 1914 and the beginning of the First World War. He had enlisted, like all patriotic young Germans, and become a private in the 33rd East Prussian Fusiliers of Graf

Roon. They wore bouquets of flowers in their buttonholes as they marched off to war.

By the time Walter returned to Germany five years later, 1919, he was a Communist. Marched in solidarity through a Berlin suburb called Mitte. Carried red flags painted with the hammer and sickle. Came to believe in the revolution. The blood of martyrs as the only true blessing. Banners exhorting the working men of the world to unite. He would sing 'The Internationale'. He even tried to learn the words in Russian.

It was accepted, at first, in the Weimar Republic. Many army veterans had become Communists. It was easy not to believe in God after all the meaningless slaughter. God just did not make sense.

Walter would also tell Tony that he was arrested in 1933, not long after the Reichstag fire. A Gestapo jailer pointed a 9 mm pistol at his head and told him to say Heil Hitler or goodbye mother. He laughed when he said this form of persuasion, coming from the National Socialists, was quite compelling.

He was also told to renounce immediately any ties or affiliations to any communist organisation. Then the Gestapo man said yes to him.

'So,' Walter said. 'I lied. I said Heil Hitler. Und hallo Mutti. Guten tag? Oh, and by the way, I said to him, tell Stalin he should go and fuck his mother.' He nodded. 'That seemed to make them happy.'

Tony laughed. 'Walter, why are you a disgrace?'

'Because.'

'You wanted to stay alive?'

'Let's talk about something else.'

'God?'

Walter looked at Tony. 'I do not believe in God, you know this and yet you also know the suffering of Christ is who we all are,' he said. 'The pain of that figure on the cross somehow becomes our pain. Thus we exist. Christ is within us.'

Tony stared at him. He wanted somehow to laugh. The German sergeant was no longer a German sergeant. His eyes were broken windows. He had become black and white. Arms outstretched, unadorned, naked and falling asleep on the floor of a non-existent cathedral. It was the floor of their barracks.

'You are not a photograph, Walter,' Tony said.

Walter ignored him. 'You are not a photograph. What does that even mean?'

He had taken off his helmet. Called it a heavy damn thing. Unbuttoned his overcoat. Lay on his back between the prisoners' bunks. He sometimes wore his medal ribbons, but rarely. They included the red and white and black diagonal strip signifying the Iron Cross 1st Class. Three wound badges. The Tannenburg medallion. Another medal of a small brass sword and oak leaves, which signified field promotion during battle. Fifteen combat clasps. The highest of honours for many. These ribbons earned the greatest respect from every German landser who had fought in World War I.

He was an old front pig, das frontschwein. They were fools for such things, these Bavarian show-offs. Prussians disavowed any ostentatious recognition. Nevertheless, he had become a Communist. It was remarkable he was even still alive. It was only because of his previous rank in the 33rd Prussian Infantry that he was not dead or in Dachau. Had become a lowly prison guard in Silesia.

He had told Tony that it was best to keep decorations concealed from some of the higher-ups, as many resented seeing such things on the chest of a mere prison guard. He referred to them as the goldfasen, golden pheasants and rear pigs, ettapenschwein. Some of them, like that chinless wonder, Himmler, who had not even fought in the first war. Keitel also once came on an inspection tour. Thought he recognised him. How could he even walk in front of such soldiers? Those good men weeping before him?

That Prussian bastard von Manstein once explained it to him. The medals and awards were the weeping, you see. To those who know about such things, it was obvious. The coloured ribbons, of themselves, signified nothing. Von Manstein understood this and remained a Prussian to the end.

'No.' Walter continued speaking from between the bunks. 'It is not an external God that speaks. It is that internal God. The voice we are born with. The God that is the ungiven heart. That ancient voice of recognition and eternal forgiveness. Such is this thing the world calls God. It is also a mother kissing her newborn child. That is God.'

'You have become a building, Walter,' Tony said. 'You are also getting fat, and I have come to love you.'

Walter laughed. 'You.'

Tony looked at the man almost asleep on the floor. 'Were you drinking beer at lunchtime again, Walter?'

Walter ignored him. 'His was the voice of the mad son Jesus of a protesting God, Friedrich Nietzsche finally heard in the Turin piazza as he hugged that coachman's beaten horse.'

'Are you drunk?'

Walter looked at Tony. 'No.'

'Walter, you are a building.'

'A building? Fuck off, a building.'

161

'A broken building,' Tony said.

The sergeant dragged himself upright. Stood between the bunks and put the square helmet back on his head. He looked at the sketch Tony was working on.

'How do you know this?' Walter whispered to him. Pointing at Tony's sketch. 'You do not even know who Dostoevsky is. Can you even read?'

'Yes. I can read.'

The painting of him as a broken building contained the image of a small oil lamp in the bottom right corner. Words above that. Tahi rua: pai tu pai hinga.

'What are they?' Walter asked. 'Those words? What do they mean?'

'One two. Good at standing, good at falling,' Tony said.

'Sometimes,' Walter said.

Tony nodded thanks. Just that.

Thank you didn't mean anything else. It was equal and honest. Where simple words mattered. Like love and respect.

Walter saw how Tony had once written *Corinthians XIII 4* below a strange church with two crosses on a hill. He hid it along with the others under the floorboards.

Walter was speaking and Tony had not heard him; besides, he was speaking in German.

'Jeder nach seinen Fähigkeiten, jedam nach seinen Bedürfnissen.'

He said this to Tony a lot. He insisted it sounded better in the original German.

'I don't know what it means,' Tony said. 'It sounds like an order to click your heels together. Obey me. What does it mean, Walter?'

'From each according to their ability,' he said. 'To each, according to their needs.' Walter nodded. He had great respect for these words. 'Do all Englishmen think like you?'

'I am not English. I am a New Zealander.'

'Is there a difference?'

'Yes.'

Walter stared at him for a bit. 'Do you think Marx would have danced with Jesus if he could?' He raised both his shoulders, palms out. 'Along Wall Street on that October day in 1929? Would they have kissed as they danced? Marx and Jesus?'

It was another moment before they both began laughing at what he was saying. It was so stupid.

The red and white village sign was circular. *Gravzano di Lucia: 2 km.*

The sun was shining and Roy was travelling in the leading Bren carrier. He was holding a compass and a map in one hand, a Thomson machine gun in the other. The vehicle was armed with the .303 Bren machine gun and a 5.5 inch Boyes anti-tank rifle. They were part of the western flanking movement undertaken by the Allies as they pushed up towards Fogglia.

Roy had acquired two of the new anti-tank weapons issued to HQ, the 32 pounder PIATs, which were indeed tank killers. He kept them with him in the leading carrier, hidden under tarpaulins.

With its low profile and powered by a strong, V8 Ford gasoline motor, the much under-appreciated Bren carrier was fast and manoeuvrable, especially on the narrow roads in the Italian mountains. Steel plates for cover. Easy to get in and out of, too.

They began to enter the village and the first thing they noticed was the beautifully made houses. Trulli houses, circular and constructed mainly from dry interlocking masonry, carefully laid with knowing fingers. Beehive-like conical roofs covered with slates and adorned with symbols of adoration and love. White crosses atop the circular roofs. One was decorated with the stylised shape of a Latin Sun. Piazza del Sol. The word *bene* written across another four houses. *Venia.* Forgiveness. The shapes of sunflowers on others. Who would not smile at such things? To be welcomed like this?

As they drove into the village, it was the children who ran out to greet them. Laughing in welcome and excited to see them. Running alongside the vehicles. Fearless, happy kids, singing and smiling in welcome. Seemed to think they were Americans.

'USA,' they yelled. 'GI. Do you have any candy? Whiskey and soda. Rock and roll...Camel, baby.'

Manny, waving back at them, could not seem to help himself. Asking his eternal question, 'Can I fuck your mother?'

David Brookes was sitting alongside him. 'Manny,' he hissed.

Manny ignored Sister and yelled to the kids. 'How much to thing with her?'

'Shut up, man,' Sister said. 'They are just kids.' Waved back to the smiling children of Gravzano di Lucia. They had such big grins. Beautiful white teeth. 'We are not Americans,' David yelled back to them. 'We are New Zealanders.'

'Get fucked, Sister.' Manny said back to him. 'I'll say whatever I like.'

Roy's carrier had to slow down as more and more of the villagers began to emerge to welcome them. Old men carrying bottles of long-hidden wine and treasured grappa. Their tentative smiles beneath large white moustaches. Raised hands and accepting nods. Hope. Flat caps. Shoulders that had worked hard all their lives.

The older women of the village, more sceptical, were not smiling and many were holding their hands across their mouths. A lot of soldiers had come through their village. They remembered them as being always hungry. And, once fed, wanting other things. They were men, they said, after all. Often violent and sometimes bestial. The old women would not forget such men.

'Parihaka women.' That was probably Urenui Bill, but what would he know, someone who looked like a walking Greek man. The most ugly Socrates, smoking a roll-your-own and hanging a towel over his erection as he walked to the shower.

'Jesus,' Manny whispered, looking at the young women. 'They are beautiful.'

Sister turned to him. He was expecting another crude remark but Manny didn't seem himself anymore. Sister frowned.

A split second of silence. Then the whitewashed Trulli houses were exploding. Roof tiles and masonry flying into the air. Towers of dust spiralling into the sky.

High-explosive shells were landing among the women and children and old men, as sudden, as unexpected, as anything imaginable.

And it is true what they say about the sound an HE 88 mm shell makes as it comes through the air. It sounds like a freight train approaching. As it comes, it sucks all noise from the air except that of itself. Exploding on arrival. Destroying everything that may have been thought. Shrapnel does that. The smiling, innocent people were singing in welcome. Asking non-existent mothers to come forward to them. To put their arms around them. Pleased and laughing.

It is the most obscene of things imaginable to see. What high-explosive shells do to human beings.

Roy's Bren carrier veered hard left into a shopfront and smashed through the display window. Glass crashing around them. The motor revving. The driver slumped forward over the levers. A young fella from Inglewood. Half his head torn away by flying shrapnel. The grandson of a dairy farmer whose first language was Yiddish. Second German, English came third.

Roy tumbled off the carrier, rolled and took cover in what was left of the nearest shop. Another shell exploded in the street.

Then he was crawling on his belly over the broken glass and masonry and bricks and saying Jesus. And fuck me Jesus, Jesus. Elbows out. Best when crawling. 'Jesus make me safe, Jesus make me safe. I will do anything You want.'

The Thompson machine gun in his hands. Scrabbling and trying to get to better cover in the rubble. His legs and backside had been lacerated in the shell explosion. Blood wet on his legs, his backside.

The ancient church bells clanged awkwardly as the Benedictus structure collapsed beneath the terrible artillery fire. The dust exploding through the falling masonry. Seven hundred years old.

Roy realised the Germans had held back their artillery fire until the New Zealand column had arrived in the village and were being greeted by the villagers.

Mobbed with flowers and singing. Greeted with love. Thinking they were free.

That is when they fired. When the Germans unleashed their howitzers. They knew what they were doing. And that it produced the best results. My Lord. Spoke for itself. The horror.

Body parts of the children and old men and women strewn about like flesh flayed and laid out in butcher shops. Mothers.

Grandmothers. Torn apart. Their innards scattered and flung and the running children thinking they came from America. Blood in gutters. Disappearing into the curtains of dust. The horror unfolding before them was overwhelming.

'Roy?' It was Sister yelling out. 'Roy?'

'Yep.'

'You all right? Where's Manny?'

Manny was nowhere to be seen. Sister had reflexively jumped off the carrier and found cover in a roadside ditch. Ensured his rifle was loaded. Fixed bayonet and taken two grenades off his webbing. Primed the fuses. Pins uppermost and ready to be pulled.

'Roy?' he shouted again. 'Call back. You seen Manny?'

Roy was unable to speak as he looked at the terrible devastation unfolding before him.

Almost the whole of the beautiful Trulli village destroyed in less than a minute. Blown apart. Some of the villagers had been carrying candles of blessing and sacred images of Saint Anthony. Flowers to celebrate treasured wine.

'I'm good, Sister.' He saw someone running. 'Is that Manny there? Going flat out for the square?'

Manny was not taking cover. He was sprinting towards the devastated bodies in the market square. Something must be terribly wrong with him. Manny would never do this. A hard and vicious man. Cruel and perverted. A perfect soldier. He must have gone mad running as fast as he could towards the piazza and the villagers who had just been shelled.

'What's wrong with Manny?' Someone yelled. 'Look out, he's gone suicide.'

The round British helmet had fallen off the back of his head as he ran. Running like the thief he was. Running like a hunted pig.

The Piazza del Sol named for the sun. Anthony, a Jesuit priest and the patron saint of all lost things, had said it felt as if he had come home when he stepped into this sun-filled place. The stigmata bleeding from his palms and eyes. Fuck me Jesus. Forgive me. Have you seen that? Bleeding priests like Saint Anthony who truly believed in these things.

The running Manny reached the woman standing naked in the middle of the town square. Streaked with blood. It looked as if she, too, was about to fall over with the others. Her huge stomach cradled in the hand she held beneath it.

Manny seemed oblivious to the ongoing German fire. Saw only the pregnant woman standing, hipshot, naked among the bodies of her family. Everything had disappeared for her in that moment of fire and dust. Her family lay strewn about in pieces of who they had been. Covered in blood. She too was obscenely naked, torn and unable to breath.

Manny had thrown his American rifle away as he ran towards her. His beloved M1.

The second shell blast had shredded the flesh of her shoulder. Her back and one arm. She stood, bleeding from her entire pregnant body. The blood gushing between her legs. A child was being born.

No one had ever seen Manny like this before.

He reached the woman and threw his arms around her. 'Sssshh,' he whispered. 'No. It's all right. No, no.'

Lowered her to the ground. Held her tight and rolled with her onto the ground. Together into the shell crater from the first explosions. Racked with spasms and contractions, the child coming. He placed his hand beneath her head and did not know what to do. Her legs falling apart. There was no stopping this.

169

Manny's arms and shoulders were streaked with her blood. No one had ever remembered Manny shedding a tear over anything in his life. Mostly he was vulgar and disgusting. Always drunk when he could be. A thief. He sneered at weakness. Now he was weeping openly before her.

One of her knees came up and she reached blindly for his face. He allowed her to touch his cheek. Said something. Torn by the shrapnel, she braced what was left of her back and hips and legs and began to bring her child into the world. He grimaced, knowing what such shocking blood loss meant. She was dying in his arms as the baby's head emerged.

Manny became frozen, unable to move. He stared at the child coming between her dead mother's legs. Her swollen face covered in mucus, choking on the blood of her mother, so badly askew in the bottom of a shell hole. Protesting. Mewling. This slippery, bloody child, grotesquely attached to her mother. The stretched, luminous, blood-filled umbilical cord.

Another New Zealand soldier was running forward. Paused when he found them. Fell onto his stomach and slid into the hollow beside him, David Brookes. Fuckin' Sister. The best fighter they ever saw with a bayonet. Manny looked away from the blood-covered woman and David grabbed the baby's feet and pulled her up and away from the pool of blood in which she was drowning. Cleaned away the mucus in her mouth and flicked it off his fingers. Found the umbilical cord, badly stretched. Blood clots falling. That red and wet newborn squalling of her need.

He placed her on the rough, dust-covered ground between them. 'Jesus, Manny,' he whispered. 'The cord?'

'Tie it,' Manny said. 'Cut it and tie the fuckin' thing, Sister.'

Manny was useless. His hands were trembling. Sister cut the cord with his skinning knife. Made a rough, bulging knot with the blood-covered cord on the baby's belly. Looked up at the mother. She was dead.

'It's all right,' Sister said. 'Bless you.'

German infantry advancing into the village from the North. MG42 machine-gun crews on their flanks. The others of each section and platoon employing their usual battle tactics of fire and movement. Fire and movement.

They heard Roy's voice. He was yelling at them from the shelter of the street. 'Manny, Sister. Germans to your front. One o'clock. About two hundred yards. Call back if you hear me.'

He was about a hundred yards away, Roy, kneeling against the shopfront next to the Bren carrier. Trying to think clearly about the next move.

'Righto, Roy.' Sister's voice came back from the shell hole.

Roy looked up as he heard the roar of the enormous panzer coming from the north to annihilate them. Black gouts of exhaust smoke erupting. The enormous bulk of the Tiger tank emerged into view at the end of the village. The grinding, the screeching of metal tracks moving forward.

'There's a fucking Tiger coming your way too,' Roy yelled towards Manny and Sister. Ducked for cover.

The turret traversing left to right and back again. That lubricated swivel, a meticulously well-oiled and perfectly machined Krupp gun, the 88 mm. Without air or artillery support, they had nothing that would stop it.

Roy immediately saw that it was impossible to get the two PIATs in the carrier. Instead, he yelled out to the radio operator.

'Get command…we need fire support…any air. Quick as you like, mate.'

The radio operator shook his head. 'We've got nothing, Roy.' Took off his earphones. Shook his head. 'Nothing.'

As he spoke the Tiger fired.

A wall exploded behind him. The radio operator was killed instantly and a driver who had been trying to clear the left track on his carrier was hit by the same blast. Him and bits of him blown all over the street. Shattered glass windows, shredded shopfront awnings. Tables and chairs. White crockery broken and scattered. Everything spattered red.

Roy looked back to where the battalion radio operator would be. He knew it would be Tommy Love. Oakura man. He was responsible for forward comms. Probably been in the third or fourth vehicle. Hopefully when they come under fire he would have taken cover. Restored communications back to brigade. Immediate battalion level.

'Comms, Tommy?' Roy yelled out. 'We got brigade? You there, Tom? Tommy?'

He saw a hand emerge, thumb up, from a Bren carrier overturned in a roadside ditch.

'Any air. Air?'

Another quick thumbs-up and then the rocking palm-down gesture that meant perhaps.

They could hear the Tiger tank moving forward. That terrible metallic squeal of the tracks. Loud bursts of radio static. The shriek of their power: a German-built V12 motor roaring heat and smoke. The ground shook as it came towards you.

Roy saw a second explosion as the Tiger fired and the last of their Bren carriers was hit and torn apart. Steel plates flying into

172

the sky. Flames erupting from what was left. The Tiger turned, almost slowly, into the wide street leading to the central village square.

Roy looked towards the bomb crater in the middle of the square. Destroyed corpses surrounded them. The body of the dead woman and the bloody bundle of her newborn child. He watched as Sister laid the baby to one side and began screwing fuses into the base of grenades. Lining them up on the northern lip of the crater.

The German Tiger panzer fired. Once again, rocked back as it did so. Recoiling. Smoke enveloped it. A house before them exploded. Christ, they seemed invincible. He had to try to get the PIATs.

Sister turned to the baby and placed his open palm on her tiny chest. She was trying to breathe. Sucking breaths in and out. A cage of tiny moving ribs fighting to breathe, coming from the eternity of her mother. There she is. He opened his fingers. This blood- and slime-covered creature. He could kill her easily. No one would know.

The rough knot he had tied holding yet. Her arms waved and her legs kicked out like she wanted to live. She squawked a high-pitched, hungry wail. Of course she was hungry. She had just been born.

Manny had taken Sister's Enfield and was firing at the approaching Tiger. That old-fashioned, fully wooded .303. The bullets just bounced off. The rifle clicked empty. Manny bent forward and reloaded, thumbing a fresh clip of rounds into the magazine. Opened and closed the bolt and continued firing.

Sister had put his thumb in the baby's mouth to quiet her. She murmured as if she had been offered a nipple and he rubbed her gums against the ball of his thumb. Jesus, he thought.

The constant rifle shots seemed to do nothing but annoy the tank and further attract attention. It turned towards them. Fired. Rocking back and forth. Fired again. That amazing bedding and recoiling gun they had. Smoke and dust enveloping it. The first shot was short and careened off the street cobbles. Howling away into the fields like a wounded beast. Machine-gun bullets began backing it up, raking the piazza.

Manny had ducked down next to Sister. Four shots.

Looked at the baby girl. Her head small enough to hold in a palm. Strong black hair on her skull. A good sign, the old people said. Wet ears like seashells. He was looking at her ears.

Anyone there. The gun was being reloaded. Back and forth, the noise and dust and screaming ricochets. And her with her wee hands. Fingernails, she has fingernails. Who knew to do this shit? Who knew how to make fingernails that small?

Sister held the baby out to Manny. He touched her chin with his forefinger. The baby reached and closed her hand around Manny's forefinger. Her first hand. Her left hand. She was left-handed. Like him.

'We have to kill her.' Sister was shaking his head as he spoke to Manny.

'What?' Manny frowned at him. 'No.' He shook his head. 'I'll take her.'

Grabbed the baby child and held her up under one arm. Crouched as if to run from the hollow.

A furious burst of machine-gun fire exploded around him and he threw himself back down.

The baby rolled out from his arm. White dust once again coating her slippery red body. Convulsing, retching like a dying pup.

Sister nodded to him. 'Kill her. Smother her. It's kinder. Quicker. From us it is kinder than leaving her to suffer. Buried alive by that bloody tank. Put your foot on her head. You can do anything. Remember?'

Manny was staring at the ground. 'No.'

'No one will know. I won't say. Kill her.'

'I cannot.'

And then, after what seemed a long time, they both ducked as artillery fire began on the northern edge of the village. More explosions: theirs. Tommy Love must have got back to brigade after all. Some called him Tame Aroha. Tommy Love knew the New Plymouth and Wellington worlds. Stayed true to forgiveness and other things.

Two Typhoons roared overhead and climbed, became vertical and turning onto their backs somehow became angelic. Looped and steadied. Unwavering wings and firing those beautiful twin .30 cal machine guns, 20 mm rockets. Jesus. They were the most welcome things to see. The RAF.

The Tiger's motor was desperately reversing. Tracks churning up mud, backing away, smashing into a whitewashed barn in an effort to hide among the debris of its own making.

'Give me her,' Manny said and held his hands out for the baby. 'Now.'

Sister looked at him.

Manny tore the baby girl from his hands. She was so weak, almost dead. Filthy. Covered in the blood of her mother. The ragged umbilical cord hanging livid from her belly.

Manny held her to his chest. Began running away from the shell crater. Zigzagging towards a side street all but blocked by broken masonry on the eastern end of the square. The shop windows smashed.

What was wrong with him?

An old woman stepped out of the ruins, shoes sliding on the broken glass. Dressed in black. Her large, peasant hands reaching towards the girl child. She was wearing a black headscarf, a black dress. Crucifix at her throat.

Manny thrust the baby into her grasp. Nothing else, he gave the baby to the old woman and kept running. He continued back towards the cover of the battalion's Bren carriers.

Manny would tell him later that her mother named her Renata. He would tell no one else this. Decided it was none of their business what her name was anyway.

'Renata.'

'That's right. And that she loved me.'

For once, Sister had no idea if Manny was lying.

The colours were mostly black and white at first. White ash mixed with water and soot scraped from the inside of wood heaters. Green came from the plumbing beneath the German officers' quarters, their copper pipes. There was some blue but it was almost impossible to get. Brown came from wood soaked for six months, and coffee grounds and discarded tea leaves. Red was particularly scarce. They had tried blood but of course that faded to brown. Tony learned to use tiny strands of red cotton, cut as finely as possible. He was told by Captain Whitten that an equal measure of yellow and magenta made red. Magenta was purple— even more impossible than red—and yellow itself was very rare.

Walter told Tony that Van Gogh, the crazy Dutchman who cut his ear off, had said that yellow represented hope. And the sun. Flowers and rebirth. Wheatfields. Yellow was almost impossible to make, he said. Yellow was impossible.

Walter had managed to get some yellow for him. It came from a Schutzstaffel unit. One of the death squads travelling to southern Russia. They told him that yellow was a Jewish colour. They had tins of it. Boasted that this was the colour of cowardice and of old bruises. Betrayal. These same men would paint the yellow Star of David on the doors of shops and barns and houses. They sold the leftover half tins to the old POW guard for two bottles of Polish vodka. It was the best. Strong Polish vodka, far superior to the Russian.

Tony would paint on the backs of plywood sheets with his black-and-white paints. The easiest colours. He would copy words from the King James Bible. Other words remembered from his childhood. The terrible violence of just being there still remained until it was held and told of love. Breathed upon and kissed by David Brookes. What then? Once he wrote on a painting: *Jesus Wept. Tangi Ihu*. He rubbed it out. Berated himself for also wanting to weep.

The plywood was salvaged by the camp carpenters, also POWs, who often risked their lives to do such things. Walter had befriended them and encouraged that slight air of defiance that hangs about any carpenter. A sort of tough indifference. Probably, somehow, because of Jesus being a carpenter having a bit to answer for. A lot of shit in his name. Walter laughing. A German soldier laughing and calling them natural socialists.

Such a small thing as to give another person something to paint on. A shitty bit of old wood. Those tough old carpenters would not deny him that.

Once he asked Tony if he knew the New Zealand painter McIntyre?

'I don't...I think he might be our war artist?'

'Rita Angus?'

Tony nodded. He had seen a photograph of *Cass* in a copy of the newspaper, 1937 in the public library in Raetihi. They had come to town to get some fencing supplies. Stores. Told Roy he wanted to read the local papers. He had almost stolen the newspaper but he didn't. Even in rough newspaper halftones it had taken his breath away. *Cass.* This painting. He was ashamed for feeling this. Who could you tell?

'I don't know her but I believe she is the best artist in New Zealand. I often wished I was her. Somehow...' Tony laughed. 'See what she saw, anyway.'

'Tony.'

Tony was shaking his head. 'Y'know red is still the hardest colour to get. Red, who would think?'

Walter came to see Tony in the middle of the day.

The sound of his boots on the wooden floor of the long dormitory hut. He was carrying two half-empty pint pots: white alum and red lac. Placed them on the wooden floor before Tony and his easel.

'These are for you,' he said.

Tony nodded to him. Looked down at the pots. 'What are they?'

Walter could not stop smiling. 'When the colours from these two pots are mixed, they become a deep red.'

Tony stared at Walter. He knew what this must have cost.

Klimt and Schiele would have known how important this red was. This wonderful red. It seemed to almost smile at you.

He wanted to say, do not risk your life, Walter. Instead, he just said his name. Then he could not look at him again.

The following week Walter brought half a tin of alizarin. It was left over from the prisoner detail that had been repainting the fire hydrants at the nearby panzer workshop.

'I heard the Russian guns last night,' Tony said. 'They are still a long way off, though. The wind carried them here.'

'Good. They are coming. At last.'

Acting Lieutenant Roy Mitchell looked up at the huge Benedictine monastery at the top of the mountain. Standing like God above the village of Cassino. A constant reminder of God anyway.

Roy was sitting in the smashed-apart front room of a small villa on the Via Lombardo, the main road into Cassino village, surrounded by broken bricks and scattered timbers. The bits and pieces of life, the things that break your heart if you let them in. Clothing. Furniture. Mirrors. Some rugs. Masonry strewn everywhere. Children's toys. A goat for milking, legs in the air and a full udder. A shoat for butchering. Photographs of weddings and grandchildren.

Cassino was distinct in its own way and yet the same as every other Italian village they had passed through in the last few months. Did not bear thinking about sometimes, how alike they became.

But no village had ever been as bad as that time in Gravzano di Lucia. When the Germans shelled the piazza and all the villagers who had come out for them were torn apart. Jesus.

Most of the original Taranaki boys had been killed there.

Replaced. Even Sister and Manny were away.

Both wounded and needing a bit of a rest too. From the things they said. That shit at Gravzano di Lucia. Nobody had ever seen Manny like that. And that was the end of that. If anyone asked him, he would say no. I don't remember that.

It was still cold in Italy that winter. The rain was steady, falling straight down. No wind. Roy was wearing a sheepskin jerkin and sitting, legs drawn up before him with his back to what was left of the front wall of the small house. He was leaning his backpack against the bricks. Holding a Thompson machine gun across the tops of his thighs. The weight of the weapon felt good. Green woollen gloves with the finger-ends cut off. No steel helmet, just a soft khaki woollen cap. Some green towelling round his neck. His long woollen pants held up with wide braces. Shearers bowyangs below his knees. His Australian boots and lower legs covered with the region's rich, dark brown mud.

A second webbing pack lay next to him. It bulged with grenades and spare magazines. The steel helmet tied to the top. Four British ammunition pouches strapped across this second pack. They contained some basic rations of hard biscuits and a tin of corned beef, a bottle of grappa and some tobacco. A glass jar filled with preserved peaches. Another jar filled with tomatoes. Wrapped in newspapers to lessen the chance of them breaking.

Roy continued to study the ground leading into the village of Cassino. He was trying to work out the best lines of advance for the young blokes in his platoon.

The Spanish cork and plane trees in the village square had been shredded. Shade trees at least two hundred years old. Now, their ancient trunks split open. Shattered branches, awkward across the road and in the gutters. Leaves everywhere.

It was a bad sign. It meant the German artillery had their range. The coordinates would be known and pre-plotted onto their target maps. They would be waiting. Reassured by their accuracy, and delay. Who would not?

Rain pouring down, hitting the cobblestones of the Via Lombardi. Dark clouds rolling down the valley and thunder rumbling. The fleeting sights of the mountain and the monastery in the sky filled with grey clouds.

To Roy's left, Urenui Bill Reid was getting a fire started in the shelter of what was left of a bakery. The tiled floor had been swept clean to his right. Next to that a fallen brick wall. A partially collapsed ceiling. It began raining and the water streamed through the destroyed roof.

'Bit damp,' Bill said from the fire.

Roy glanced up at him. 'Yeah, Bill.' Nodded and smiled.

When they first arrived in a new town or village in Italy, Bill would often walk into any house and take whatever he wanted to feed his boys. Jars of preserved tomatoes. Pears, peaches, olives. He knew where all the hiding places were.

Ignored all objections.

He was known once to have punched an old woman in the face when she tried to stop him. Stood in his way and grabbed his arm. Bill did not seem to care. Many of the victims of this plundering said he was a thieving bastard. Sometimes they wept and screamed. He simply stepped around them with his arms full of their food.

Before what had happened at Gravzano di Lucia, Manny often accompanied Bill on these foraging expeditions. Ostensibly it was for Bill's protection but Manny said it offered other opportunities. He would smile at Bill's actions and almost invariably ask the outraged women for sex.

And he said he could not stop laughing at their reactions. Hands on his knees, but always carrying the M1 carbine .30 mm semi-automatic. Lightweight. Easy to carry and, being American, reliable in a fight. Grenades also in his pockets and belt. Manny carried a lot of grenades with him.

He would say that at least he had not killed them—make a throat-slitting gesture—like the Germans would have. So be grateful. Turn around, lift up your dress and show me your shaking arse. Open your legs. Be grateful.

Some did. He had terrified them. That was him. Believed nothing. Thought of as an animal by many, including his fellow soldiers. Even those he called brother.

'Have you got any more salt, Roy?' Bill asked from the fire.

'No.'

'We need more salt.'

'Righto mate.'

'Roy?'

'What?'

'You ever have times when you think we are somehow part of something that lasts forever? Like the monastery that looks like a mountain up there and how the sun sometimes comes through the rainclouds?'

'No.' Roy looked at him. The Urenui fisherman. The sleeves of his battledress were pulled up to keep them out of the food. He made their bread with the potato-water yeast he had carried since Sidi Rezegh.

Onions and a lot of salt were the secret to good food, he said. Curry too, covers up the bad tastes. Wash the old meat with malt vinegar, cold water, cut lemons squeezed into the water if you got them. Methylated spirits work too. Make sure you wash it well and cook it for a long time.

In Serrano he once made them fish and chips. He boiled some stolen potatoes and when they had cooled, cut them up and fried them. The fish was freshly caught bonito. Filleted and dipped in raw egg, flour. Fried in the same pan as the chips. Bottles of white wine. Beer. It was a Friday night after all, Bill said, and we always used to have fish and chips on a Friday night. From the takeaways on Ngakoti Street.

For pudding, bottled peaches and a rice pudding with sultanas. He made a yellow custard with stolen cream. Someone found a ukulele and they began singing. It did not feel like thievery. Their food. What they did. But it was.

'We all die, mate,' Roy said. 'You know that better than most. Seen it a hundred times.'

'I know.'

Roy was looking at his friend, who nodded back to him. 'Rains like this sometimes in Taranaki.'

'It does.'

German white phosphorus smoke bombs began exploding in the street. Granatewerfer 34s. If any phosphorus landed on you it would burn your flesh down to the bone.

A thick, blinding fog began to cover the road. German high explosives and anti-personnel mortar rounds began exploding among the houses. Stone walls shattered, wooden support beams splintered.

Roy was flat on his back. Covered with fallen bricks and

smashed terracotta tiles. White dust. The roof had all but collapsed on top of them.

'Jesus Christ, Bill,' Roy yelled; he didn't know. 'Hang on mate.'

He was trying to get to Bill and found he couldn't move. Wounded, trapped by the fallen masonry, he was losing blood from his chest and belly. The more he tried to free himself the more the wounds bled.

He could hear the German soldiers as they advanced along the street. Throwing grenades and clearing what remained of each house.

Roy dug the heels of his boots into the rubble. Managed to sit up and push some of the masonry and timber off his chest.

A wooden-handled grenade came spinning in through the doorway. Exploded. Followed by another.

Two German soldiers, both carrying MP40 submachine guns, appeared in the doorway. They wore brimless paratrooper helmets. Same soldiers as the bloody Fallschirmjäger of Crete.

Roy killed them both with the Thompson gun. One burst. Changed magazines, the gun slippery with his blood.

'Bill?' Roy called again and even as he called, he knew Bill was dead. That strong metallic smell of blood and opened guts and meat in the air, mixed with cordite from the shooting and explosions.

More rapid bursts of the dreadful 7.62 mm MG42 gunfire. The whole front wall of a house fell into the roadway.

Then he heard two Bren guns firing. A slower cadence, almost a hammering sound. The sounds of .303 rifles. A Wairarapa company was counterattacking, pushed forward from brigade to support the Taranaki boys.

Entering the outskirts of Cassino, where Roy and his men had been attacked, they quickly cleared and secured the area. Retrieved the Taranaki wounded and set up defensive positions.

The freshwater eels Roy's grandmother caught in the Mimi Creek came for the chook guts she threw in. They would come for the blood and she would gaff them. Throw them up onto the bank and then put them into a galvanised bucket she kept there.

Eel meat was good to eat. Skinned, boiled, cut into small pieces and served on the table with salt and malt vinegar. Watch for the small bones. Smoked eel was better. It could be exceptional if poached in fresh milk and the smoking-wood was old manuka.

Urenui Bill.

That is what his opened belly and chest looked like as he died. Eels squirming in a bucket.

The Russian soldiers came to liberate the POW camp at Myslowitz in January 1945. They were part of the great southern advance of the 7th Soviet Red Guards, 3rd Tank Regiment, Chuikov's 1st Ukrainians. They were accompanied by three brigades of mechanised infantry. Upper Silesia had become an area of enormous tactical importance for the Soviets. It represented the security of their western flank as they advanced towards Berlin. They had learnt this at the encirclement of Stalingrad and earlier on the Kalash front.

The first thing the Soviet infantry did when they broke down the gates of the Stalag was to kill any Germans they saw. Anyone standing in their way. Food and alcohol after that. If there were women there were women. But killing came first, and most enjoyed that part.

It had been a long war and they would never tell their mothers what they did. Their wives., their children. There was no need. They would never say that many of them had come to enjoy the savagery they had been licensed. No. Their taking of German girls and women. No. Who would tell such stories?

For many, it became natural to do what they did. Like the Cossacks of old. Every old standard of decency was mocked. The highlight of taking a German town became raping their women to death. Justifying their savagery by humiliating the haughty blonde bitches.

There was always, of course, a line between doing it and enjoying it.

Shooting a badly damaged woman in the head when she had been raped by many men? Sometimes a blessing, in the end. That was doing it. Getting by.

Laughing at an emasculated SS soldier trying to eat his own penis to stay alive, that was hilarious. That was enjoying it. Boiling their feet. Boiling their hands.

This is what these men had become. They looked forward to what they could do next. To the very next German they encountered, with their white feather beds.

Nobody cared except God. And Stalin had told them fuck God anyway. So they came to Germany instead. Millions of feathers from their beds were blowing along the streets. Up to the soldiers' knees in places, like snow.

And who had not wanted to do this at some point in their lives? Kill all the corrupt citizens? Torture their deceivers and hang them in the main square? Who, in their right mind, has not wanted to do that? Decide who decides.

More than twelve thousand Russian children were born in Berlin during 1946. Many more were aborted. Twelve thousand babies is a lot. They were often the most beloved of babies, and who would think? Geliebte Kinder. Many were born in January and February 1946, a most wonderful year.

When asked of rape, many in the 16th Shock Tank Army simply said, yes, of course. And as many as we could. The older German women would often step forward, trying to save the girls. It did not work. The men raped them too. That was the point. The brutality. The cruelty. The ultimate humiliation of the entire country.

If they objected, we killed them. If they did not, we let them live. Sometimes we killed them anyway. Because we could.

Tony had heard the Russian guns months before and he began to hope, just a bit, that they might be freed. The Russian artillery seemed relentless in attack.

The sounds of the T34 tanks in the freezing mist brought him absolute confirmation. He knew the engines were not German engines. The Russian motors ran on diesel, which froze at a lower temperature than petrol.

A very different sound from the petrol motors of the panzers. It meant the war was over.

Sergeant Walter fell to his knees in the snow and raised his hands in prayer. Tony watched him and laughed. This man who had disclaimed and ridiculed God, and yet now thanked God.

Tony was laughing and clapping his crutches together in applause for him.

The leading elements of a Russian reconnaissance unit emerged from the surrounding birch forests. Three T34s, painted white and seemingly unstoppable. Relentless.

Walter had laughed. Said white angels have emerged from the east to free us all.

And now, out of the birch trees, they were coming fast along the road to Krakow. Snow flying from their tracks like angels.

To their left, a long rail siding and goods sheds. The lead tanks bumped over the crossing lines and stopped at the front gate. Rocking. Waiting.

Tony could hear the roar and steady rumble of idling motors. Those fine V12 engines. After a few more minutes, the motor roared again and the tank lurched forward and drove straight through the front gate of the camp, smashing it down. Drove straight into the middle of the central parade ground and began circling in celebration, turning on one track. Ripping up the earth. Mud flying. A terrible desecration of the parade ground with its carefully drawn white lines. The place where they had called the attendance roll sometimes three times a day, every day for three years. Sacred ground to the German guards.

Another much larger formation of T34 tanks was approaching the camp from the east. They belonged to advance units of the assault front: 5th Guards Tank Army.

Soviet infantrymen were running beside the tanks. They wore brown caped uniforms. Some wore helmets, others did not. Carrying machine guns and running beside their tanks. Almost like hunting dogs. They would let nothing hurt their tanks.

Tony watched Walter Schmitt walking towards the advancing Russians. He called to him but Walter would not stop. This kindest and most decent of men. This communist. This fool who had lost everything because he was honest about who he was. This coward.

He would laugh for days at what they had said to each other. He had said you must never stop painting, Tony. No matter what. Look at me when you agree, New Zealander. It is real. Promise me.

Now he walked towards these remote and wonderful beasts

coming out of the white forests. Like angels with a red star on their foreheads. He was unarmed, his hands held out in welcome. Smiling. Tony was smiling at this German man who had brought him red paint.

Walter was calling out to the Russians how he loved Karl Marx with his entire being. He was being deliberately expressive, and had told Tony that is what they will understand. Have you seen their dancing? he had said. The men singing? Their love for us.

Tony urged him to be careful.

But Walter continued speaking to the advancing soldiers in Russian. To make them feel more welcome, he said. He did not know he was speaking the language of 1905 and it was the language of a German conqueror. Tony learned this later from the Soviet soldiers. He had badly mangled the words, which were couched in the Czarist inflection of superiority. The terrible, embarrassing pronunciation of rulers.

He had announced to them that he wanted to have intimate relations with Marx and Engels. Read their Communist Manifesto with his entire being. My fellow workers, do you feel as I do? In your testicles?

Seeing their frowns, their confusion at his words, he began to sing 'The Internationale' to them. It was almost funny but it wasn't.

They shot him anyway.

Central North Island. Aotearoa.
New Zealand, 1946

The black-and-white Gibson bus stopped at the bus stop on the main road opposite the Valley Road turnoff. A yellow signpost.

Roy got off the bus. He still wore his old khaki battledress jacket. It was thin and unbuttoned at the throat. Chevrons unstitched. Medal ribbons gone. Red diamond gone. New Zealand flashes gone.

Best for the start of a new life, the staff sergeant behind the stores desk told him at the Trentham demob. They would send him the campaign medals if he wanted them. Care of the valley where he and Tony had grown up. He said it didn't matter, really. He kept the boots.

Roy looked up. It was a clear October day with high white clouds blown up from the south. The wind was cold with a mountain chill in it. The hills around him were green. Everything seemed wet. There must have been a rain shower in the morning.

He walked to the rear luggage compartment of the bus and began unloading his pack. A new shovel, axe and slasher.

The bus driver came up behind him to ask if he needed help. Her name was Catherine Hall and she was a far better driver than the man she had replaced from before the war. Ken Hatherley, the old bastard. Bad temper and worse breath.

Ken had enlisted in the Div Cavalry, became a tank driver. Had all his rotting teeth removed by an army dentist at the Linton military camp. Sent overseas as a replacement. Killed in North Africa on Operation Crusader, his remains buried at the Heliopolis war cemetery in Cairo. His mother sent a memorial to the Allied War Graves every year until she died.

The bus company, short of drivers with most of the men away, hired women. Catherine Hall had been taught to drive at the age of twelve by her father on the farm. For haymaking mostly. Roy also remembered her from the Clifton Sports Club near the river. She played for a Northern Taranaki netball team. Defence, he thought. Strong-legged player. Wide feet and good hips and would later wear Taranaki colours. Deserved a silver fern. Finest person you would want to meet.

'No, thanks Catherine.' Roy turned from the bus with a shake of the head and she held out her hand.

'Good luck, Mr Mitchell. Welcome home.'

'Thank you.'

'I watched Tony play rugby with the firsts. I am so sorry we lost him.'

He nodded.

She got back on the bus and sat in the driver's seat. For a moment Roy thought she wanted to weep. But she just smiled and turned to look at him. 'Mr Mitchell.' Wet eyes.

She released the handbrake and checked the rearview mirror. All the while standing on the clutch plate and shoving the old Commer bus into first gear. Frowned then as she concentrated on what she was doing and pulled the vehicle out onto the road.

Changed gears. Graunched them a little but carried on.

Roy watched the bus until it disappeared towards the bush-covered bulk of Mount Messenger. He heard her changing gears once again.

Across the road from him, the Butter Factory. A corrugated-iron red roof, upon which a pound of butter had been painted. Behind that the sun and the mountain took up the remainder of the roof. The factory had double loading bays facing the road with wooden stop-planks bolted into the cement to guard against the milk carts banging into them.

Along the boundary fence, leading to the factory, two round troughs for the horses. It was where the farmers would wait every morning after milking to unload milk and cream cans from their carts. A common enough sight before the war.

Next to the butter factory, the 1920 Memorial Dance Hall and beside that the rugby field. That revered flat space. Divided with white lines, twenty-five yards apart. Faded now. Always remembered for its soft green grass, scattered with sheep shit and shrouded in misty morning winter rain. Lichen had grown on the cross-poles during the war.

A small mob of full wool Romneys were grazing in the dead-ball area. Unshorn for two or three years now. Long, dung-caked locks of wool hanging dry from their rear ends, they would rattle as they ran. When the NZEF soldiers were told to hurry up, they were often told to rattle their fuckin' dags.

Paint had faded on the scoreboard. However, the result from the last game remained: Valley: 18, Visitors: 3. They were proud of that score so they left it up.

It must have been around lunchtime because Roy could hear the shrieks and laughter of children in the district primary school across the road. A hand bell being rung and a young woman calling out to stop running. The sounds of their feet on wet asphalt and a bouncing ball. They were safe and alive and laughing and that was enough, really.

No bombs. No dead mothers. No dead children. It is forever with them, y'know? Tears only for a skinned knee. Hurt feelings and disappointments. The children were all right. That was the main thing. Roy stood and looked at the old school building and yard for a few more moments. He and Tony had once played bullrush rugby in that same paddock.

Jesus, Manny would have said, where are their mothers? I want to fuck someone. Sister would say, shut up man, what is wrong with you? Urenui Bill would be getting the cooking fire ready.

He saw again Tony's reflection in the big windows of the schoolhouse. The tennis court next to the schoolyard was enclosed with rusting wire mesh. High enough to catch the wild shots. Tony trying not to laugh as Roy missed the return of serve again.

The general store on the main road had Mobil pumps now, a red pegasus horse prancing and flying on each of them. A drive-through verandah. Red and white Coca-Cola signs. Park Drive tobacco. Pocket Edition from Blenheim. The painting of a smiling young woman wearing a sunhat and holding tobacco leaves.

The weatherboards of the nearby blacksmith shop were unpainted. Birds' nests now in the rusting gutters. Grey windows and dirt smudges. Probably going broke. Not so many horses needed on the farms now.

He and Tony used to take the old school horse there to be shod.

Mr Horrie Cole, the blacksmith. He was a bent-over old man now. Him with his black woollen singlet, leather apron and leather gloves. Once-powerful hair-covered shoulders. A burning kiln always in the middle of his open-air shop. Thick sawdust on the ground and his great bellows, a fire-filled air. The four-pound hammer he seemed to be endlessly smashing onto the anvil. Flying sparks and the memories of that regular clanging as he formed horseshoe after horseshoe. The smoke and smell of burning hooves as he fitted the glowing red-hot iron.

Someone said he walked around the place now bent over like a half-open pocket knife.

When he was twenty-three, Horrie Cole played rugby for the King Country. Known as a good tight-head prop. He could run like a first five with a broken nose. Motorcars will not last, he had said. I will stick with what I know.

The first half-mile of road up the valley was made of crushed white shell-rock, graded level and compacted. This road-fill came from the quarries made by the Construction Division of the First United States Marine Corps. They had been based in New Zealand before beginning their terrible campaign through the Pacific islands. Those tall American boys with their bulldozers and graders. Their smiles and their wide, well-made roads.

They were as welcome, the old people said, as the flowers in May. That was an old saying from where they came from. Flowers blooming in May was the welcome sign that winter had ended there. In the southern hemisphere spring came in August. In New Zealand, flowers usually died in May.

They were so very pleased these American boys had come. They saved us, you know. From the Japanese. They would rarely speak of how the young Americans also seemed to make their daughters want to climb over fences to be near them. They were good-looking young men with wonderful manners. Showed great respect, the Americans, extremely courteous. They had also had gramophones with records of Glenn Miller and the Andrews Sisters.

They began to find a lot of girls' underwear abandoned in the fields beside the main road. At the edges of the flattened grass. Where they had probably been dancing with those American boys.

Many of those same fine young men would be killed at Tarawa, Peleliu, Saipan. Iwo Jima. Okinawa. Twenty-four thousand of them. Those smiling boys. But by God, they could dance to those records in the leaves of grass. Those barefoot American boys, dancing with erections, smiling away at the Kiwi girls climbing fences with their wonderfully lifted skirts.

Hard to imagine twenty-four thousand of them being killed.

Roy began walking up the valley road. To his right, the old All Saints Church. White-painted weatherboards and red roof. Crosses on both steeples. Stained glass.

A simple wooden door with a plain step-up entrance from the pathway through the memorial lychgate. On one side, the names of the men from the district who had served in the First World War. On the other side, a mason had begun to list names of the war just ended. It was not finished.

The names were in alphabetical order on the plain stone, flat tablets bolted to either side of the gate. A cross next to a name meant that he had lost his life.

He saw his own name: R. M. Mitchell. Tony's name was above his with a cross next to it. A. J. Mitchell. Anthony, but he was always called Tony. Rowdy after they joined up. Tony had died of his wounds on Crete: A. J. Mitchell. DOW. 1941. Roy had buried his foot at the Whangamomona listening post.

Seashells and tiny pebbles in the cement of the gate. A small lawn surrounded the church, fenced off as close as possible to the building edges. This allowed any stock to graze to the gravestones. Nothing, after all, should be wasted. A large rhododendron had been planted in the front. A yew along the side. Jesus dwelt within.

Roy had stopped and was staring at the church. It was tiny. Measuring just four yards by about twelve long. You could barely swing a dead cat in it.

Some said it was so bloody small because this was how they felt when they arrived. They looked at those hills and this became a place of safety for them. Offering a sanctuary of sorts from the wilderness outside, the unknown horrors. Many people would be married there. Baptised.

Roy was still staring at the church across the road they had attended as children. He reminded himself that it was 1946. And that he was twenty-six. Returned from the war. He had left Tony in Crete.

Remembered holding hands with his brother at that same church. Being terrified the first time they attended. They had been baptised in that very church. Made God's children. Roy turned and continued walking.

The troopship *Dominion Monarch* from Trieste had docked in Wellington harbour and he was demobbed at the old Trentham Camp, where it had all begun six years earlier. Sure enough. Their father once said the reward for his service was stolen earth, would you believe it? This scarred land, with its cobalt deficiency, a lot of scrub and pumice. Perfect for returned soldiers.

Another twelve hundred acres had been added to the original allocation. Raupatu. Confiscated during the troubles, they said. What they had begun to call Crown land. Large surveyor's blocks in the wilderness. Covered in old bush, blue and white bush. Threads of red kawakawa in the oldest parts. Tony had said once that it was the best land anyway. Because nobody else wanted it. They all looked at him when he said that.

Tony had always been a fool about such shit.

After another half-mile the valley road reverted to a muddy track, as it was before the war. You would sometimes have to lead a horse up it on foot. Could not ride it.

Rising steadily up into the bush and disappearing over the old ridges towards the mountain in the east, Ruapehu. Directly behind him, to the west, the silver ribs of Taranaki. Tony told him the old story of how they had quarrelled, separated. The river, Te Awa Whanganui, was not the path but that which always lay between them.

Two long white lines from the slipstream of an aircraft appeared above Ruapehu.

One hundred and forty-five American B-17s dropped their bombs on Monte Cassino and almost everyone cheered as the ancient Benedictine monastery blew up.

David Brookes did not. Tony was dead on Crete by then and Sister was still weeping for him when he was alone.

On the valley road, he adjusted the pack further up his back by leaning forward at the waist and shrugging it higher. He had done this countless times. From Greece to Crete. North Africa. Through Sicily and up to Cassino where he was knocked. It was after the repatriation hospital in Taranto that he got back to the battalion in Trieste just as the peace treaty was being signed. May 1945; back to NZ on the *Dominion Monarch* not long after that.

Every infantry soldier knew that leaning forwards and shrugging the pack higher onto their back seemed for a while to make it easier to keep walking. It was in Serrano that the battalion became fully mechanised for the first time. Their role as infantry soldiers remained but it meant they did not have to walk so much. Got to the front line more quickly. Got to be killed faster, Manny said.

Roy continued holding the axe and spade just below their heads in one hand and the slasher in the other. The pack and those old ammunition pouches settling onto his back.

He had always carried extra grenades. Spare magazines for the Bren. Tobacco and coffee. Four British canteens. Since they landed in Italy, brandy or grappa in one, water in the other three.

The bush-covered hills rising up before him. Hold my hand and see what I am seeing, Tony. But that was a stupid thing to think. Tony was dead.

It was about another hour before he stopped and rested. Caught his breath. His back and shoulders hurting. His knees. Hips too. Sat and rested the pack against the base of a tree. Looked downhill, the way he had come.

Remembered Sergeant Niania speaking to them during Trentham training about what it meant to be an infantry soldier from Aotearoa. He said New Zealand too. But he used another voice when he said that.

'First day out,' he said, 'everything hurts. Second day, same.

You are hurting everywhere. You are sore. Your feet and your back. Your arse. But.' He walked back and forth before these young men. 'After another day it begins to get easier. The weight has not changed. The mines and flares and ammunition still being carried by you, and rightfully so—they have not changed. The rations and water bottles on your back. The weight of the rifle you carry in your hands has not changed. The weight of the bayonet has not changed.'

Sergeant Niania waited another moment before he said: 'But you have. You have changed.' Sergeant Niania was a traditional man.

It would take a few more years before Roy stopped searching for minefields. Snipers, machine guns. But that was all right too. Happened to a lot of the older men. They would sometimes yell out in their sleep for no reason. Embarrass themselves. Many would laugh at anything you said. Anything at all. It stopped the thinking too much. Singing together, that was also good.

The land beside the road was boggy and filled with islands of harakeke and raupo. Pukeko swamp hens were stalking koura, the delicious freshwater crayfish. Their one lifted foot poised above the water. Insects flew above the reed-filled pools. Second growth manuka fringed the roadside. No stock. The paddocks were bare.

It would be dark before he reached the farm. All the rest of the day on the road. That was all right. Walking at roughly five miles per hour with a half-hour rest break every three hours, must be fifteen miles. It would be dark when he got there. The sun set at about five-thirty and if he could not see to walk, he would sleep in the long grass and fern on the side of the road. Roll up in a groundsheet, sleep even through the rain. That was easy, they had done it a thousand times. Bivvi up, they called it. Make tea in the morning.

Roy continued walking. He kept his eyes to the east. Behind him the mountain he knew as Egmont.

'Have you ever just considered it for a moment?' Tony had once asked him. 'About the name of the mountain? Egmont?'

'Yes. I have.'

'Named by Cook for his boss. The First Lord of the Admiralty.'

'So what?'

'He never even came here.'

They had argued and Tony would not talk to him for a while. Refused to. Would turn away at the table. Their father was asleep. Drunk as usual, snoring and groaning. Yelling out in his sleep. Their mother looking at them and smiling a lot and holding the edge of the blanket that separated their bedroom from the kitchen in the one-roomed hut they lived in.

It lasted a month. Them not speaking over the name of the mountain. Eventually, Roy said sorry to his brother. This was a rare thing.

Tony immediately forgave him. 'About time,' he said, and laughed. Relieved they had stopped ignoring each other.

Roy was looking at his feet as he walked. His legs were becoming tired.

The old infantry joke: why why are my waewae so sore? Waewae were his legs. Memories of being a soldier. Running again...Come on boys. You can do it, keep going. Keep running.

Spread out and keep running, you ugly bastards. The things his mates would yell to each other in the minefield. They said it was good to be laughing as you were blown up. That terrible adrenaline rush of laughter was like not eating breakfast before an attack. In case you were shot in the guts. More likely to survive a stomach wound with an empty belly; clean intestines heal quicker. Older soldiers knew about this. Another mine kills another New Zealander. He had eaten breakfast.

Roy had been standing still on the road, looking down, as the memories came over him.

He looked up and opened his eyes to see an old man astride a draught horse harnessed to a flat-bed trailer. It was stacked with dark split firewood. Rubber wheels. Tyres with chalk marks on them.

Roy stepped back to allow them to pass. Nodding and raising his hand in greeting.

The old man stopped. 'You Roy Mitchell? Michael and Louisa's boy?'

'I am.' Roy nodded. 'That's right.' He had seen the man before but could not remember quite where. His face was familiar.

'Well, I'm your neighbour from the old days. Nick McCarthy. You probably don't remember me, son. But I remember you boys. My word I do. You bloody twins. Jumping out of your skins if I recall. You and your brother. Tony. He's not with you? No?'

'Mr McCarthy.' Roy nodded. 'Of course. Your farm was next to ours, up the back. I beg your pardon.'

The man leaned down, offered his hand. They shook.

'I only manage it now,' he said. 'Sold out to the Fields. You will too if you know what's what.'

204

Roy stepped away. 'But it was your place,' he said.

'No, no. Just the same. The scours and the bush sickness. Old man Field reckons there'll be another depression after the war, though. Like the slump we just had, he said.'

'No,' Roy said.

'Demand dropping off, see. No more wool for the uniforms. Meat for the soldiers. Makes sense. I sold it out to him. Took all the pressure off as well.'

'I see.'

'You just back?'

Roy nodded.

'That twin of yours. Not with you?'

'No. He is not.'

Nick lowered his eyes after a while. 'Want a ride?'

Roy nodded, smiled and threw his pack and shovel, the slasher and the axe onto the trailer and climbed up. Moved some of the firewood blocks to make a rough seat behind the swingle bar. Braced his feet against the front board as the old man kicked the ribs of the horse he was riding and the trailer lurched forward.

Roy noticed a black-and-white dog behind them. A bitch, by the narrow bones in her face, and showing some white eye. She was running slightly behind them. A shy dog, it looked like she had been badly hurt somewhere along the line.

He looked closer. She was outstanding. A wounded treasure.

'She any good?' Roy said to Nick's back.

Nick glanced over his shoulder. 'Who?'

'That black-and-white eye bitch you got back there? The shy one following us.'

'You mean our Floss?' Nick said. 'Best bloodlines there is. Her mother had two champion pups. Boy was the sire, from

Otairi Station over near Hunterville in the Rangitikei. Owned by one of the Lillburnes or the Duncans, I believe. The Blinkhorne brothers knew what they were doing with working dogs. The head shepherd, Jim. Finest stockman you ever saw. You heard of him?'

Roy was nodding. 'I have...he won the North Island trials three years running before the war. Strong heading dog name of Boy. Sire a champion before him, and the mother was one of the old border dogs, I was told. Brought over by the original Scottish musterers. Understood only Gaelic commands.'

'There you are,' Nick said. 'Many of the old southern dogs only knew Gaelic. A foreign tongue for many. Almost had to shoot them when the owners died. But how could you kill a dog like that? Just for not knowing what you were saying to it? Teach them English, I say.'

'She for sale?'

'No.' Nick shook his head. 'No, these old dogs are like gold. You cannot sell them.'

'Righto then.' Roy replied. Refusal was the first custom for all such sales.

They both fell silent.

Floss was running beside the trailer's back wheel. Long, pink tongue falling wet and naturally from her mouth. Ears cocked. Occasionally blinking but with that fluid running action of all good working dogs. Her easy balance over the rough ground was remarkable. Strong, liquid shoulders. There was also that silence about her as she ran. A sure sign of worth. When she looked at you, the entire world slowed down. Strong eyes.

She was priceless. All she needed was respect for who she was, and her loyalty would be given forever in return. Such as this was by its very nature unquestioning. He knew he would buy her within the hour.

The old land was unfolding before him. It was all those places he recognised most. Somehow touched with their laughter and disbelief and wonder. A hand on a fence post. The land, filled with wild bush and those sheer greywacke faces. White bluffs and papa slips. Many razorback ridges yet. Moko te whenua, Tony said of their place. Scarred land. Their father's land.

Roy closed his eyes. What he remembered most about their childhood was that it rained a lot and there was not much food. After she left, even less.

Walked out during the Depression. Their Depression. Make you laugh if you wanted it to.

The higher they travelled, the more the land seemed to relax around them. It became more all right somehow for it to be what it was. Covered in bush. Untouched. Uncleared. Rough. Happier too, somehow.

A mournful singing noise coming from the man on horseback. Nick, humming away at an old-fashioned gospel hymn. After a few more moments, some words. 'Ooooh...What a beau...tiful thought I am thinking...concerning a great speckled bird.'

The horse's eyes had widened at the noise. Sometimes Nick would slap his own leg as he sang. Cry out to his dead mother.

Floss just kept running and did not break stride, opened and closed her mouth once or twice. Pink tongue dripping.

Nick continued. 'Remem...ber her name is recorded....on the pages of God's holy word...'

He paused, trembling, and fell silent. Wiped the heel of his palm over his eyes. Sighed.

They began descending the track towards a shallow creek bed with a green-laced and slippery papa crossing.

'Nick?' Roy was concerned at the steep angle of the track.

'Roy?'

The trailer began sliding, veering to one side.

Nick was pulling back as hard as he could and Bill the horse was digging his heels in and sitting back on his tail to try to slow them down as much as he could. The trailer shafts, straining and pushing against the harness collar.

'Jesus,' Nick whispered. 'Hold on, Roy.'

They were being propelled sideways by the weight of the firewood. The swingle bar chains snapping against the pressure. Still sliding and unable to stop. Rocking, almost about to turn over, both hanging on and leaning.

It was a full minute before the trailer slid, jackknifing to a stop at the water's edge.

'Jesus fuck me,' Nick whispered.

Roy had not said a word. At least nobody was dropping mortar bombs on them. Machine-gunning them. No one was being killed.

'That was a bit bloody close, mate,' he said.

Another minute passed and old Nick had still not replied. He was gaining his breath. Laughing as he breathed. 'Yeah. It was. It was.'

Roy decided he would change the subject. Try to make him see sense about the dog.

'You sure that dog's not for sale?'

The creek water reached up to the axles of the trailer. The horse blew air through his nostrils while bending his head to drink as he walked through the creek. Nick and Roy had crossed and resumed their climb up the steep track on the other side. That was all they could think about for now. Getting up on the flat.

It was another two hours before they reached the new land the government had allocated to him for his overseas service. It was marked on the track frontage by two timber stakes driven into the ground. A cross brace. Blocks 363/364/.NZDVLD.

Nick turned and put his hand up to shade his eyes. Looked out over the high bush and rough country. The sounds of cicadas in the trees. Shrieks of fleeing birds. Distant in the valleys.

'Here you are young Roy,' Nick said as he slid off the horse and indicated with an open hand. 'Your new place. It's right next to where you boys grew up anyway if I am not mistaken.' He was pointing to the south. The burnt trees. 'The old house, over there. You must remember?'

'Yep.' Roy was staring at the land. He nodded. Block 362. Their father's soldier settlement farm from the first war. Now his from the second.

'You all right?' Nick glanced at him.

'Yep, good.'

Roy remembered how he and Tony had laid possum traps all around here when they were young. It was pretty much untouched country. Some of the older trees had been taken for timber and there was a bit of regrowth along the paths where they had been hauled away with bullocks and chains. But these paths were marked anyway with mostly mahoe, kawakawa and raru. Ancient wheel ruts.

The bulk of this country was, as it had always been, good for nothing but what it was. The best of reasons, Tony would say, nobody else wants it.

Bloody Tony, he would say things like that.

So much, Roy thought, had been touched by his brother. He could still sometimes almost see him near a tree. Hear his voice. Especially, for some reason, whenever it rained. Walking next to him, going home. A dog with them. Possum traps over their shoulders. Whooping like Red Indians as they ran down ridges after wild pigs.

Floss had crept closer to him, silent in her movements, Unnoticed, she lay with her chin in the grass and lifted a tentative, white-edged eye towards him. A reminder? A question? This was the truth of such eye dogs. They allowed you to know yourself better.

'Any idea what you'll do?' Nick waved his hand at the thick bush of his new farm.

'I'll work something out,' Roy said.

Nick nodded. 'As I said, the Fields will buy your place if you want to go and live in town.' He cleared his throat. 'Get a job at the freezing works over in Waitara. Borthwicks down at the river mouth there.'

'I'm right at the minute, Nick.'

'Railway workshops in Whanganui East will always take on someone looking for work.'

'I'm good.'

'Those old union shops never turn anyone away. Especially the returned blokes. Forestry Department too. Always hiring.'

Roy was shaking his head, smiling but ignoring him and looking at the ground.

'They own my old place now.' The longer Nick spoke, the louder his voice seemed to become. 'Like I said,' he yelled.

'Righto.'

'They got the biggest station in the district now, the Fields. Must be over sixty thousand acres altogether they got. Hundred thousand.'

Roy knew old Nick was not even speaking to him anymore.

'Oh yes,' Nick yelled again. 'At least ten bloody musterers work for them. At least. Even got their own fencer, for Christ's sake. Their own cook. They must kill five sheep a day just to feed the fuckin' shepherds. Over three hundred horses. Blood stallions. Thoroughbred brood mares, I heard. Hundreds of dogs. Ten shepherds with ten dogs each. Ask yourself.' Nick was shaking his head and trying to smile at Roy at the same time.

It was a few moments before Roy replied. 'You got a price for her over there?' he said. 'That dog there?'

Nick frowned at him. 'What?'

'She for sale? That dog there?' Roy nodded towards Floss in the grass. 'What's her name? Floss?'

'Floss.'

'Looks a bit shell-shocked to me, Nick,' Roy said. 'She been hurt? Kicked by a horse or something? Run over?'

'No.' Nick shook his head. 'Sound as a bell. Just a little timid is all. Clever as you would ever get. Good blood. Well bred.'

'No, mate.' Roy coughed. 'She's a damaged animal. We can both see that. Anyone can, just looking at her.'

'Good blood,' Nick repeated.

Roy remained silent. He looked at Nick, unsmiling. Shaking his head.

Nick looked at him. 'You are a harder man than your father ever was. No. She is not for sale.'

It was a full minute before Roy spoke again. Changed the subject. 'I have ordered supplies.' He was examining the accumulation of mud on his boots. 'Fencing wire. Posts and corrugated iron. Some cement. Nails, milled and creosoted timber. You got any idea when the deliveries come up the valley, Nick?'

'That would be with Freeman R. Jackson's Thursday truck,' he said and scratched beneath an armpit. 'They generally come though once a week. On Thursdays. Bring the mail, any supplies you ordered. Day after tomorrow, that would be.'

'Any idea of the time?'

'Oh, it depends.' Nick crossed back to the horse and trailer. Made a show of checking the leather harness and a broken chain connection. 'Round midday generally. Give or take an hour. Depending on the going.'

'The going?'

'Yep. Like that blessed creek we just crossed. A sinner of a thing, that creek. Especially if it's in flood.'

'I have fifty-five pounds,' Roy said. 'My final pay at demob down at Trentham. All the money I got in the world. I'll give you five pounds for that dog right now.'

Nick stared at him and repeated what he had just said as if it was bad news or a question that he had not heard correctly. 'Five pounds...'

'Yep. I'll give you five pounds for her,' Roy said. 'Right now.' He was holding out a banknote.

Nick laughed. 'You would get five pounds for her first pup alone, young Roy. Jesus. She will have six at least with her first litter. That's thirty pounds. I'd want twenty for her.' He looked out at the bush-covered hills. The new farm.

Roy shook his head. 'No one will breed from her, mate,' he said. 'No. She will go any male dog put near her.'

'You reckon?' Nick said.

'She is frightened by the sound of a raised voice. Jesus, man. A cough? A hard sound? If it wasn't for her bloodlines she'd be gone already. Dead. Yeah? Shot her if you felt generous.' Roy nodded once and shook his head.

Nick looked at him, folded his arms. He knew it was the truth. 'You need a start?'

'I do.'

Nick nodded, cleared his throat and turned his back. Crossed to where a silver disc had been nailed into the lichen-covered trunk of an old kahikatea. A mass of bracken fern at his feet. Hanging branches of lichen in the tree. A strong tree.

'Lot L45918. Mitchell. Waimarino Lands and Survey. Lots 363/364.' He was reading the disc nailed to the tree. 'Is that you?'

Roy nodded. 'That's me.'

Nick was standing at the edge of the road. One hand still leaning against the kahikatea. 'The creek's down there,' he said. 'The Mangawhero.'

Roy stepped forward and again held out the banknote. 'Five pounds for Floss there? Right now. What do you say?'

Nick smiled and looked at him. Took his hand and shook it. 'Well done, young man. I am giving her away for that price but you do need a dog.'

'Thank you.'

'She will have fine pups for you. Put quality over her, mind.'

'Nick,' Roy said. 'I told you. She will not take any dog for a long time. Here.' Roy gave Nick the five pounds.

They shook hands again. 'You all right, young fella?'

'Dunno. What do you reckon?' Roy looked at him.

'I reckon you're all right.'

The dog had come closer to Roy. She seemed to know somehow that he was hers now. Sensed he was a good man. Her feet moved as she sat. Pink tongue lolled. She leaned into his leg for just a moment. Pulled away and her eyes half closed. Ears forward. Waited. Lay down at his feet.

'Stay here, the Floss,' Nick growled at her. 'That'll do.'

She opened and closed her mouth. Looked away. He had always been a cruel old bastard towards her. Her ribs and backbone showed plainly through her coat. Sharp, hungry eyes. A line of hair growing back over the welts on her spine and hips where old Nick had whipped her when yarding some in-lamb ewes. Thrashed her with a fencing chain.

Roy would come to know and detest the way he treated animals. Consider him someone to avoid at all costs. It was also true that old Nick had become more vicious after he had sold his property to the Fields. All landless men become madder and more terribly cruel as they age.

The horse blinked as Nick returned. Braced his legs in anticipation of the old man's weight. Nick mounted. The trailer rattled and lurched forward. He kicked the horse in the ribs and raised a hand as they moved off. He did not look back.

Roy watched him as he disappeared around a rising bend leading to the property that had once been his farm. Once his place before he sold it to the Fields. His land. It had been the smart thing to do. Financially. And so he became the manager of what used to be his. In his bones he knew something was wrong, but it took the worry away. Whisky helped. And he had all that money in the bank. Not as much as he hoped after the mortgage got paid but at least he could go to the races as far south as Awapuni and

Otaki. Trentham for the Wellington Cup. Began to beat his wife. Despise his children.

'Good luck, young Roy,' Nick yelled out. 'You know where I am if you need a hand? I knew your mother. Your father too, though we didn't get along too well.'

It was true that many had disliked their father. Tony had always loved him. Forgave him all things.

Roy did not.

Their father was just a fool since the war. Useless. Tried twice to kill himself and drank sherry in the morning. Called methylated spirits 'fix bayonets'. Rum was gunfire. He would often look away when he was trying to speak. Stutter. He once wet himself at a funeral in Waitara. Wept all the time, the damn fool. Sang hymns at the most inappropriate times. Outside the schoolhouse, the classroom. When everyone else was silent. He would sing and they would look at each other. It was almost like he was trying to be mad. Broken was his heart—a poem he once recited. Jesus.

Floss lay down in the grass and waited. Roy pushed the spade he had been carrying into the ground and was holding the handle. It was something his father used to do. Just standing on the side of the track and leaning on the spade, unable to move for a moment. He looked to where the old farm had been. The swing bridge over the Mangawhero. The track to the old house. The fruit trees their mother had planted. In spring the white blossoms were pears. Apple flowers, pink.

He could not see it but there was a broken trellis holding up what they called the Chinese gooseberry vine. It had spread over the outside long-drop toilet. Next to the toilet there was a white mulberry tree. It brought the tiny silver-eyes in spring. Every year, like new arrivals with ancient memories, they would come. Tony said they were also called tauhou. The waxy eyes.

She had walked out in 1934. Their mother. She had planted all those beautiful trees and vines and then walked out. They couldn't sell their little bit of milk or wool and their father was almost constantly weeping by then. Drinking away whatever money they managed to get.

There was not even enough to pay the mortgage. The Valley store had stopped their credit. The owner, Mrs Smith, held a hand over her mouth. Closed her eyes and shook her head. Looked away. Could break your heart if you let it. He remembered their mother going outside and vomiting with shame.

So, in the end, down the track Mum went. Swayed over the swing bridge. Wearing her church hat and carrying a brown suitcase. Once she was on the main road she did not look back and she did not come back. It was, she would say, pretty much downhill from there.

Their father had trouble getting out of bed after he found out about her leaving. Turned his face to the wall. High shoulder. Told them to go and find what work they could.

There was little paid work for them. It was the Depression, what many called the bloody slump, and they were barely fourteen.

They eventually found work in a bush-clearing gang. It was just for their keep. They worked all day helping the tree fellers for their food and a dry place to sleep at night. But they were also taught many practical things in those gangs. Best way to use an axe. A spade. Make a bush hut, a whare, in an hour. How to build stockyards and fences. Kill and butcher animals for the table. And begin to work with the dogs. Handle horses, not only to haul timber but to ride into town for supplies. Because they were light, being so young, they often got the riding duties.

After another year, they were taught by an old Scottish shepherd to work with stock. The same old musterers showed them how to break in horses. The slow way and the not-so-slow way. He was a convicted stock thief from the South Island but a magician with dogs and horses. He appreciated their help and saw they both had a facility.

It wasn't long before they had reputations. All right, those Mitchell boys. Quick learners and cheerful when the going got tough. They went on to become good contract musterers. But it was known in the district that Tony was a bit like his father, a little touched. Would often weep, and at the strangest things. Like a foal being born.

The local men said that that old Mitchell had never punished his boys enough. He had been gassed in the war and hissed when he spoke. Couldn't raise his voice to them. Never punished them either. A weak man. Coughing his guts up most mornings. A drunk. His wife took off to Australia.

Tony had asked him once, 'What is the unbeaten child spoiled for, Roy?'

Roy had shrugged. 'Obedience?'

Tony looked at him. 'Do you think we held hands as we swam together in our mother's womb?'

'Fuck,' Roy exclaimed and stepped back. 'Don't ask me that sort of shit, Tony.' He was shaking his head. He looked like he wanted to be sick.

Tony blinked. 'I'm sorry,' he said. 'I shouldn't have asked you that.'

Roy pulled the spade out of the earth and then drove it in again.

The betrayal on Crete. The abandonment. The guilt he felt

because of the terrible moment when he was just too bloody frightened to go back. Knowing that white flush of relief as he ran away from his brother. It was true. Who would you ever admit that to? Such a secret being your utter cowardice.

Being terrified and running from your twin brother as he lay and died in the dirt.

Floss opened her eyes and then closed them again. Ignored him.

Roy was still holding the spade handle, and suddenly sat, almost collapsed, on the ground. A bewildered look had come over him. Floss sensed that this was unlike him. She was almost embarrassed for his bewilderment.

In 1936, he and Tony were cutting bush up on the Matahiwi Track when a police sergeant rode down the Parapara track from Raetihi on a white-faced horse he called Rocky. It was because, he said, that is what his arse felt like after riding the white-faced horse for more than ten minutes. It had a bony back. A mule's attitude. And he had developed rocks in his arse.

He found them and told them their father was dead. With their mother gone now for over a year it was up to him to let them know.

'Your dad lasted not much more than a year after she took off. Left everything to you boys. It was a soldier's block from the war, did you know?'

They nodded.

'They say he was drinking bad in the end.' The policeman looked at the ground after he said this. Then he said, 'I am sorry, you boys. For your loss.'

The farm had been left to them and their mother had not

contested it. She cabled a reply that the boys were old enough to look after themselves and wished them well. The farm was theirs. Given to them by the government anyway. She said she just wanted to forget everything about New Zealand. The mud. Rain. Him. The depression. Her children.

Tony would sometimes ask Roy why their mother did not want to see them. Why she didn't come home.

'We make her feel weak, see,' Roy said. 'Like how some people in prison don't want to see their kids. She loved us but we were the other life she left behind. Doesn't want to think about again. The mistakes she made. So she took off. Can't blame her, can you?'

She had replied in the cable that if the boys did not want it, the ownership of the property could revert to the government.

The old house and yards had burnt down and what stock there was had run wild, died or been stolen. A magistrate in Whanganui held the title deeds, government authorisation for the land and their father's will.

As usual Tony said nothing. He walked off to a nearby fence line, held the top wire and looked away over the high ridges. The place they grew up on was about eighty miles to the east as the crow flies. That meant in a straight line, he supposed. There were no crows in New Zealand. Keruru flew in straight lines, though. You could hear the whooshing of their wings as they passed between the Puriri. The wood pigeon, with their big white breasts, were easy to kill. Beautiful to eat. She took off like a bird.

Roy told the sergeant of police holding the white horse they would keep the place for now. Asked if he would please inform the local justice of the peace.

'What about you, Tony?' the policeman asked. 'How do you feel about this, son?'

219

Tony nodded. He was looking away in the direction where their farm had been. He did not turn around. Simply raised a hand in agreement. What could you do? That sort of gesture. A raised hand with your back turned.

In the first winter after their father died, it rained every day. As a result of this, they travelled down to the coast and looked for work in the towns. They were only sixteen years old. Boys. They tried the meatworks and the fertiliser packing sheds. Nothing. They sought casual labour at the railway yards. Unloading the wagons. Sometimes they had to sleep rough. Woodsheds behind houses were good, apart from the rats and mice, which also came indoors during the winters. Sometimes possums in the rafters. Old newspapers kept you warm.

Poor people would feed you if they could and the rich would often tell you they had already called the police. The wives were frightened of you. A natural enough thing, Tony said, to Roy's outrage. When the warmer months returned, they went back to the valley and found work in the district with the biggest bush-clearing gang. It was just for their keep.

Three years later, the boys were nineteen and up on the Waiouru central plateau when the war broke out. Early September 1939. Spring. A fencing and a tree-planting contract for the New Zealand Railways. Pack horses and sleeping in a tent but they felt lucky to have it. Good regular money.

A union official came up from Wellington and called a meeting for all members and associate members at the recruiting office that had been set up at the Memorial Hall next to the Ohakune Public Swimming Baths.

There were a few introductions, then they were told that they were at war with Germany and they should, if at all possible, join up and do what they could for the country and for Britain. The union man didn't say the Empire, he just said Britain. Our trading partner. He sounded like a politician. He insisted that this war was much, much different from the last one. He also assured the engine drivers that all essential services on the railways would be maintained.

He finished with the words 'not a backward step', and received a loud ovation. The clapping went on for quite a bit. So he repeated it: we will not take a backward step. Cheers.

It did not seem to bother the audience that the same bloke was a waterside fighter of some repute who had come across from Melbourne and went to the state farm Weraroa near Levin with Peter Fraser for three years. Stood behind him with his hands crossed. No one would touch a hair on Fraser's head without going through him first. And he could fight like the Ulsterman he was. Union through and through.

Then they went inside.

The Mitchell boys were immediately signed up into the New Zealand Infantry Brigade, 22nd Battalion. The Wellington/ Taranaki Battalion. Their father's old battalion. The smiling recruiting officer sent them down on the night train from Waiouru to Trentham. They were nineteen. Turning twenty in 1940.

When they arrived at the training camp near the racecourse, four very angry NCOs told them they were showers of ugly shit then began screaming at them.

'Just do as you are told, you ugly worm people, or I will kick you up your fucking arses so hard you will taste boot polish for a week.'

From the edge of the station platform, a grey-haired, sergeant major was watching them. His hands held behind his back. An old model lemon squeezer firmly on his head. Leather chinstrap beneath his bottom lip. 'What did you ugly people expect? Paradise?' he whispered, and chuckled to himself. 'Forgiveness for what you will do?'

He had been watching them. They had begun to become soldiers. They might be all right.

Roy whistled to Floss as he got to his feet. He didn't know how long he had been sitting on the side of the road like a fool. Holding on to the spade, just like their father often would.

He lifted the army pack up onto his shoulder. It was still heavy; scarred and utterly familiar. Retrieved the axe. The slasher. Waited until his head cleared. The things he thought sometimes.

After a few more minutes, he stepped through the fence gate and began to make his way into the new land the government had given him.

Lots 363 and 364. Floss followed. She would stop when he stopped, walk back when he walked back. He pushed on through scrub and regrowth manuka until the rising ground underfoot became clearer. Cooler. The older forests on higher ground. Moss and green ferns beneath the canopy. The earth, made muscular with exposed tree roots. Above him, sunlight filtered through old rata trees, rimus.

The sheer beauty of these trees had sometimes stopped the first loggers from cutting them down. Breathtaking stuff. But not often. They had to be outstanding. Their bark flaking to the touch and rough leaves. Red flowers in decoration like the edges of a well-made kakahu cloak. Who would have thought about such things when you cut them down?

Floss sniffed at a path that wild pigs had used to get down to the creek. He began to follow her downhill. A single cheeky piwakawaka fantail danced and challenged their progress. The sounds of the running water increasing as they made their way to the bottom of the spur. Running over rocks, beyond the clumps of toi-toi. The Mangawhero creek. You could smell the water.

It was only three feet wide now. Flat and fringed with a flood plain of about a hundred yards on its western edge. Filled with rocks and banks of stranded driftwood. Fallen and tangled logs. The creek where Tony had saved him during that terrible flood of 1933. The old man tree his brother had pulled him from still lay entangled along one bank. Limbs like hands. The high green face of the opposite bank above him.

Floss bent her head and drank, intent, her slow tongue lapping. Roy waited and listened. Knelt, one leg parallel. Another old war habit: to be still and wait. Ready to move. Listen through the silence, man. He could hear the sound of the dog drinking. Water running across the stones of the Mangawhero. Somewhere a tui called, that wet creak of a song, followed by her chuckling. He waited. Began to smile like a fool.

The late afternoon and the lengthening shadows of the bush around them. Roy found a place they could camp for the night. He took off both his packs and gear. Placed the axe and spade laid out as he would the machine gun and grenades. Gathered some old dry manuka twigs and leaves. Lit them with the waterproof wax matches, watched and blew on the leaves as they caught alight. The flames catching onto the twigs. The crackling and smell. Done it a thousand times. He gathered larger pieces of near-dry wood and leaned them against the fire in a cone shape. Drying them out to use later. The fire flared and blew sideways as a night-wind came in from the west. Sparks flew up. Thick embers were beginning to form in the base.

He set up the fly tent upwind of the fire. It was lightweight, made from old parachute material. An old Fallschirmjäger groundsheet and a Liebstandarte sleeping bag, both made of quilted nylon. Some of the German military gear was very good in the cold. Especially the SS and Fallschirmjäger kit. They say Upham would not allow a German-made vehicle on his place after the war.

The groundsheet was dry and warm. Roy crawled inside the small fly tent, got into the sleeping bag, rolled up a towel for a pillow and lay down. Whistled to Floss.

'Good girl.'

She came and lay at his feet. Good as a hot water bottle, having a dog on your feet on a cold night.

As he fell asleep, he could hear the water in the creek. He was on a bit of flat ground above it. Could build the whare here.

He was woken by a fine rain and the *pock-pock* of larger drops falling from the trees overhead onto the stretched nylon of the old fly tent.

Floss had progressed from his feet to curl up warm against the small of his back. He had been reminded of the sharp bones of her spine when she moved in the night. Her breathing coinciding with his. It was common for shepherds and musterers to sleep against the blood heat of their dogs. Especially on cold nights in the bush and high country.

Roy crawled out of the tent. The ground was wet and the air was filled with that high country, almost distilled, mist. The sun coming through the morning haze. It would be a fine day. Floss followed him out of the tent and ran off to squat.

He found some wood shavings and rekindled the fire. Once it was going, he watched the flames. Wiped his eyes with the back of his wrist. The smoke.

Floss shot him a furtive look.

He knelt and began unpacking his 08 pack. Laid out each of the four British ammunition pouches, almost as if there was an inspection. His hands were shaking for some reason. His mouth was working. Soundless, yet it was opening and closing. He removed the rest of the pack's contents. Three flat oval tins of mackerel in tomato sauce. A towel and a small bar of Pears soap. Gillette safety razor. Comb. A bottle of iodine, two bandages and a tourniquet. Zeiss binoculars engraved with the Luftwaffe eagle. Three pairs of woollen socks. Two tins of corned beef. Four blocks of military-issue Cadbury chocolate.

There were no more flares or extra magazines. No grenades or loose bullets. He always carried six grenades. Have you ever seen what a grenade can do to someone? What they reveal?

Room for more rations. He tried to whistle an old tune and could not. Roy never wept. He would not.

Ten boxes of wax matches. Striker paper. Some loose tea in a screw-top tin. A pair of linen shorts and two shirts. Three candles and matches. An ex-Wehrmacht mess kit and fork, knife and spoon combination. A can opener. Two larger spoons and pint bottle of Hennessy brandy wrapped in a hand towel. For emergencies.

Floss raised her head and looked at him. And then looked away after a bit. He had become silent.

The last thing he took from the old pack was an oilskin pouch. His discharge papers and record of service. His paybook. The legal deeds of ownership to the land adjoining the block that had been allocated to him from the World War I agreement for returned soldiers. A copy of their father's will.

He dropped two handfuls of black tea leaves into the teapot. Stared at the boiling water for a moment before lifting it off the fire with a stick through the wire handle and poured it into the teapot.

While he waited for it to cool, he paced out the dimensions of the whare he was going to make. His bush hut.

Dug his heel into the ground to mark where each of the corners would be. Hammered stakes into those corner marks using the back of the axe. Stepped back and nodded. Seven yards long by five yards wide. There would be a verandah and a corrugated-iron chimney. He would install a rainwater runoff tank. Gutters and pipes to and from.

He dug foundation channels between the stakes with the spade. The lines of future walls. Cleared away a few remaining small trees and bushes. Planned where the front and rear doors would be. The placement of any windows.

An old musterer's advice, put your doors and windows in first, boy. Build the rest of your hut around them. Saves a lot of time. And make sure there are two doors. One in and one out.

It was nearing midday when he stopped working. Floss had stayed close enough. She was a silent companion, lay still and watched him constantly.

Like all good working dogs, she had begun to anticipate what he wanted. When he was holding a longer pole to mark where the front doorway would be, he said, 'Axe.' She looked at him, not understanding. Ran to where the axe and spade were but did not know what he wanted.

Roy lowered the pole, walked over and showed it to her. Rubbed her ears and said axe. He said it again, axe. This is the axe. It's a Fiskars axe. Best axe in the world, my mate. Axe, Floss. Axe.

The next time he needed it, he just said, axe, Floss, and she went and got it. Dragged it by the handle. The heavy head in the grass.

'Good girl.' Patted her twice.

Lunch for them both, that first day, was a can of bully beef. Fray Bentos, South American meat from Uruguay. In North Africa they would sometimes call it desert chicken. Hah. Roy twisted the key and unrolled it over the metal lid. Pulled it away. He spooned out about a third of the fatty mess onto the grass for Floss.

She looked at it and then at him.

'Go on,' he said. Floss began to eat. She did not look up as she ate, which meant she trusted him. That he would not kick her or take food from her halfway through.

Roy ate the remaining bully beef. The greasy, familiar meat. It was cold and there was a lot of fat. He had eaten it every day for four years. You could mix it with other things like rice and vegetables. Onions. Tomatoes when you could get them. Even fruit—raisins and slices of apple. The South Africans liked to do that. Sometimes peaches. Still, a layer of fat seemed to always stick to the roof of your mouth.

After lunch, Roy began to clear a track from where his whare would be, down a small gully and up the track to the gate on the valley road. Floss watched as he cut away the fern and scrub they had pushed through the previous day. He levelled the ground the best he could and dug narrow drainage hollows into the sheer sides of the drop-offs. Squaring the sides. Remembering the strength of the high country rain, slips and floods, allowed for the possible placement of drainage pipes while measuring the track being roughly two paces wide. Wide enough. Laid rough timber supports of cut scrub on the falling edge of the track.

He had been working on this for about two hours when Floss barked twice. Twice was warning him someone was coming. Her nose quivering as she raised her head and barked again.

He listened.

'Hello.' Someone was calling out in his direction. 'Hello?' Same voice. 'Are you there, Mr Roy Mitchell. Mr Mitchell?'

Two men had ridden up to his gate on the valley road. The older man was standing in his stirrups and shouting in Roy's direction. He was wearing an old-fashioned hat with a shiny brown band. A woollen suit and tartan tie. White shirt and broad leather belt across his growing stomach. English riding boots.

His face had a whisky flush about it and was tinged purple on his upper cheeks. A thin white moustache. He looked like what he was: the district's wealthiest land owner.

'Are you there, Mr Mitchell?' he shouted again. 'My name is Jack Field and we own the Tahatia Station. Backs onto your place. I knew your father. Your mother. Went to school with your mother. We heard you were back and just wanted to let you know we are bringing a muster through later today. Two thousand head, more or less.'

Roy knew who he was. Owner of Tahatia. Best grazing and finishing country in the entire district. A lot of sheltered plateau country, perfect for lambing and calving. Seven or eight natural ponds and three runoff creeks. A lot of natural springs. Finest grazing land you ever saw.

Some said it went back a while. To the old muru raupatu. The confiscations. Eaten land, Tony called it. But he was like their father in that regard. A bit of a sook.

It had been in the Field family now for three or four generations. Started with over one hundred and thirty thousand acres and wide tracks leading to a river jetty. A twelve-stand woolshed and covered yards. They said paddle-steamers would come up the river for the bales of wool before the tar sealed roads.

The Field family had benefited from every wool boom since 1870. Became wealthy and invested in Broken Hill Australian mining stocks and the Bank of New Zealand. Became even more wealthy. New Zealand Breweries. Fletcher Construction. An abattoir in the Lower Hutt Valley and a hotel in Masterton called The Commercial. Wellington's tramways. Auckland gasworks.

But Tahatia Station was the source of it all. Wool and frozen lamb. Rivers of gold for a bit. They had flourished ever since, in this new world. The original five-hundred-thousand-acre block had been gifted to them by the grateful New Zealand colonial government, which did not ever call it Aotearoa. The colonial government believed that New Zealand was just New Zealand. What the lost Dutchman Abel Tasman called it.

Roy could hear the faraway sounds of barking dogs coming down from the hills. High-pitched whistles ordering them to behave. To get away back. To come on. To come to me. Sit down there.

Jack Field smiled and glanced over his shoulder as he heard yet more sheep coming up the road. Spilling down from the high ridges. 'There we are.'

Roy saw that the entire hillside was moving with mustered yearling lambs. Must be three thousand head spilling over the slopes towards the road.

Bold shepherds were following this enormous mob. On horseback for the most part. Alternately sitting and standing in their stirrups. Whistling at their teams of dogs running behind the great mobs of young sheep. They would be shorn again before being sent to the freezing works. Ten stock trucks at least. Mustering dogs running everywhere.

'I remember you boys well. Your mother,' Jack Field yelled again to where he thought Roy might be. They all seemed to remember her. The tone of voice changed when their father was mentioned.

Roy stepped out of the bush line and greeted the older man. 'Mr Field.' Walked up the slope towards the gate.

Jack Field sat back on his horse. 'Roy,' he said, a little surprised at his sudden appearance. 'My word. Roy.'

'Mr Field,' Roy repeated.

'How do you do, son?' Jack Field smiled. He had a full set of dentures. A gold left incisor. It was popular at the time to have a gold tooth. A sign of success.

Roy noticed that the other man who had accompanied him was much younger. A boy, fourteen or fifteen. Probably had not begun shaving yet. Dressed the same as Jack, he too was mounted on a fine blood horse.

Jack Field followed Roy's glance.

'This is my son. Wiremu,' he said. 'I call him Billy. The wife, she calls him Wiri. Wiri Field. The fourth generation of our family. She adopted him from somewhere up the river. Wiri came from Sister Aubert's orphanage up near Pipiriki. I don't even know half of what she says.'

Wiremu had European features, a thin nose and Scottish freckles across his pale skin. Narrow lips. Blue eyes, reddish hair and an apologetic smile.

Roy said nothing. The old man had said a lot and was still going.

'She tries to speak it to me sometimes,' he said. ' In the Maori lingo. But I say no. Only one language in New Zealand, I say, that's English. What do you say, Roy?'

Roy was thinking about the bayonet charge at Maleme. The rising sound of Ruamoko at dawn. The courage no one knows about. His lost brother Tony who had loved the truth of the te reo language. He ignored Jack's question.

'How do you do, Wiremu?' he asked very respectfully.

Wiri gave Roy a startled nod. Bright eyes. Tony's eyes. The most, intelligent, knowing eyes. Such men often made the best soldiers. Naturally humble.

He raised his hand towards Roy. Whispered, 'Good, thank you, Mr Mitchell. Good.'

Roy wanted to cry for some reason. Jesus. Would not. Tony would have wept. He said, that's good, instead.

Jack urged the tall bay forward with his knees. Leaned down, extended his hand to Roy across the gate.

232

'Roy. You don't mind if I call you Roy, do you?'

Roy took his hand and shook it. 'No, I do not mind that, Mr Field.'

'Call me Jack. And, by the way, sorry for your loss. The brother on Crete. Tony was his name?'

Roy nodded.

Jack watched him for a bit longer. 'As I said before, I run into old Nick yesterday.'

'You did?'

'He told us you were back. Give you a ride and sold you that well-bred bitch, I understand. Name of Floss? Five pounds is a good price for her.'

Floss had sunk into the grass about ten feet behind Roy. Hidden. Chin on her paws. She disliked the man on the big horse. Sensed the cruelty in his voice.

Jack's mount walked back two or three more steps.

'Stand still,' he growled. It blew air out of its nose, swished its tail and threw its head back and forward. Roy silently watched the animal's objection to the enormous disrespect on its back.

'Would you like to come and work for me?' Jack asked. 'You can sell the place to me if you like.'

'Sell the land?'

'I'd make you farm manager if you want. Take all the pressure off. There will be another depression, son. Now the war is over and the Americans have left. Britain's broke anyway. Sell your show to me. Much easier.'

Roy stared up at him.

'Nothing would change,' Jack continued. 'Take all the pressure off, son. Old Nick sold up to us and he's much happier now. Just ask him.'

Their father had rarely spoken of the Field family's large station bordering their place. Only said once that old man Field was no better than a damn thief. A standover man. A bully and the son of a killer.

The Field family were held in high regard by many. Jack Field himself was the local justice of the peace and chairman of the district roads committee. It had been reported that he was considering standing for the National Country Party in the next election. His photograph was often seen in the daily newspaper during school prizegiving week. Rugby games. Cricket matches. Had a good smile, Jack. That gold tooth.

Jack Field's father, Albert Field, had given four hundred live bullocks to King George V and the Empire as a gift at the outbreak of World War I. As a gesture from a grateful nation, Your Majesty, he had said in the cable.

His great-grandfather, Colonel William Field, had been a battalion commander in the Royal Irish 33rd of Foot at Pukerangiora.

'No,' Roy said. 'I'd rather not work for you, Mr Field. Or sell the place to you either. Sir.'

Jack Field watched him for a moment longer. No one he treated as an equal called him sir. Not even the accountant. Nodding, he knew this was a certain disrespect on Roy's part. He looked for a weakness in the young man standing below him who'd just said no to him. Twice. The old man snorted and cleared his throat. 'Call me Jack,' he said again and widened his smile.

Roy looked up at him. Nodded.

'Well, anyway,' Field said. 'We just came by to tell you of the muster we got coming. And to welcome you home, of course.'

'Thank you,' Roy said.

It was a year after he returned that the letter came.

He woke in the dark of predawn and lit the candle beside the bed. The light threw shadows around the interior of the whare he had completed in a little over four months. A single-room hut with a bed at one end, a sitting area with a sofa and a kitchen with a table and two chairs. Newspapers spread on the table to serve as a tablecloth. A tea mug. Packets of Saxa salt. A container of sugar.

Along one outside wall, he had constructed a verandah to sit on during sunny days, the soft evenings. He had discovered a natural spring in a bluff above the creek and had piped water to the washstands outside his hut. Would bring the water indoors next year. It had only taken him a week to build the catching yards and the dog kennels above the north-facing track. Floss, however, remained his only working dog and she still slept inside.

Roy had settled into a familiar farming routine of clearing the land: mainly slashing and burning the bush to make a living from farming livestock. He received a small monthly war pension from the government that had been deemed a development loan.

He rose from the bed and carried the candle into the kitchen area. Washed his face in the basin he kept there. Lit the kerosene lamp, blew out the candle. Raked the fire, added newspaper and kindling to it. Once it began to catch, he let Floss outside for a run.

He lit another lamp in the middle of the hut and waited for the water to boil. Thought about the farming supplies he had ordered the previous week. The truck should turn up at eleven that morning. Thereabouts. It meant mail and supplies. Often loaves of freshly baked bread. Stores. Farming equipment. The same truck had brought the doorframes for the whare and sheets of corrugated iron for his roof.

Occasionally he received letters and information pamphlets from the agriculture department or the government. Their stock sales and projections. Newspapers too. The Empire Games coming to Auckland in 1950. Who would have thought?

More wire and battens and strainer posts. He already had enough staples. Lot of people forgot the staples. He had ordered another wire strainer. Another jenny. Three sets of wirecutters.

The kitchen smelled of woodsmoke from the fire.

As the sun rose and the light improved, Roy looked at the interior of his whare. On a kitchen bench, the base of an ancient totara strainer post had been fashioned to serve as a knife block. Ladles and spoons on the walls. Herbs hanging from the ceiling above the indoor chimney. Rosemary. Koromiko. Matai and wild parsnip. Bunches of parsley in a jar. Another jar filled with wild mint, roots turning white. A set of false teeth.

Breakfast was griddle cakes, just flour and eggs and with salt and baking soda mixed into a batter and fried in beef dripping. Fried some eggs in the dripping. Took a leg of bacon from the chimney interior hook and cut off three slices. Once this was cooked and eaten, he drank two large mugs of black tea.

He looked at the pocket watch he kept hanging from a nail above the fireplace. Ten past seven. He could still get some scrub clearing done before the truck arrived.

For the next three hours, Roy steadily cut the manuka covering a paddock near the hut where he thought he could develop a fine covering of grass. Once burnt and sown with grass seed it might, as they said, come away. He only stopped to take a break to catch his breath, take a drink from the bottle of tea he carried or sharpen the slasher with the whetstone he kept.

The Freeman R. Jackson Mail and Rural Delivery truck could be heard coming up the valley road from about a mile away.

This weekly visit had become something of an event in the valley and many of the people looked forward to its arrival. Every Thursday. Some even planned their whole week around it. Church on Sunday. Mail truck on Thursday. Fish and chips on Friday.

The driver's name was Errol Murphy and the women along the road had taken to calling him Hairoil because of his beautiful black hair, which he kept combed and neatly parted with the help of what he called his secret weapon, Layrite hair oil.

Beneath the neatly combed hair, Errol always seemed to have a half-inch roll-your-own cigarette in his mouth, rarely lit. Blue Zig-Zag papers, the slow-burning ones. He had seen the American films where the Hollywood stars would light each other's cigarette and these had somehow become symbols of smouldering sexual desire.

Errol knew each of the farmers and each of the farmers' wives along the valley by their first names. When he stopped the truck at their gate, he would take his comb and, looking at his reflection in the side mirror, run it through his shining hair while smoothing his other palm behind it. If it was a woman who was waiting for him, he would make three or four sweeps of the comb. Flick off the excess oil before he put it back in his top pocket. Wink. Sometimes he would also kiss the comb as he did this. Wink again. This time with the other eye.

Roy was standing at his mailbox. One hand resting on the old empty twelve-gallon oil drum. It had been laid on its side and nailed to a post. *R. Mitchell. 361 Valley Road*, written on it in white paint. A sugar bag covered the front.

He was granted one sweep of Errol's comb as the Bedford truck came to a stop.

A dust cloud caught up to the truck and blew over them.

'Letter for you, Roy,' Errol said and turned to search through the stacked rows of envelopes and packages arranged on the passenger seat. 'From the government by the look of it,' he said. 'Addressed to a Sgt Roy Mitchell. Ex 22 Btn. 2NZEF. 361 Valley Road? That's you, isn't it?'

'That's me. The old me anyway,' Roy said.

'I'm sorry, mate.' Everyone had come to hate such envelopes during the war. It was most often bad news. Cables were worse. Those wavy blue lines.

Roy thanked him with a silent nod and took the letter. Cleared his throat and gave Errol the list for the following week. There was no good going on about these things. The hand holding the letter from the government began shaking so he put it in his pocket and began to go through the list with Errol.

Drench and creosote. One bag of sugar. Two bags of flour. The fresh bread, of course, two loaves and some agriculture department catalogues. Four books he had heard about: *Farming for Profit in New Zealand Hill Country. Growing Pinus Radiata in*

Hill Country: CSIRO. *War in the Desert with the Div* by Brigadier (ret.) Henry MacLaurin. Another one titled *The Bright Future of Top Dressing in the North Island*.

'I got your list, Roy,' Errol said.

'Any newspapers?'

Errol often brought him the *Dominion* and the *Daily News*. *Wanganui Chronicle*. The *Dominion* was usually a week old. Sometimes he managed to get it sooner.

'No, mate,' Errol said. 'No papers this week. Look, I better get going.'

'Righto,' Roy said and stepped away. Embarrassed he had been talking too much. Jesus.

Errol put the truck into gear, winked at him again and drove off.

Roy tried not to touch the letter in his top shirt pocket as he walked back to his hut. Imagined somehow that it was heavier than what it was and reasoned with himself that that was a stupid thing to think. Nothing could be heavier than what it was. Nothing could be other than what it was.

Took off his boots at the door and sat down at the kitchen table. Opened the letter.

From the government, as expected.

The Defence Department's embossed title. The Ministry of War. Service: Army. OHMS. On His Majesty's Service.

The letter was addressed to him as the nominated next-of-kin of Anthony Robert Mitchell: and it was their most welcome duty to inform him that Anthony, in spite of earlier reports, was still alive.

Roy stopped reading. He had buried Tony's foot at Maleme.

At the listening post they called Whangamomona. Wept for him. Believed he was dead. Died of his wounds. That strange sense of relief, shame and sorrow sweeping over him.

The letter went on to explain that due to the heavy losses of the battalion in 1941, many casualty reports were inaccurate. Subsequently, lists posted to Maadi Camp were also often inaccurate.

However, they were delighted to inform him that Tony had survived the war.

Roy stopped reading. Jesus Christ. Jesus Christ. Tony was alive. Floss had snuck inside and was lying in the spill of white ash near the fire, watching him.

He cleared his throat and continued to read. Touched the embossed crest at the top of the page. A raised shape beneath his fingertips. A Rangatira holding a taiaha and a pakeha woman holding the flag like she would defending a child. There were stars and sheaves of wheat and ships. Crossed mining hammers and a golden fleece. A crown.

Sitting there at his kitchen table, the letter of his brother being alive in his hands.

Strangely, he thought of that young English man from the Fleet Air Arm running towards him. The one he shot. What a strange thing to think. Holding a letter from the Crown. The way the newspaper flew out of his hand as the .303 ball hit him in the chest. Knocked him onto his back. You could not say such things after the war.

And that naked Australian dancing unknowing on the roof of a Cairo latrine. That 9th Div boy with a burning newspaper pushed up his arse and no idea what he was doing.

He ran away from that listening post. Returned to bury his brother's foot above Maleme. He had believed Tony was dead. It was easier and he did not have to tell the truth.

It could be funny if you wanted it to be, Roy.

Now the letter was saying that there had been a mistake. That his twin brother was alive. Had not died of his wounds. Was living in a hostel called the Gallipoli in Auckland. Grafton.

He stared again at the opened letter in his hands. And then he sat back.

Why had Tony not written to him?

Why had it taken a government letter for him to know his brother was still alive?

It was a fine day in spring 1947 when Roy arrived at the Hobson Street Bus Station in Auckland.

Auckland/Bombay Hills/Hamilton/Te Kuiti/Pio Pio/ Awakino/New Plymouth/Stratford/Hawera/Wanganui on the vertical sign above the slatted waiting seats. The wartime covers long removed.

He left the bus station carrying a small suitcase and walked onto Symonds Street and a carpet of fallen red flowers. Paused and realised it was the beautiful lines of Pohutukawa trees. An earlier shower of rain had slicked the asphalt pavements and a northerly wind was coming in from the Hauraki Gulf. The sun shone bright as a milk token and there was the hot tar smell in the air. Behind him, he could hear the tram bells clanging outside the Farmers building on Queen Street.

He continued up the slope of Symonds Street until he reached the old brick tram shelter at the end of Karangahape Road. Turned left and crossed the Grafton Street bridge.

Below him, the old cemetery. A gully filled with ponga trees. They looked like a thousand green umbrellas at Eden Park. The ancient headstones and a narrow creek below him.

Once he had crossed the bridge, he turned right into Park Street. Continued walking for about another twenty yards and stopped when he saw Tony. Anthony. His twin brother.

He was where he had said he would be. It had been eight years. All those long war years. The last time was on Crete. Maleme airfield. Whangamomona listening post.

Tony's left trouser leg was pinned up. A pair of crutches propped up into his armpits.

Roy had written asking if he could come up to Auckland and see him. Tony's reply had come after a week or so. A defensive, cursory tone. He could not meet Roy at the bus station, he said. It was difficult for him to walk very far now. It would be best to meet at the Park Street shops. Matter-of-fact terms.

He wrote that he could not afford a taxi and could not ride a bike properly yet. Because of the leg. I'll be at the shops at four o'clock. Your bus gets in at half past three. Time enough to walk up to the Grafton Street bridge. It is at the end of K Road.

Then, almost bizarrely, the ending of the letter in a different tone. Please come and see me, my brother. It has been so very long and I love you. And then something that Roy did not understand but it instantly reminded him how deeply strange Tony could be. Why he was considered an outsider.

You asked me why I had not contacted you? Well, I don't know except I am terrified of you. With much love and respect: arohanui: Tony.

Tony had not yet noticed him. He was staring instead at a commercial artist working on the windows of a greengrocer's shop opposite.

The white writing on the window sure and fine. Confident tails on the *g*s and old-fashioned *r*s with saddles.

Rangitikei Spuds, 2/6 a sack. Pukekohe cabbages: 2d each. Ohakune carrots: 4/6 a 10lb bag. Keri Keri cauliflower. Hawke's Bay apples.

There were tables topped with boxes of fruit. Bags of potatoes stacked on the pavement. Freshly dug purple kumara in wooden crates stacked on each other.

The commercial artist was using a maulstick to steady his hand as he worked. A damp cloth to clean the edges of the words. A paint-spattered canvas drop sheet was spread along the pavement under the windows.

Tony was leaning back against the window of a Billings Menswear, crutches loose in his armpits. A worn suit, frayed at the cuffs and covered in paint. Narrow-brim hat tipped to the back of his head.

Roy could not move as he watched his brother standing there. Unable to speak.

One-legged men were common enough on the city streets after both wars. Nobody even took much notice. They were often angry men, though. Some were embarrassments. On crutches with empty trouser legs. Become drunkards and bothersome. They would fall over all the time, often seen sleeping between the gravestones in the cemetery. Warm there, with the sun on the stones.

If you woke them, sometimes they would tell you to fuck off. No one spoke about these things. It was better to close your eyes and sing 'God Defend New Zealand'. Or even 'Pokarekare Ana'. My love will never be dried by any God. It will always be watered by my tears.

244

'Tony,' Roy whispered, he cleared his throat and raised his voice. 'Tony.'

Tony turned and smiled. Stood up straight.

'Roy? My brother.' Smiling. Swaying. As always, completely helpless before him. His paint-covered hands, palms up, came out towards Roy. Looking at him as if there was nothing else in the world but him at that very moment.

Roy was trying to say something. Covered his eyes, in shame, to hide them. Sobbed. He could not speak for weeping.

Tony, staring at him, lifted a finger up to his lips. His terror had evaporated. 'Sssssh. No matter, Roy. My brother,' he said. 'Nothing. Say nothing. You have snot coming out of your nose.'

Roy smiled, nodded. Waited a moment before he took his hand away from his face. That was enough for now. His voice was shaking and all he could say was: 'Snot?'

'Yep.' Tony pulled Roy close and hugged him. 'It's all over your fucking face, Roy. Jesus, it glistens in the light.'

'It glistens? The snot?'

They were laughing as if they had not been apart for the past eight years. Had never been apart.

They walked along Park Street and Roy slowed his pace to match Tony's awkward swinging gait. It was just after four in the afternoon with the warmth and damp smell of early evening in Auckland. An old cry of alarmed blackbirds.

They stopped on the corner of Park Street and Rangimarie Road outside a small fish and chip shop. *Ithaca Golden Grill*, it said on the window.

'Here we are,' Tony laughed, 'the house of Epictetus and Stavros.'

A small bell tinkled as they walked through the blue and white plastic strips. That strong smell of old fish, new fish, lemons and hot lard. Cut potatoes and cigarette smoke.

Tony was a regular customer and the owner, Stavros, never mentioned his missing leg. Did not look at it. That is why Tony always came back to him. Stavros smiled when he saw him.

'Mr Tony. How are you?' That was it. He looked at Roy. Frowned. Roy and Tony were still almost identical.

'Stavros,' Tony said.

Stavros had been taught good manners by his grandfather on Ithaca. That island of coming home after long absence. He remained silent.

Tony held up two fingers and put a shilling on the counter.

Stavros took the coin, rang it up and then placed two individual sixpences back onto the counter. The chips were free. His grandfather would have approved.

Tony nodded. 'This is my twin brother, Stavros. His name is Roy.'

Stavros smiled at this. Good manners. He smiled, tilted his head slightly to one side and wiped flour from his hands on his white apron. Held out his hand. 'I am very pleased to meet you, Mr Roy,' he said. 'You are twins, all right. He looks just like you. Didyma?'

They both nodded.

After a moment, Stavros turned back to the cooking. He lowered the wire baskets of chips into the bubbling fat. 'You in Greece during the war too, Mr Roy?' His back to them. 'Killing the Germans? Both?'

'Yes,' Roy said to his back. 'Both.'

Stavros nodded and lifted the wire baskets from the vat and, with metallic clanks, hung them up to drain.

'Good.' He shook the last of the fat from the baskets and heaped the chips onto two squares of white paper. A tall stack of newspapers below that.

Sprinkled salt over them and held up a dark plastic bottle.

'Seevee?'

They both nodded.

He splashed vinegar onto the hot chips and wrapped them quickly into two separate newspaper parcels.

'There you are, Mr Tony,' he said. 'You already paid.' Nodded towards Roy. 'You too, the brother Roy.' A huge smile. 'Good on you both. Fighting for Greece.' He said something in Greek and made a fist.

They took the chips and left the shop through that same clattering of blue and white plastic strips. Parsley in the fish shop window. Catch of the day: trevally and gleaming, rose-coloured schnapper on trays of ice. Price tags written upside down. Some of them in Greek. No one except Stavros could understand the numbers.

Tony could not eat and walk at the same time. They found a bus shelter and sat. Tore holes in the newspaper packets. The smell of vinegar billowed out. Fried chips. Rising steam and printers' ink.

They ate this remembered treat with relish, smiling, and did not speak. When they finished they licked their fingers and put the old newspapers in a bin.

An unspoken and immediate grace existed as they made their way along the road. They were unaware of it except for the ease, the comfort, they had with each other. The silent, undeniable knowledge. Tony lurching slightly on his crutches and Roy walking slowly beside him. The most natural and unthinking of things, it was almost as if it had always been so.

Blessed are the twins, the oracle said, Castor and Pollux. They think not of the other. They are the other, don't you see? I and thou. Had they swum together in their mother's womb? Held hands as they swam? He did not say: what a gift that would be, my beloved.

They stopped at the front gates of Gallipoli Lodge on Rangimarie Road. It was an old Auckland house. Two-storeyed, 1880s, set above and back from the road. A cement ramp recently added up the side. The original wide steps at the front remained. Nikau palms growing on either side of the steps. Six letter boxes, newspapers spilling out of them. Wet letters on the bricks and the grass.

The house windows were set well back from the balustrades. Upstairs, filigree ironwork and handrails. Another inheritance house from parents who had lost their sons.

Tony had been moved to the Lodge from the Red Cross repatriation ward at Papakura Military Camp.

Most of the tenants yelled out in their sleep and were known as being bad-tempered. Old men, deformed from the war. Most drank a lot of cheap northern wine. All were amputees. One was blind as well. String lines tied up around the ground floor to find his way about. Red Cross braille cards pegged to the cords like washing on a line. Another had lost both legs and yet another, multiple amputations, was incontinent. Unable to sleep with the night terrors.

He would hang himself with a coathanger in the kitchen within the year. Left a note that that simply read: I shit myself again today fuck this.

Since both of his hands had been blown off too, he hanged

248

himself by leaning forward onto the wire length of the coathanger on the kitchen doorhandle. Got a tea towel for his neck and rotated his head as he did it. It is easy if you have no hands to save yourself. Simply fall forward off the wheelchair. He had written the note with a pencil clenched in his teeth. He had not learnt to use his toes from the one foot he had left.

Nobody else cared if he had shit in his pants. Newborn children did it all the time. All children of God.

Iron lacework on the front porch. An odd-shaped lump of gleaming kauri gum as a doorstop. Windows open for any cool breezes coming up from the gulf. Wooden floorboards. Rangimarie spelled out in copperplate in the black-and-white marble pattern of the front entrance. The same name of the road. It meant peace or, for some, a peaceful view of the sky and the sea.

Flanking the entrance, two 25-pounder brass shell casings. Tall and polished, they held an assortment of walking sticks and umbrellas. Wide bay windows stretched around the front of the verandah.

The entrance hall was lined with dark wooden panels. Worn Persian-style runners on the floor. Several more pairs of crutches leaned against the wall. Coats and hats in an alcove alongside three wheelchairs. Blankets with bold tartan patterns draped over the wheelchairs. They were to put over what was left in public. Especially for the Anzac Day parades when the other veterans came over from the Mount Eden RSA to get them. Lemon squeezer hats with brass badges. NZ flanked by ferns. The black berets of the Armoured Brigade. That smell of old men hung about them and about the entrance.

Roy could hear soft music coming from the floor above them. American jazz piano. It stopped abruptly. A bump as if something had fallen over. Tony was holding open the door to his small and modest flat. Next to the entrance way, there was a small kitchen. A bathroom and a single bedroom at the end of a short corridor.

Roy stepped into the front room. It had once been the main drawing room of the old house. He stopped. The entire southern wall of the apartment had become a painting.

The wallpaper and sarking had been stripped back to the original rough-sawn rimu boards.

The enormous figure of a man had then been painted directly onto these boards. Parts, as clearly represented as a photograph and other parts, outlined, unfinished.

It was of a large muscular Te Atiawa man dressed in Borthwick's Freezing Works white overalls. The sleeves had been removed at the shoulder to reveal his powerful arms. Tattoos of crosses and dots, an eagle and a dragon. Some prison attempts at ta moko. Attempts at truth. His journey to here.

The man was working on a beef carcass which was hung from a metal hook and suspended on a conveyancing chain. The legs and head had been cut off the body of the animal and it was covered in white fat. Mottled flanks and veins, long tendons and strong, red muscles. It was the top chain. The legendary beef chain. Dozens of such hanging bodies aligned behind it.

Roy could not speak as he stared at the painted figure on the rimu boards. He barely heard someone calling out. It was coming from somewhere near the front door of the house. The verandah.

'Tony? Hello, Tony? Are you there?'

It was a familiar voice, remembered as with a hint of good humour and forgiveness. Strength in it yet. That beautiful voice coming for you would make you smile. Laugh, even. Sister.

'Tony? Has Roy arrived yet?'

You would be safe with this voice coming for you. And this voice would never give up until it had got to you. In every action, in every fight, Roy had heard this man. Yelling out that he was alive. Reassuring him. In Greece and Crete. North Africa. Sidi Rezegh and El Alamein. They both turned towards him.

Sister. It was David Brookes.

Sometimes, Tony once said, I was weeping so much I could barely paint.

On Monte Cassino, Sister had come for him. He had bandaged him up, stopped the bleeding and carried him down the mountain to the wonderful Polish doctor, Samborski. Said nothing. He had also carried the body of Manny Jones to the regimental aid post below Casa Elto. Wept for him also. His tormenter. You would not find a better man than this man.

Someone had told him once, when he was young, that the kumara never speaks of its own sweetness. He did those things but would never speak of them. Sister.

Roy also knew they had given him that name because it was an insult. A name to humiliate him. Manny yelling, 'Take your hands away, Sister Boy. Show us your cock.'

Made his life miserable, the poor bastard. Especially Manny. Relentless. It became more than humour.

David forgave them somehow. Silence, acceptance and often just a bloody grim smile.

Then they saw him in action. Sister. They stopped then. Everyone except Manny, of course. And it was with the bayonet that he was the best. The most primitive of all their weapons. Unbelievable in his protective savagery. Never seen anything like it. Surprised by the boy, the CSM, Mother McCready, said how good he was. The best bayonet fighters were often like that, though. Quiet and terrible.

He was standing in the doorway. Dressed in civilian clothing now. And smiling. A sleeveless Fair Isle pullover. Open shirt. Jacket. Soft leather shoes. He had let his hair grow slightly longer from the war and he looked like an older student trying too hard to belong. Holding books under his arm. The most capable and ruthless bayonet fighter he had seen.

This same man, awarded the DSM and having morning tea with the King and his Scottish wife at Buckingham Palace. One lung had been shot away from him on that night at Casa Elto, and a kidney too. David said nothing of such losses as he carried the others down to the regimental aid post. Went back twice. Covered in their blood. His blood too. It embarrassed him.

'Hello, Roy.'

Roy stepped forward and held his old comrade close. Hugged him. They patted each other's backs.

'I thought he was dead too. My God, it almost broke my heart. I have always loved him.'

Roy heard the tenderness in David's voice.

'Hold on.' He frowned. He took two steps back. His hands on his head as if to think.

Tony ignored him, looked at David instead. Smiled. 'I'm not dead, you bloody fool. I am here, and I love you too.'

David crossed to where Tony was standing on his crutches. They looked at each other for a moment, and Tony touched his cheek with his fingers. Reached out, held the back of David's head and pulled him closer. Kissed him with his wonderful mouth, open and smiling. His trembling lips.

Sometimes, when he was sleeping, Roy saw again that 9th Div boy on the latrine roof near the Clot Bey brothel. And then the Northern Transvaal Horse Artillery, already dead and scattered in the sand around the mosque of Sidi Rezegh. They had played rugby against them on Freyberg's field at El Maadi. They were such bad losers, the Springboks. The South Africans called it Carisbrook on the bloody Nile and said the All Blacks would do anything to win at rugby, anything. Called them shameless and laughed as they said it. They knew themselves to be like them.

He heard the roaring of panzer motors and saw red and green tracer rounds floating above Ruweisat.

Tony was calling out from Crete, where are you, my brother? And have the horses got water? Where are the dogs? Aim at their boots as they fall, man.

A weeping nurse from the 4th Indian Div was opening the back doors of a Red Cross ambulance. Blood spilling from it as if a bucket had been kicked over.

Wounded New Zealand soldiers were being carried back to the triage tents at El Alamein. Torn into pieces.

It was raining in the Waikato. That beautiful, gentle rain falling softly over the flat land.

The sound of his beloved twin brother's voice calling out as he left. Walking out of the Lodge on Rangimarie Road. The memory of their kissing.

'Don't go, Roy. My brother,' Tony called out to him. 'Please. This is why I did not...' He was still in the arms of Sister, who held him tight.

Roy sat in the bus and stared out the window at the farmland as they drove south. He saw Waikato dairy farmers feeding their calves. How they were surrounded by white buckets and in paddocks of high green grass. Poplar trees in rows. Weeping willows. Raised tractor roads. Electric fences. Once known as the place of ancient and legendary kumara fields. Peach orchards. Such was the fertility. The local Jerseys were spoken of with much admiration.

He watched the moving reflections of his face in the window. The passing land beyond. The memory of that village in Italy. Gravzano di Lucia, where the German artillery had waited for all the villagers to come out to greet them. It was Sister who had gone to help Manny in the piazza.

Va bene, bello zozzo...va bene. Bello. It's all right, my beautiful boy-child. She'd said that to Manny.

Zozzo is what she called the little ones, her toddling children. And she said the strangest of things to Manny as she died. She told him she loved him...ti amo. How could she say that? She did not even know him. And he was a terrible man.

Then he thought of Tony. Tony would know what to say. He would understand it. Make sense of it for him. Why his memories had become like the moving pictures in the cinema. Tony kissing David.

In the room with them in each other's arms, he was unable to reply. Their love might break his heart.

An agriculture department pamphlet he had read emphasised that the Jersey was known for the high butter-fat content of its milk. Much higher than the Friesian, which had, it must be acknowledged, a substantially greater yield of milk. Per animal, that is.

The title of the article was: 'The Future of Dairy Farming in New Zealand'. Roy did not have cows but plenty of people in the district did. Their father had tried to become a dairy farmer. But it was no good. He was useless at everything he tried. Their father. The hopeless bastard.

The Friesian was a solid cow on flat ground. The Jersey tougher and more adaptable in the hills. The rough scrub country of early Taranaki. They were naturally suited to this tough new land, it seemed.

However it should also be noted, the pamphlets warned, that the Jersey bull is a nasty fellow. The male. He will try to gore you to death if he is any good. Kill you.

Put a copper ring in his nose as a yearling if possible…if you want to keep him anyway…soon as you can. Attach a chain to the copper ring. Or, if not, cut off his balls as a calf. That works too. Sell them as steers with their fat shoulders and rumps for the abattoirs. The old men in the district often laughed as they spoke about them.

He had seen those uncut Jersey bulls with their heavy-set black shoulders and slim yellow hips. Savage horns. Taranaki bulls looking at you with bloodshot eyes. Lifted noses and smelling the air of you. A formidable fellow and their desire to kill you is as important to them as breathing or fucking. Do not forget that.

There were red and green tracer rounds above the Ruweisat Ridge. Every fifth round was tracer.

He was going home. Through Te Awamutu; Te Kuiti. Piopio. Along the flats before the Awakino. To cross the bridge over the evil river. And then rising up into the first winding turns of Mount Messenger. Passing through the tunnel and falling into Taranaki.

It had been a long night, a long day. His head nodding onto his chest. A moment of silence, of sleep.

Then the popping of parachute flares above them and that white sand below them in the swaying brightness. Soft beneath their feet as they ran and the Taranaki boys being blown apart in that white minefield. That ancient terror of being unable to help them. The cries of his friends in the dark. The agitation as he woke, his hands coming up to protect his face. The bus had slowed and almost stopped as it turned into a tight bend on the mountain. Billy McKay saying, I am a cowboy and an Indian from the King Country.

He looked around but no one had noticed. The bus was turning close to the sheer papa banks of the mountain. The dripping ferns.

It was becoming dark as the bus reached a plateau along the North Taranaki coast. For a moment or two, there was a view along the coast all the way to Nga-Motu and Pari-tutu, the islands, the sugarloaves of New Plymouth. The glittering sea in the bay between them. To his left, the cloud-caped shape of the mountain rising. High up, on a dark shoulder, a small yellow house light came on.

Roy began to slowly relax into the sound of the hissing tyres on the wet road as the bus navigated the last of the mountain's bends. The steady rain and the rhythmic pull and return of the windscreen wipers.

The New Zealand Government Department of Agriculture had said that rain is one of the reasons the grass grows so well in New Zealand. The other is nitrogen. And this comes in the most natural form as ancient solidified seabird manure from a small island in the Pacific called Nauru. This wonderful source of natural nitrogen will be widely broadcast across the New Zealand countryside from airplanes. It will be called topdressing. Other trace elements will be added to improve the soil and eliminate all disease.

The locals on Nauru believed that the mining of their land would last forever. They had so much to sell and give away, you see. If not, they believed, something else would come along.

The pamphlet also suggested that cyanide sprayed over the New Zealand farms could eliminate grass grub. Cyanide will kill most things you don't want. Some farmers had already sprayed cyanide on their paddocks and got rid of that damned grass grub. In a heartbeat, they said.

He had always known they were close. Sister and Tony. He had once seen them holding hands as they walked along a seawall in Cairo. Fingers interlocked like children. Laughing, almost dancing between the rows of palm trees.

They smiled and looked at each other. Manny had said it was like they were in love and wanted to fuck each other. But that was Manny and it was before the battalion was sent to Greece. It was before Crete.

And it is true that the blood of all people is formed by the land itself. That is all the painting on the rimu boards was about, really. He had found his brother again. How Tony smiled as he placed his fingers on David's cheek and kissed him.

Acknowledgments

Liam Robert Daisley. Above all others.

Albie H: to you and your never ever forgotten koha. I thank you.

Aotearoa New Zealand VA. SM. LW.

The Randell Cottage Writers Trust and Creative New Zealand. This novel was extensively edited and shaped at 14 St Mary Street, Thorndon, Wellington, New Zealand. I will remain eternally grateful to Creative New Zealand for the place that is the Randell Cottage.

My agent Lyn Tranter: 'Get your skates on.'

SD